RED KNIGHT

DANIEL COLEMAN

VORPAL WORDS PUBLISHING

Copyright © 2018 by Daniel Coleman

www.dcolemanbooks.com

Interior illustrations by E.K. Stewart-Cook

estewartcook@gmail.com

Cover art by Antonio Jose Manzanedo Luis

dibuja2@gmail.com

Cover Design by Stefan Mark and Jodie Coleman

Editing by Daniel Friend and Nancy Felt

All rights reserved. This is a work of fiction. Any resemblance to persons living or dead is entirely coincidental. No part of this book may be reproduced in any form or by any electronic or mechanical means, including information storage and retrieval systems, without written permission from the author, except for the use of brief quotations in a book review.

Published by Vorpal Words Publishing.

ALSO BY DANIEL COLEMAN

KNIGHTS OF WONDERLAND SERIES

Jabberwocky — Book 0

Hatter — Book 1

Red Knight — Book 2

White Knight — Book 3 (forthcoming)

A NOTE ON THE KNIGHTS OF WONDERLAND FROM THE AUTHOR

Jabberwocky was the first novel written in the series. It comes first chronologically as well, and includes many of the same characters as the rest of the series. Hatter starts the storyline of Chism and Hatta. *Jabberwocky* and *Hatter* can be read independently, but since *Hatter* is the launch point of the rest of the series, it became book 1 in the series.

Daniel Coleman also writes award-winning Contemporary Fiction

Gifts and Consequences

To Reece

A boy who is kind
a boy who dreams
a boy who understands Hatta even better than I do

1

"I never asked to be a leader."

Chism handed the letter from the Queen of Hearts to his new commander.

Lieutenant Serrill's grey eyes slid along the words. "Don't want to lead? Simple—don't be the best man for the job."

"I've never been able to, Sir."

"Able to what?" Lieutenant Serrill looked up, leveling his heavy gaze on Chism. From his seated position, their eyes were almost level.

"I can't not be the best. It's not in me to be something unless it's the best I can be of that thing."

That was a major part of the reason Chism didn't want to lead. No soldier would ever follow him. He was great with a sword, but goats would follow a bandersnatch before soldiers would follow an unsocial runt like Chism. It made no sense to desire something he'd fail at spectacularly.

Lieutenant Serrill stood up from his folding camp chair and smoothed his rough beard. "Remind me just what it is at which you are the incontestable best."

Chism couldn't tell if the order was sincere or mocking.

Reading what people meant versus what they said required social aptitude that Chism would never possess. Just like using his tongue to defend himself. The Elite who Chism had always admired as a kid—Sir Trevik, the Voiceless Knight—had never been one for talking either. Chism's sword, Thirsty, had talked loud enough for people in two kingdoms to hear.

Chism drew Thirsty and laid the flat of the blade across his free hand. The cool metal hummed in a silent, satisfying way. In the blade, Chism saw the reflection of his own dark eyes. Steel was simple, strong, and predictable. Everything Chism tried to be.

Lieutenant Serrill looked down at Thirsty. Then back into Chism's eyes. "Let's see, then." Lieutenant Serrill walked out of the tent, straight to where the rest of the squadron milled around.

Ander, Chism's Fellow, stood in the center of the group, shrugging and apparently deflecting the questions of the other Elites. His white hair matched the other Elites' unkempt beards in shagginess. Voices cut off when the lieutenant approached.

"Elite Chism has been assigned to Scaled Tiger Squadron."

No one reacted. They'd obviously figured it out; why else would he and Ander show up out of nowhere? At least there hadn't been any talk of *Sir* Chism.

"Orders of the Red Queen herself. I am to respectfully demote the current sub-lieu and replace him with our new member."

Chism met Muehner's eyes. The large, bearded man's glare was so dark it should have been accompanied by thunder. *I didn't ask for it*, thought Chism. He kept Muehner's gaze even though, physically, he was a coyote facing a lion.

"I, for one, want to see if he can handle a sword like they say." Lieutenant Serrill looked to the back corner of the gathered Elites. "Mave!"

A young man, a couple years older than Chism, stepped forward and offered a wide, friendly smile that made Chism like him immediately despite himself. His impressive pale beard matched his hair. Probably blond, but Chism's colorblindness prevented him from knowing for sure. With so much prettiness, Mave belonged in the Merchant's Guild, not traipsing around with soldiers. The rest of the group had enough ugly between them to offset Mave, but only through sheer numbers.

In a rapid voice, Mave said, "If you want to test his sword, you might want to pick someone else, Sir. I'm the least prolific."

"Proficient," corrected the man at Mave's side, probably his Fellow.

The day didn't have enough light left in it for more than one decent fight. Chism muttered, "Why waste our time?"

Lieutenant Serrill looked questioningly at Chism.

"I'm living on fate-granted time, Sir." Chism never should have survived childhood, much less his two run-ins with Duke Jaryn. "It's irresponsible to waste that time sparring with your handsome young soldier."

"An oddsmaker would give a scraggly kid like you three-to-one odds against him."

"He'd pay for the misjudgment," said Chism. "Give me a real test, Sir."

"Mave *and* Gorman, then," said Lieutenant Serrill. "Fellows, gather some shroudtree bark to wrap the blades."

As a few Fellows scattered to get the bark, a dark-haired giant stepped forward. Gorman was taller than Muehner and as big as any two of the other Elites put together. The huge tunic Gorman wore was tested by his sheer size and when he pulled it off, Chism saw that he was puffy with muscle, not fat. Gorman's Fellow, an average-sized soldier, struggled under the weight of his sword as he retrieved it from a tent. Gorman drew the sword as easily as Chism drew Thirsty. The hilt was big enough for both of Gorman's huge hands and the blade was as long as Chism was tall.

"Even odds now?" asked Lieutenant Serrill.

"Not on their best day," said Chism flatly.

Some of the Elites growled and most of their faces went dark.

Lieutenant Serrill faced Chism. "Belittling the men you are supposed to lead is a poor way to avoid leadership."

"Are flattery, underbluffing, and time-wasting better, Sir?"

Lieutenant Serrill crossed his arms and stared down his nose at Chism. "Muehner, Mave, and Gorman against *Sir* Chism. If he'll condescend to spar with lesser soldiers."

It hadn't been Chism's intent to alienate his new squadron, but he lacked the skill to fix it with his tongue.

As Chism worked on an appropriate response, Muehner stepped up next to the other two and said, "No more talking, Chism. Shut yourself and show us." As opposed to Mave and Gorman's friendly smiles, Muehner's face was an impatient scowl.

Most Elites would never talk to their sub-lieu like that. Nor would they talk like that to a Knight, unless the Knight was Chism, apparently. He didn't care; he'd provoked it, although not on purpose. It was just more proof that he didn't belong at the head of any group.

The Fellows returned with flexible sheets of tough bark. Ander wrapped Thirsty's blade and the other Fellows did the same for their Elites. Without practice swords available, it was the best way to make sparring safe.

Road dust still covered Ander's face, etching the fine wrinkles around his eyes. They hadn't taken time to settle in and clean up after weeks of searching for Scaled Tiger Squadron.

"Bung and bights," said Ander in his chastising tone. "Just because their blades are covered doesn't mean a good blow can't kill you."

Chism nodded.

Ander wasn't done. "That giant's got two mountains of muscle behind his sword, and Muehner already had reason to hate you before you opened your slapdash mouth."

"Did I say anything I can't back up?"

"Only a fool says something simply because it happens to be truth." Ander pulled the final knot tight then added, "You had a chance to earn respect today, but now all you'll do by beating them is earn their contempt."

Chism smiled and asked, "Have I ever told you how much I love late advice?"

Ander muttered more curses under his breath then joined the rest of the squadron and began looking for bets. As Chism faced his opponents, he heard Ander getting very favorable odds. Only a fool would bet on a boy as small as Chism against three healthy Elites. Unless that fool had seen Chism and Thirsty work together before. Chism blocked everyone out, focusing on the upcoming match.

"Fight!" said Lieutenant Serrill.

Thirsty purred.

Chism smiled.

His three opponents tried to form a triangle around Chism, so he charged and slipped around behind Mave, using him as a shield from the other two. The giant and Muehner wasted time regrouping, and Chism tested Mave's skill.

Not impressive, for an Elite. Chism parried a clumsy strike, got past Mave's guard, and landed a blow to the groin that was hard enough to send Mave to the ground.

"Cheap shot!" shouted one of the Elites.

"In a three-on-one fight?" Ander yelled back. "No such thing!"

"Just stay away from the head," said Lieutenant Serrill.

He didn't need to say it. Strikes to the head were always illegal in sparring and led to automatic disqualification.

The other two continued to spread out, attempting to take positions at Chism's front and back. Chism engaged each briefly, always circling to keep one of them between him and the other.

Gorman was a great shield—slow enough in his footwork that Chism circled him at will. But the air hummed like an angry beehive when Gorman swung his sword. One wrong blow would easily crack Chism's skull or break a bone. Chism focused his attack on Gorman's solid midsection, attempting to take the giant's wind away while he accumulated points, but he had trouble getting close enough to land anything significant. Not only did he have to maintain a safe distance from the huge sword, but he had to constantly circle Gorman to keep Muehner away.

Chism began circling to Gorman's left again, then spun and came around his right side, swinging Thirsty at shoulder level. Gorman got his sword up to block, but his feet tangled and he began to tip. With a kick to the back of the knee, Chism helped Gorman to the ground.

While the giant attempted to get his hands underneath himself to push up, Chism laid Thirsty against his throat. Gorman let his sword fall and held his hands out to his side.

That left Muehner, the one most motivated to beat Chism. Without giving Chism time to recover from beating Gorman, Muehner lunged forward, striking once from the left, then immediately from the right. His sword flicked as quick as a whip. Chism parried both blows. To finish the combination, Muehner thrust straight for Chism's chest. By instinct, Chism deflected it, but Muehner's blade slid across his forearm as he stepped back. Without the wrap, it would have sliced through skin.

The former sub-lieu was obviously the best swordsman of the trio. However, Chism now only had to focus on one man. He put Muehner on the defensive with a combination twice as long as Muehner's had been. Only one of his blows landed—a glancing shoulder strike. Chism took half a step back and to the side as if the short offensive was finished but the moment Muehner relaxed, Chism spun and came at him again.

The first swing caught Muehner across his lower back. Without the shroudbark it might have been a paralyzing blow. While Muehner was still squaring himself, Chism brought Thirsty down hard on his thigh.

Instead of blocking, as Chism expected, Muehner swung two-handed. Chism ducked under the sword and brought Thirsty up to slice across the larger man's armpit. As Chism retreated he jabbed Muehner in the ribs.

As they faced each other momentarily, sizing each other up, Chism felt a happy tingle in every part of his body. It felt like a smile, but had nothing to do with his face. Months had passed since Chism's last good fight. Maybe longer. As enjoyable as his morning routines with Thirsty were, he lived for the duel. It was more satisfying than bread and sweeter than pure honey.

Muehner didn't seem to be having as much fun. No smile showed on his face, and his heavy breaths came through clenched teeth. While he and Chism were still separated, Muehner worked his sword arm in a slow ark, getting it ready to fight, but he didn't rub or touch any of soon-to-be bruised parts. Chism knew how hard he'd struck. For days, Muehner would feel the injuries, but he wouldn't let them affect the fight. Muehner was an Elite; Chism didn't expect anything less.

They came at each other again. It took all of Chism's concentration, but he was able to give and not receive blow after blow and touch after touch.

Twice more they disentangled to face each other, take a breath, re-engage. Muehner was fast and imaginative, but Chism was more of both. As the fight went on without Muehner gaining any points, he became more desperate to score, thereby leaving himself open, but Chism waited for the perfect time to make a kill strike.

When they separated again, Muehner stepped back an extra step, breathing heavy. Chism held his ground, and watched. Something about Muehner's posture wasn't right. It wasn't relaxed enough. If Muehner truly was out of breath—

There! Muehner sprung. Chism spun without thinking and brought Thirsty down hard across Muehner's back.

The older Elite had expected to meet resistance, but Chism was in a new line of attack while Muehner was in an empty one and he sprawled to the ground. Chism was on him as tight as a shadow, and brought Thirsty down toward Muehner's face, which was looking back over his shoulder.

Only through sheer will of Chism in opposition to that of his sword, Thirsty came to a stop a blade's width from Muehner's nose.

"Enough!" shouted Lieutenant Serrill. It had to be obvious that Muehner was getting desperate and one of them was likely to get seriously injured. Since the first combination when Muehner had landed a mock slice of Chism's arm, his sword hadn't touched Chism. By Chism's count, he had landed twenty-two.

A nice even number. A good place to stop.

Chism pulled Thirsty away from Muehner's face, took a few steps back and began untying the knots that held the shroudbark in place.

No tapping or snapping came from the rest of the squadron—only the stark clink of lost coins falling into the hand of a new owner. Ander had done very well. But it sounded like there were two separate jangles happening. Chism looked up to see who else had been crazy enough to bet on him and saw an Elite he didn't know drop some coins into Lieutenant Serrill's hand.

"Like Chism always tells me," Ander explained, "it's a sword fight, not a size fight."

While the coins clinked, Chism considered offering Muehner a hand up, but that would require touching him. Chism never touched anyone; it was nothing against his squadmate. Instead, he finished unwrapping Thirsty.

"Change of plans," said Lieutenant Serrill, stepping forward. "I'm adding Chism to the reconnaissance mission tomorrow."

Rubbing his collarbone as he stood, Muehner said, "It'll be a year before he has enough beard to pass as a Domainer."

Chism doubted a year would be enough. The rest of the squadron hadn't used razors for months in preparation to infiltrate the Western Domain. They had cultivated some impressive facial hair. Chism hadn't used a razor since ever.

"Shave Mave's beard and glue it to him," suggested Gorman, earning some laughs.

"No fake beard necessary," said Lieutenant Serrill. "He'll be invisible."

Wot, the oldest in the squadron, said, "So that's how he became the Red Knight? Magical powers?"

Perfect, thought Chism. *More Red Knight nonsense.* His reputation had spread to the far corners of Wonderland after all. He ignored the talk and examined Thirsty's edge for damage.

"Chism will walk behind the wagon," said Lieutenant Serrill. "Those backwards barbarians make children walk while the men ride."

"Chism the child," said one of the Elites.

The other Elites chuckled, but Chism kept his eyes on Thirsty's edge and ran his pinched fingers carefully along the cool blade. He had always preferred Chism the challenger. Unlike Chism and Muehner who both breathed heavy trying to catch their breath, Thirsty was ready for more. In their years together Chism had never known his friend to grow tired, hesitant, hungry or sore. Thirsty was not only the perfect friend, but the perfect soldier.

Out of the corner of his eye, he saw Lieutenant Serrill shrug. "If the barbarians want to ignore or underestimate Chism, we'll shove it in their filthy faces." With an almost hidden grin he added, "Like he and his Fellow just did to all of you."

"Why bring him at all?" snapped Muehner, who was even more tempestuous after being drubbed. "You've said a hundred times there won't be any fighting."

"No, there won't be. But if there is, which there won't be, I'd be a fool to leave behind a soldier who can soundly beat three Elites. Even though there will be no fighting."

"No disrespect to the new sub-lieu," said Alendro, a senior Elite who Chism recognized, "but we've all heard how rash he can be."

Even if Chism was in a talking mood, he wouldn't argue with that. Anyone who knew his history would be crazy to bring him on the mission. But Chism felt as if he'd changed in ways he couldn't put his finger on. There hadn't been any situations to prove he *wasn't* the same hotheaded kid who put a sword to Duke Jaryn's throat—twice—but Chism felt more in control than ever. Maybe Hatta had broken that impetuous part of him when he'd fixed the kingdoms. It might be a healthy improvement, but Chism wondered if the potential loss of spunk would do harm or good in the long run.

He felt the lieutenant's eyes and looked up into them. They had shifted from grey to silver, and they were as penetrating as Thirsty. Maybe it was the fact that the lieutenant had bet on him. Maybe the lingering thrill from sparring was affecting him. Chism had the feeling that Lieutenant Serrill knew him better than Chism knew himself.

When Lieutenant Serrill broke the gaze, he said, "We don't need to worry about Chism."

Muehner wasn't convinced. "Four months we've been preparing. He just shows up and tags along?"

Chism didn't speak. There was no rush to prove anything. He was the youngest Knight and maybe the youngest sub-lieu in the history of the Elites. He hadn't asked for leadership or titles, so it didn't make sense to fight for them. Let the lieutenant decide. And fate. It was fate after all that had granted him time when he should have been dead on half a dozen occasions.

"Chism's coming," said Lieutenant Serrill. "Along with the six originally slated to go. Enjoy your last civilized night, men. Tomorrow we become barbarians."

2

If judging a man by the hair he grows on his chin was as petty as judging a woman by the fairness of her face, then the Western Domain revolved on a platform of pettiness. And by those standards, Chism was as worthless as a three-legged racehorse.

With only one night to prepare for the mission, Chism stayed up late by the firelight learning all he could from Wot about the Domain. Wot was even older than Ander and seemed to know something about everything. Somehow Chism managed to learn next to nothing.

By the time the Elites were three days into the Western Domain, he had learned very well what to expect as a boy along for a journey with a group of Domainer men. Or as the Maners called themselves: the Indomitable. None of the men would talk to Chism, so there hadn't been any overt lessons in barbarian culture. But the Elites always stayed in character, even when there were no Maners near, which meant pushing Chism around whenever they felt he wasn't acting enough like a peon. A single slip could derail the entire mission after all and forfeit their lives. Chism couldn't complain; they all needed as much practice acting like Maners as possible before reaching their goal—the largest city in the Domain.

The six Elites and one Fellow were either better actors than Chism expected or they took satisfaction in maltreating and ignoring him. With the exception of Chism, they had grown the six most impressive Scaled Tiger beards and were included in the mission for that reason alone.

The most frustrating part of the journey was being unable to do his morning routine with Thirsty. How would it look if someone witnessed the worthless boy performing perfect, complex sword routines? Thirsty hadn't even come along. Again, the sword just didn't fit his disguise as a worthless boy. Leaving his only true friend dozens of miles behind didn't make the journey any easier.

On the sixth day in the Western Domain, towers were the first part of the city that came into view. Phaylea, a capital of sorts, was surrounded by a crude timber wall that stretched a half mile in either direction. The thick logs were sharpened to a point at the top and buried at the bottom. A dry moat in front of the wall made it half again as tall. A few soldiers patrolled a walkway behind the tops of the timbers, showing only shoulders and bearded faces.

In front of the city gates was a roughly-milled drawbridge. Fatherless families loitered, holding out a forest of filthy hands to every crosser of the bridge. Women wore small metal rings and rods through their nostrils, eyebrows, all parts of the ear, and even their cheeks and lips. Many of them wore clothes made of feathers and haggard scales. Boys wearing old wool clung to their mothers' hips. Some looked as if they'd taken handfuls of dirty fleece and matted it to themselves.

A shirtless boy next to a gaunt, leathery woman looked up at Chism. The pitiful eyes could have belonged to his brother, Hatta, ten years earlier.

You're better off, thought Chism, *with a mother who can't provide than we were with a father who could provide only cruelty.*

Chism and Hatta had no business surviving childhood. If not

for the townspeople of T'lai, they would have starved. As much as he wanted to help the beggar boy, there was nothing Chism could do, and it wasn't right to spend his fate-granted time feeling sorry about things he couldn't change.

Chism looked away from the pleading eyes that reflected a lifetime of suffering, distracting himself with the release mechanism of the bridge. Under an assault, one rope could be cut to send the bridge crashing into the dry moat below, preventing would-be attackers from gaining easy access. The fall wasn't far, but the collapsing timbers would easily crush the bones of anyone unlucky enough to be on the bridge at the time—soldier, horse, barbarian, or beggar.

Eventually the bridge and its crowd of mendicants ended as the disguised Elites passed through the wall into the city. Phaylea's streets were packed dirt passages between huts and patched-together shops. Here a corral of sheep. There a shack barely big enough for a woman to sell decorated walking sticks. Next to her, a baker.

The aroma from the baker was overpowered by much worse smells. Puddles of sewage were mostly restricted to the narrower passages that were basically alleys, but the odor permeated everything.

Muehner stood in the wagon, holding a plain, darkish flag. Red, Chism had been told, and the symbol of tribute for the war effort. With the longest beard, Muehner had to play the part of leader.

Not far from Chism, a shaved-headed man in a tanner shop raised a small cane and yelled, "Hee!"

Chism reached for Thirsty without thinking and felt only the handle of his belt knife.

Muehner wasn't startled. He raised the small flag and answered, "Hee!"

The man with the shaved head turned his attention to a scrawny man who was stretching a skin in the shop. He said something Chism couldn't hear and hit the smaller man across the back with his cane.

Chism was almost out of sight, but he strained his eyes to see the sufferer's feet. Sure enough, he was missing his big toes. A slave. The Domainers sold many of the slaves they took to faraway lands. The very unlucky ones had their toes cut off and were kept in the Domain. Even the orphans and widows on the bridge were better off than slaves.

"Hee," said a very old woman with cloudy eyes and a cloak made of feathers. More rings circled her ears than Chism had ever seen.

Muehner responded to her salute, as well as every other greeting offered by the Domainers. Lieutenant Serrill and the other Elites rode in silence, looking for all the world as if they'd seen such a rambling city every day of their lives. From crusty Wot, with grey streaks at his temples, to fresh-faced Mave, they looked every bit a group of men from a Maner outpost doing their patriotic duty.

The mission was all but assured.

The Elite spies wound down the curvy street for nearly a mile with Muehner maintaining the false display of public spirit. Somewhere near the center of the city, they reached the gathering ground and Chism finally saw some civilized buildings. Four stone silos, each wrapped with a wooden staircase. Sparse streams of men carried bags of what had to be grain to the top and emptied them into a chute, then wrapped the bags around a pole and slid to the ground.

A few wooden buildings surrounded the silos, all with men and women busying themselves in and around them. A low fence separated the gathering grounds from the rest of the city. A short-bearded man stood with a leather-bound ledger at the entrance. The administrator was an anomaly in a city of barbarians.

"Name!" he asked, raising his voice over the clatter of a nearby smithy.

"I be Ririe. We come from north," said Muehner.

"What bring ye?"

"One bushel beans. Three bushel white wheat. One bushel barley. Dozen waterskin. Gross arrows."

The food in the cart could feed the city's widows and orphans for a month, but the Maners would store it all away for the war efforts.

Filthy barbarians. They were more like animals than men.

The man wrote as Muehner spoke, then turned to the last page of the ledger and moved his mouth as if making mental calculations. He reached into two separate pouches hanging from a strap on his neck and handed over about a dozen small metal chits.

Muehner grunted appreciatively and tucked them into his own pouch. Chism didn't know much about chits since there hadn't been any opportunity to ask questions as they traveled. From what he'd seen, the more important a Maner was, the more chits he wore in his beard.

In a dismissive voice, the man said, "Skins and arrows to building with black roof. Beans to cellar behind building. Wheat in second tower, barley in third. For next three months, bounty chits for cookpots, boot leather, honestones, catgut and barrow raths." The recorder had probably done this a hundred times today. He turned to the next man in line but didn't look up at him.

Muehner signaled, and Wot urged the horses forward. The first structure they passed was nothing more than a beamed roof supported by pillars at the corners. A bevy of blacksmiths hammered, quenched, poured, and stoked. Three forges, eight anvils, and mounds of raw materials were all being put to work, priming the Domain for the next invasion.

As he walked behind the wagon, Chism did calculations in his head. A blacksmith with helpers could turn out at least five axe heads in a day. The hafts could be produced ten times as fast. The finished weapons wouldn't be anything fancy, but good enough for an invasion force. That meant that the smithy he'd just passed was turning out twenty-five weapons every day, and that was only one workshop out of who knew how many. In addition to weapons, every other Maner throughout the Domain worked their individual manner of war preparations.

In another building, men and women twisted flax into bowstrings. In an open workshop, coopers pounded staves into metal jigs to make barrels. The giant war-making machine echoed through the city.

How could Wonderland hope to stand against a civilization that was nothing more than an invasion factory? Nothing in Wonderland came close to the Domainer efforts. Hopefully Scaled Tiger's reconnaissance mission could change that, once they returned to Palassiren to report.

Wot pulled the horses and wagon to a stop in front of the black-roofed building. Without speaking, Muehner motioned to Wot and Chism. Wot hopped down from the wagon bed, then reached back over the side and pulled a dozen waterskins, bound by coarse twine, onto his shoulder.

Chism had to climb onto the loading board at the back of the wagon in order to reach in. He laid his walking stick across the sacks of grain. The arrows were tied into four bundles. He swung two onto each shoulder and jumped down from the wagon. The weight pulled him off balance, and he fell onto his backside. The nearby Domainers laughed. So did his squad, except for Mave, who jumped down from the wagon and took a step toward Chism.

"Aylen," barked Muehner, and pointed at the bed of the wagon where Mave had been riding. "He'll sprout no hair if ye treat him like babe."

Mave flushed and climbed back into the wagon.

Mave's Fellow, Kilven, gave Muehner a dirty look for chastising his Elite, but kept his thoughts to himself.

Chism climbed to his feet in silence and kept his head down as he walked into the warehouse. The wagon rolled on.

Another clerk of some sort sliced through the twine of one bundle, sending thirty-six arrows clattering to the ground. He picked one up, tested the tip, and flexed the shaft until Chism wondered if it would break. It was Domain made, as were all the contents of the wagon.

The arrow held up under the scrutiny. The clerk picked up another one and inspected it as well. Mave had suggested sabotaging the arrows and poisoning the food or filling the sacks with weevils. Lieutenant Serrill had refused, unwilling to put the mission in jeopardy over something so petty. Mave agreed with the decision after he took a moment to think it through.

The second arrow was as sound as the first, and the third as sound as the second.

"How many arrows?" the clerk asked Wot, even though Chism had carried them.

"Gross," said Wot.

"Put arrows there, with others." The clerk pointed with his beard toward the wall on the far side of the huge warehouse. He moved back to his table and picked up a porcupine-quill pen.

Chism scraped the unbound arrows into a stack and wrapped them up in his arms. As the clerk talked to Wot, Chism headed down the aisle he'd indicated. It was lined with ladders along the left side. Scaling ladders, most of which tested the height of the store, were stacked by the hundreds. The depth of the stack made it impossible to know exactly how many hundreds, even with Chism's knack for counting. Chism counted thirty-one rows of ladders. Even at only twenty ladders in each row, that was six hundred twenty. Enough for most armies, but the target-line painted a few feet out from the ladders on the floor told a different story.

When all the essential supplies reached their target line—war.

Across from the ladders, torches were stacked, though not as high. Seven hundred forty-one visible, with three times that many behind. The torches were mere inches away from the target line. A few days more would fill that quota.

Spades next, perhaps seven-tenths there. Cookpots next to the spades, not even close to the halfway point. That must have been what the first recorder meant about bonus chits for certain items, including cookpots.

As Chism passed each commodity, he made a mental note of its progress. Only tent stakes were all the way to the target. None were as deficient as the cookpots had been. But as supplies reached their target lines, the invasion-factory would direct resources toward those still lacking.

Along the far wall, he passed weapons of all sorts: axes, maces, sheathed swords, polearms, bows, bowstrings … and arrows. Some in quivers, others tied with twine or rope, some stacked like firewood. Chism's contribution made no measurable difference. Forty-one thousand, he estimated. Instead of retracing his steps, Chism continued along the aisle. Vicious-looking crossbow bolts, followed by towers of crossbows.

Catapult parts were piled next. Winches and winch pins, skeins and slip hooks. Opposite those were thousands of bandage cloths, battle insignia, boot soles, spools of thick thread, and needles. It was the most impressive stockpile Chism had ever seen, a quartermaster's fantasy. He had to focus to keep from gawking.

In front of stacked wagon wheels, Chism stopped for an accurate count. It might give an indication of how many troops to expect. Thirty-four stacks of twenty-nine each equaled—

"Vaylee's beard!" a booming voice announced. "They've turned my stores into nursery!" A huge man with angry eyes and seven beard chits walked up the aisle. His thick eyebrows continued unbroken from one side of his forehead to the other, like a giant black caterpillar that might crawl off his face at any moment.

Chism didn't know what to say. He thought of taking the man by surprise and hiding the body. There was a good chance it wouldn't be found until the Elites were safely away. But Chism didn't think he was doing anything wrong. Better to wait and find out what the Eyebrow had planned before doing anything that would draw more attention.

Calloused fingers scraped across Chism's chin. Chism took a small step backward to keep from lashing out at the man's touch.

"I do not feel whiskers. Do you?" He had a drawn out way of talking.

Before Chism could reach his own hand up to his chin, he saw the man's frying-pan hand coming toward him. He could have ducked. He could have blocked. He could have drawn his knife.

Chism gritted his teeth and took the blow. His head swam into darkness and back, but the smack was easier to take than the touch had been. It was the kind of physical contact he was used to.

"Go find yer mom-may and stop skulking in my stores, stu-pid boy."

Chism took a slow step past the Maner, still gaining his balance, and was helped along by the man's boot.

"Come back when ye have chits—and beard to put them in!"

His foggy mind made the next few steps difficult, but Chism took in as much of the warehouse as possible while he hurried out.

Wot was waiting outside and barely glanced at Chism, who did his best to imitate a Domain boy trying to become invisible in the longshadows. Chism's faced throbbed, but he tried to ignore the pain by rehearsing the numbers he'd picked up in the warehouse.

The rest of the squadron arrived with an empty wagon. Wot climbed in and tossed the walking stick onto the ground. Chism grabbed it, and then took up his spot alongside the rear wheel. They rode away from the city center minus supplies and flag-waving, and plus one black eye and bruised bottom.

The outer walls came into view, men still patrolling and the beggars carrying on. Horses, wagons, and people moved in both directions through the gates, anxious to be on the desired side of the city walls when darkness fell and the gates closed.

The Elites' wagon passed through without incident, casting a tall shadow onto an even larger crowd sprawled along the bridge than when they had entered the city. Fifty-eight people, including the infants bundled onto mothers' backs. Every child old enough to stand presented their palms, waiting for alms. In trying to find a path that didn't require touching anyone, Chism fell further behind the wagon. He kept one eye on the Elites and one on the people closing in around him. At least the distractions kept him from noticing many of the individual beggars.

Wheels creaked along the timbers of the bridge. Most of the Elites ignored the urchins with the same airs with which they ignored Chism. The tiniest kid, a boy covered in dirt, was trying to say something but his words were one long chain of stutters.

A bigger boy next to him mocked him saying, "D-d-d-d-d-d-d."

From his position at the rear of the wagon, Mave pulled out a coin and tossed it in front of the stuttering kid.

No matter how pitiful the boy was, it was a stupid move by Mave, however harmless. A coin would feed the boy for a day, but what about the rest of his life?

The bigger kid was quicker. He butted the tiny beggar out of the way and pulled copper from between two of the massive slats which composed the walkway. After wiping it on his own filthy trousers, which probably just made the coin dirtier, the boy scowled at it.

"Mommay," he demanded. "Is this a money?"

A flat-faced woman with a baby bundled on her back and another on the front tore the coin away from the boy and said, "For love of Vaylee!" She hurried to one of the gate guards with the coin outstretched. "Filthy Wonderlandercoin."

Trouble was coming for sure. Chism searched the area for defensible positions and escape routes. The archers on the wall would be the biggest problem, but he could scale the wall and dispose of them. At close range, their bows were as useful as a bow in a girl's hair—merely decorative. Chism wouldn't survive in the long run, but it might give the other six a chance to escape.

"Halt!" shouted the guard, a young man with only a bit of chin and cheek scruff. His tunic looked like coyote skins, but it was old and mangy. A carved stone hung from his neck, similar to ones he'd seen on officials at the gathering grounds.

By the time Muehner looked back at the guard, Lieutenant Serrill had scanned the crowd of beggars, guards, wall with archers, and path in front of the wagon. He gave Muehner a nod only perceptible because Chism was watching closely. Muehner reined the horses then stood. The wagon was still on the bridge, but all four horses stood on the solid ground on the far side of the bridge.

"Talking to me, chitless toad?" yelled Muehner.

The guard unconsciously rubbed his thin scruff and took a small step forward, barely meeting Muehner's eyes.

"Woman says your man gave her this." He pitched the coin.

Muehner snatched the coin from the air and looked at both sides. Traffic on the bridge plugged as beggars and others gathered at the commotion. People pressed on Chism from every side, touching him with shoulders and legs. He moved back, away from the wagon, to where there was space to breathe and to be. He didn't stop until his back touched the city wall. Only a few in the crowd wore the stone that was the closest the Maners came to a uniform for soldiers, but the group had taken on the feel of a mob, ready to erupt.

In the front of the wagon, Muehner spat on the coin and hurled it into the dry moat. He stepped over the back rest of his seat, into the bed of the wagon, and loomed over Mave like a thunderstorm.

"Where did ye get filthy coin?" Spittle flew from his mouth, some of it catching on his beard.

Mave didn't shrink as Chism expected. His chin came forward. Mave's vanity would let him take the punishment that was coming. "I just—"

Muehner backhanded Mave as hard as Chism had been hit by the Eyebrow then glared at Mave, who rubbed his clenched jaw.

Kilven, Mave's Fellow, stared daggers at Muehner, but the scene was too tense for anyone to pick up on the Elites' dynamics.

"Thank ye for alerting me," said Muehner to the guard. "Him

and me'll have words later." He motioned Lieutenant Serrill to nudge the horses.

"I can not let ye go," shouted the guard over the noise of the crowd.

Chism didn't know what the issue with the coin was, but it had to be important for the young guard to challenge Muehner.

The crowd filled the bridge, and curious people from the city approached through the gates. This far into the Western Domain, the people probably hadn't seen real fighting for quite some time. They appeared hungry for it.

Bare-chinned and swordless, Chism stood at the corner of the bridge, looking over a wall of his enemies' backs, only able to see his squadron because of their elevated position. One hand rested on the hilt of his small belt knife. The other held the walking stick, which was a poor substitute for Thirsty.

Muehner leveled a wicked look at the guard and asked, "Do ye see this?" He pinched a gold chit at the bottom of his beard.

"Aye," said the guard.

"And this?" A silver chit this time, but larger than the gold one. As if it settled everything, Muehner said, "Chits and beard and ne'er afeared."

"Still, your man broke law."

Muehner jumped down from the wagon and a ripple coursed through the crowd as he pushed toward the guard, shouting, "Question is, can ye make me stay?"

Chism couldn't see either of them, but their words rang through the crowd.

"Panjandrum will have my beard if ye leave." A gulp was implied in the tone of his voice.

Chism had no idea what a panjandrum was, but it was obvious that the situation was going to get worse before it got better.

Muehner shouted, "I'll have your beard if you delay us! Fields and animals waiting for us. Warm beds and warm women three days nigh. Ye'll pay in skin if ye make it four."

Chuckles flowed through the crowd, but somehow the guard resisted Muehner's barrage. "Talk to panjandrum in morning, then on your way."

Relative silence came from the site of the confrontation. Chism glanced around for something to stand on, but he saw only the release mechanism to collapse the bridge in case of an assault on the city.

Simple. One cut rope would drop the bridge into the dry moat. It would plunge the area into chaos, take the attention off his squadron, and make escape possible. Muehner might not survive, but some of the Elites could sneak away and carry reports back to Wonderland. It was the only move that made sense under the circumstances.

It would likely kill a dozen children and maim two more dozens.

But Chism couldn't see any other hope for his men to escape. Already, hundreds of potential soldiers stood ready, and that number could swell to thousands. Six men against thousands was impossible, even for Elites.

Seven, thought Chism, drawing his knife. *Seven against thousands.*

3

On the wagon, the Elites were standing, swords and cudgels held, but not raised. Indistinct murmurs rose from the crowd.

If someone doesn't do something soon, somebody else will, thought Chism. *Better to be the one who acts.*

Taking out the bridge was still the obvious option—the only one that gave the mission any sort of chance.

And take away what little chance any of those beggars ever had in life.

From day one of his life, Chism had been a kid who never had a chance. Even if it meant the worst outcome for the Elites, he couldn't take everything away from the kids on the bridge.

Other options.

With his walking stick, he could incapacitate eight or ten Domainers before they even fought back, but where to start? The woman to his right? Her ten-year-old son?

I hope someone has a better idea.

Apparently, Lieutenant Serrill did. He sheathed his sword, and the other Elites followed. Surrender. Of course. They could fight off forty, but a hundred times that number would take their place.

Still looking angry enough to fight four thousand, Muehner took his spot on the wagon. Someone on the ground turned the wagon back toward the gates. A bridge full of gawkers made it a slow process.

With Lieutenant Serrill captured, Chism had command of Scaled Tiger Squadron. All of the options belonged to him and him alone. There was no room for confidence, fear, or anything else—only for action.

He could slip away, go back a hundred miles, locate the other nine Elites in Scaled Tiger Squadron, and attempt a rescue. Of course, anything could happen to a boy without a beard traveling alone in the Domain. And even if the six Elites in Phaylea were alive when he returned in a week, what would he do? Storm the biggest city in the Domain with ten Elites, seven of which were Fellows? A suicide mission wouldn't save anyone.

The odds of the panjandrum letting them off were worse than slim. Muehner had a good accent, but the rest of the group was fair to poor. One short interview with each man would convince anyone that they were not Maners. Even without considering the accents, there was too much ignorance in the group for the panjandrum to miss.

As invisible as the beggar children, Chism trailed after the captives.

A kid in front of Chism asked an older brother, "They going to Pit?" He sounded hopeful.

"Not until panjandrum judges."

A grey-haired lady added, "Is probably nothing. Misunderstanding. They'll be on way home tomorrow morn."

"No," said the first kid. "Pit!"

"I seen them when they keem in," bragged the older boy.

Chism slipped through the crowd to avoid being recognized. Most of the accents were mild enough that he understood what was said. He continued to overlisten to as many opinions as possible.

Everything from a year in the Pit to getting off with the guard's beard as an apology. No one guessed the truth.

But Chism knew. With the exception of Muehner's minimal interactions, the mission shouldn't have required speaking or passing any scrutiny other than visual. The only possible solution was to spring them in the next twelve hours before they went to the panjandrum.

The building to which they led the Elites wasn't far. The city wall served as the back wall of the prison; the other walls were stone and mortar. The building was one story, long and narrow, with a torch burning on each corner. Buildings in the area had roofs of pitched thatch, wood shingles, and even mud and fronds. But the ceiling of the jail was constructed of timbers as solid and seamlessly fitted as the city wall.

Some children snuck into the jail but were shoed out within seconds, suffering smacks on the ears or kicks in the behind for their attempts. Chism, thankful for the wool he wore and his whiskerless chin, watched for another hour. The building had a few windows, but they were too high to see into and too narrow to crawl through. A few men went in and came out, but Chism couldn't make sense of their purpose. A guard at the top of the city wall walked past every six or seven minutes.

Night forced the crowd to disperse. A jailed Domainer sang songs in an accent as thick as the jail walls. Chism only understood one word in five.

Jailbreak and escape were impossible without supplies. Muehner and Lieutenant Serrill carried Maner money in their pouches, but that did Chism no good. Bread or weapons he could steal anywhere, but to procure what he needed, he knew only one place to go.

The main road was lit by irregularly placed torches. People of all ages walked in both directions, but Chism was the only kid who walked alone. Each woman who passed asked a hundred questions with her eyes. Chism kept his head down and walked as if he had somewhere to go. If he wasn't careful one of the women would try to bundle him up like the babies they carried and take him home for a hot dinner and a blanket on the floor. It was the first time he'd seen any form of tenderness from a Domainer.

Luckily, no one spoke to him. When the supply compound came into view, he took a side street, then slipped down alleys that led him closer to the low fence. The half-moon gave more light than he wanted. A cloudy, moonless night would have held enough light for his eyes and obscured him from countless others. Near the fence, he stood in the shadow of a dark mud building and watched.

No motion anywhere. The same for sound. And eyes, as far as he could tell, except his own.

A cloud encroached on the moon, and Chism crept forward. The wooden fence was taller than Chism, but the crossbeams made for easy climbing. He paused in the shadows on the other side of the fence. Still no motion or sound.

He'd circled far enough around from the entrance that the warehouse where he'd deposited the arrows was straight in front of him. Fifty paces of meadow separated him from the back wall. The autumn grass was brittle, and to Chism, every footstep sounded as loud as the blacksmith hammers from earlier.

Slow footsteps, sliding feet into the grass instead of crunching on top of it, carried him to the warehouse. He slipped around to the darker side of the building, watching for a way in. Around the first corner, he lucked upon a side door and tried it. Unlocked.

A flood of moonlight filled the room when Chism pushed open the creaky door. The man who'd hit him in the warehouse, the Eyebrow, shot up in his bed.

After half a moment the Eyebrow said, *"You."* He threw his blanket aside.

In two steps, Chism closed the distance and opened the man's forehead with his walking staff. The huge caterpillar on his forehead was the first part of the Maner to hit the wooden floor. The chits in his beard clinked as they slapped along side. Blood trickled into a small pool, but not enough to bleed him dead. Chism could solve that. He pulled the knife from his belt, bent down, and put it to the Eyebrow's throat. Mave, at least, would be glad for a little destruction in their wake.

Perfect. I'm thinking like Mave now.

If for no other reason than to avoid acting like the greenhorn, Chism let the quartermaster live and tiptoed further into the room. Another door, with hinges as creaky as the first, led into the warehouse. Almost none of the light from the moon reached the huge storage room. Anyone else would be entirely nightblind. For whatever reason, while he couldn't see colors, Chism had night vision like a bat.

Chism wandered two aisles until getting his bearings. If he remembered correctly, ropes, twines and cords were just down ... yes. He wasn't picky. The first two lengths of cord strong enough to hold a man's weight went around his shoulder.

He backtracked to the quartermaster, trussed him like a hog, tore a strip from the blanket to gag him.

With the rest of his stolen rope over one shoulder and his staff leaning on the other, Chism closed both doors and walked quickly into the moonlight. At any moment, lights and alarms could call a torrent of willing soldiers. Step by step, he hoped for some background noise to cover his paces.

Noise didn't happen, but neither did discovery. Over the fence he climbed, then crouched in the shadows and considered: side streets or main road? His knowledge of the Domain was too limited to predict how people would react to a boy who appeared short of his teen years carrying a rope *and* a walking stick in the middle of the night. The fewer people he saw, the less chance of another slap across the face, kick in the backside, or worse. He started down the crooked streets, using the moon as a compass. It hung dangerously low. If he couldn't get his men out of Phaylea by sunrise, there was no point in trying.

Every street Chism walked was dark. If light shone ahead, he turned to another path. Many of them couldn't even be called streets, just alleys and passages, some so narrow he had to turn sideways.

And the moon continued to sink.

At one intersection, not only light but also music came from a doorway ahead. Chism turned left and stepped into a pair of short-bearded men—dregs of the lowest standing.

"What's this?" asked one of them, latching onto the rope.

"Rope," said the other, a fat, scruffy man with dull eyes. "We can't buy nee a swallow burnwater with rope."

"Vaylee's beard, I knows that." As he turned his head to look at the other man, Chism dropped him with one knee to the crotch then another to the face.

"Hey," protested his friend, raising fists the size of small buckets.

Chism ducked under the slowest haymaker ever. He spun for momentum and slammed his staff, one-handed, into the man's temple. The ground shook when the man fell at Chism's feet.

Only half of the half-moon showed over buildings to the west. Chism avoided any more run-ins and made it back to the city wall and the jail. The singer continued to croon, and Chism realized that madness, not drunkenness, must be to blame. If it was the other way around, the prisoner would have fallen asleep long since. Chism hurried to the side of the jail furthest from the front gates and dropped the rope into a puddle of shadow next to the city wall.

With nothing more than the staff and belt knife, Chism strolled into the jail, his eyes as wide as a young girl's at a Sixteenery. The setup was simple—barred cells along one side and a corridor along the front. A small desk was crammed into a corner that would have been a cell had it been barred. Two guards, one with his head down on the desk and one pacing in front of the cells. The Elites' weapons lay in a heap by the door.

"What's this?" asked the standing guard from halfway down the corridor. A scrawny, balding prisoner in the first cell stopped singing and staggered up to the bars.

The other guard's head shot up. His eyes bleared puffy and red. "Thought I told you cretins! Don't be as gentle with this one, Reyal."

The guard who had been pacing, Reyal, came toward Chism, slapping his palm with a cudgel and smiling cruelly. Chism backed toward the desk, doing his best to shrink. His walking stick wasn't as sturdy as the guard's club, but its length did the trick when Reyal got close enough. Knee, gut, face and Reyal wasn't smiling any more.

"Hee! Breaking jail! Hee!" It didn't come from either of the guards. The mad singer was using his voice again.

The guard stood behind the desk with his hands raised in a calming gesture.

"Oh help! Hee! Hee! Hee!"

"Shut yourself!" shouted Chism at the prisoner. He pulled his belt knife and raised it.

"Citizens! Soldiers! Indomitable!" His voice grew shriller. "Aymatungula! Arms! To arms!"

Chism's knife flew, and the man fell. A lingering squeal reverberated through the small jail. The plan hadn't involved killing anyone, but there was no time to mourn over it.

The guard behind the desk paled and reached slowly for the keys, which sat in a puddle of drool. Chism motioned him toward the cells, and the man obeyed. Still no sounds of alarm from outside.

A pair of hands waited outside the fourth cell and accepted the keys from the terrified guard. In moments, the Elites were out and the guard was in, bound and gagged with strips of his own sheepskin. The injured guard and one other prisoner were given the same treatment, each in their own cell.

Five Elites and a Fellow grabbed their weapons and lined up at the door in a matter of seconds. Chism motioned for them to wait.

He walked into the street as if he hadn't just killed a man and broken six others out of jail.

The night was empty. Just like Mave's head had been at the bridge.

With a wave, Chism summoned the Elites and led them toward the dark corner on the far side of the jail.

"Boost me up," he told Lieutenant Serrill.

At the lieutenant's signal, Muehner and Gorman cupped their hands under Chism's feet.

"Strong work," whispered Muehner, then he and Gorman tossed Chism upwards. Chism caught the walkway with his elbows and heaved himself up.

He sat and waited. One minute. Another.

A guard finally appeared. When he noticed Chism, he put a hand on his axe haft and walked forward.

"What are ye doing here, pigboy?"

As usual, being underestimated was annoying, but useful.

"I'm lost."

"Lost? Vaylee's beard. I'll show ye to poke around where ye don't belong." He grabbed Chism by the collar and began to turn back the way he'd come.

With a sweep of the ankle and a shove, Chism sent him down. The sound of his body hitting dirt replaced his surprised grunt, and Chism heard nothing more.

Gorman heaved the rope upward, and it reached Chism on the first attempt. He secured it to a pointed wall timber, and it immediately went taut.

Chism looked up and down the rampart. No sign of approaching guards. There shouldn't be for at least six minutes. He peeked down and saw Muehner halfway up the rope. Wot had just started climbing. Lieutenant Serrill was at the base of the rope, directing the others.

Mave stood at the back of the short line. He kicked at the dirt and looked over one shoulder, then the other. Perhaps he heard a noise, perhaps he just grew antsy, but Mave turned and walked to the street side of the jail.

Muehner pulled himself onto the walkway.

After checking both directions, Mave disappeared around the corner and reappeared carrying a torch.

No, Mave. Don't do it! Chism thought. He snapped his fingers, trying to get Mave's attention but they were too far apart. Yelling would be just as bad as whatever horrible idea Mave hadn't stopped to consider.

Serrill had noticed the flickering light and stepped to grab Mave, but he was too slow. As Wot came over the lip onto the walkway, Mave flung the torch end over end. It settled onto the roof of the hut across the street. Pitch and thatch flared, casting light like a sunrise onto Chism and everything else.

Gorman made it to the walkway just as the first alarm sounded. A single, shrill whistle that traveled a hundred miles through the empty night. The night didn't stay empty long.

Men and women swarming out of buildings like hornets. Whistles joining and amplifying the first; shouts and orders reverberating through the city. Light, blinding and hot. Kilven, joining the others on the wall.

Mave was on the rope; so was Serrill, bringing up the rear. Chism couldn't throw the rope over the outer wall until they were all up. Ten paces was too far to jump down and still hope to be able to run.

With the commotion on the ground, no one had noticed the Elites. The first Maners to the scene didn't seem to care about the fire. They surrounded the structures on either side of the burning building.

Mave pulled himself over the lip. One more to go.

The wooden building to the west of the fire collapsed all at once, even though the fire hadn't touched it. Maners with buckets of water arrived moments later. They poured them not on the fiery building, but on the rubble. Their only goal was to keep the fire from becoming a conflagration.

Lieutenant Serrill joined the rest of Scaled Tiger Squadron and Wot hauled in the rope.

The building to the north of the fire folded, and the focus of the churning anthill turned to other nearby structures. No attention was given to the fire, only to stopping its spread.

Just as Wot found the end of the rope, guards arrived on both sides of the catwalk. Wot threw the rope over the wall and gave Kilven a small push. The Fellow hurried over the wall.

"Hee! Wall breach!" yelled someone from the city below.

Ladders were pulled from buildings one or two removed from the fire and slammed against the walkway. Chism ran to the first ladder and shoved it back into the street, climbers and all. A guard ran to him along the walkway, but Chism was prepared. With two blows from his staff, he sent the man groundward.

Another guard followed and went down on the walkway instead of into the city. Another. And another. Fire filled Chism, crackling and fierce. Each time a partner in the dance went down, another one came forward to meet Chism's smiling face. Thrown objects, hard as rocks, bounced off without denting his concentration. Maybe they were rocks. Chism couldn't spare the attention it would require to check. The narrow walkway made the dance challenging, and therefore that much more enjoyable. A roaring fire and a roaring crowd were the perfect accompaniment.

Happiness, which usually eluded Chism entirely, had arrived in bulk. Chism wanted it to never end.

Chism looked up for his next dance partner, but the guards held back. Arrows nocked to bows stared at Chism. Maners had overrun Gorman and Wot, holding them at sword point. Archers approached on their side as well.

The lieutenant and Muehner were still pushing ladders away from the walkway. Mave had his hands over the wall, on the rope, ready to follow his Fellow down. Some archers aimed at the Elites while others leaned over the wall and fired. Kilven was down there. Mave screamed and reached down into the empty air.

If Chism rushed the archers on this side and Gorman and Wot surged against the Maners on their side ... they would all die, and the squadron would be no better off.

Lieutenant Serrill held a ladder, but didn't push it over. He slowly let it fall back against the walkway. With a two-handed gesture, he called down the squadron.

Chism ground his palms around his staff. He'd never been in full-scale battle, and he still felt like he could take on every Maner in the city. By his count, he'd already beaten nineteen of them, and had no desire to leave the count on such a prickly number.

Lieutenant Serrill must have known what Chism was thinking because he pointed directly at Chism and said, "Drop it."

Chism ground his teeth and let the staff fall.

Mave had left the rope and drawn his sword. He tried to push past Muehner and Lieutenant Serrill to get the archers who fired at his Fellow. The Elites restrained him and took his weapon. The city wall prevented Chism from looking down at Kilven. It didn't matter. Even if Mave's reaction hadn't told Chism everything he needed to know, the Maners had fired more arrows than Kilven could possibly have avoided.

The volley of rocks and debris from the ground ceased, and two more ladders appeared nearby. Something trickled down Chism's jaw line, and he wiped at it. Blood. A dull ache above his ear explained where it came from.

A pale-haired giant stepped forward through the ranks of archers and approached Chism. He was easily the largest man Chism had ever seen—as tall as the sky itself and wider than Gorman. His beard was twisted in a braid that hung like a giant tusk down to his gut. The sheer weight of metal in the Maner's beard was enough to account for his massive neck.

Sky Tusk came to Chism's mind instantly. *Skytusk.*

"This is boy ye could not kill?" The huge Maner's voice shook the timber walls like thunder. Skytusk turned to the men behind him, roared a laugh, and added, "Chits and beard and ne'er afeard."

It wouldn't be hard to send him down to the rooftop below and bring the total count up to an even twenty. Chism quickly realized the idea's foolishness. Better to leave impulsive thoughtlessness to Mave.

The nearest guard said, "If that is boy, then I am girl still strapped to mother's bosom." A couple of others grumbled angry support.

"Hmpf," said Skytusk, pulling a dirk as long as a short sword from its sheath. He lifted it to Chism's neck and said, "Last words, Boy?"

Last words? How could you sum up a life in one sentence? Chism's entire—short—Elite career was his last words. The Circle and the Sword was his life.

"Long live the Circle and the Sword!"

"Ha!" The man smiled and looked over his shoulder at his men. He bent over to bring himself face-to-face with Chism and said, "Booger on your SwordCircle, but you've got as much beard as any of us." The giant turned to the crowd below them in the streets. "Behold, manifest wonder. Boy is dead!"

In one motion Skytusk jabbed the dagger toward Chism. It slid between Chism's skin and shirt and arced down, slicing the shirt in a single motion. He did the same with the pale wool trousers and even Chism's unders.

Humiliation before execution. Something else Chism didn't know about the Domain. He turned his back to the wall and covered his front parts with his hands, ready for the next blow.

The fire simmered, ember-bright below in the ruins. The buildings around the fire had all been collapsed, and everyone in sight was looking up at the wall. The crazy Maners were cheering.

The giant shouted, "*Man* is born!" He turned to the guards behind him, and between them they came up with a pile of furs and leather. He shoved them into Chism's hand and said conversationally, "In lateryear ye'll have beard to match clothes." In a more commanding voice he ordered the Elites, "Rest of ye, down ladder.

If ye want to be ransomed, cooperate. If ye want to die like other one, resist."

The Elites filed down the ladder while Chism stared down at a goatskin tunic. Like the fire in the building, the fire inside him was mostly extinguished. Fighting was pointless. And he stood naked and unarmed on an enemy wall. In the end, he decided to do his best to make the clothes fit.

4

Before the sun appeared, the Elites were marched to a dirt field surrounded by a low patrolled wall deeper in the city. A row of twelve wooden platforms, each with its own trapdoor, stretched across the field in a single line. Some Maner guards opened the first trapdoor and dropped a ladder in. Lieutenant Serrill, who stood at the front of the Elites, looked down into the opening.

The giant commander, Skytusk, stood in front of him. "Welcome to Pit. Length of stay will depend on how soon ransom arrives."

Lieutenant Serrill glared up at him. "And if it's never paid?"

The giant shrugged casually. "At end of one year, those still alive will be sold."

"After they cut off our toes!" snapped Wot.

"Is your decision," said the giant. "If you attempt escape, you lose foot thumbs. Now, down. Pit waits."

Lieutenant Serrill went first, fearlessly. Chism held back, hoping that by the time he had to descend, the sun would appear and somehow the first—and last for many days—lucky rays would find him.

It wasn't even close. The other five Elites went down way before the sun came up. The sun itself made sure he knew there would be no luck for a long time. Chism pointedly ignored Skytusk and the other Maners as he went rung under rung into the ground.

As soon as Chism stepped off the ladder, it was raised up. The trapdoor slammed the Elites into darkness.

"Great horned spoon in the sky," muttered Wot. "I can't see a thing."

Lieutenant Serrill had his hands out, feeling one of the walls. "Chism. I've heard rumors that you have the eyes of a bat."

"Something like that," said Chism. Muehner's arms had been close to touching him, but they diverted at the sound of his voice. Chism kept the others away by talking. "Stay away from the wall on my right. It's made of thorns and brambles that look like they've grown around a metal frame. There are a few gaps in it, but none bigger than a man's arm."

Bigger than a man's arm if that man was Chism. He might not have the beard, but he'd been given the clothes. The goatskin tunic had been poorly tanned and was more abrasive than burlap. But what could Chism say? Apparently he was a man now so he couldn't really complain. For once, he faced an enemy that didn't underestimate him. He felt, somehow, that something he'd been due had finally been given to him. Why did it have to come from his enemies?

"The walls in front of me and to my left look like the same timbers as the ceiling. They're tight. You'd have a hard time fitting a knife blade between them." He didn't need to tell them to stay away from the trench to his back; their noses told them that.

"That's a latrine over there?" asked Lieutenant Serrill.

Chism stepped closer to examine it. "Not a hole, a trough. It comes from the cell next to us and slants down to a drain with a grate. Looks like we get to enjoy what everyone upstream sends down."

"All the cells are upstream," said Mave quickly. He always talked as if the words would get lost if he didn't get them out fast enough.

"Shut yourself!" snapped Gorman. He was stooped like a huge ape. "It's your fault we're in here."

True as that was, the words were sharp for a man who had just lost his Fellow. Mave didn't dispute the words, and Lieutenant Serrill didn't step in.

The Elites settled to seated positions in silence. Whether considering their own fate or Kilven's, no man's thoughts made it out of his head.

Eventually, a new type of light began to pierce the ceiling—an array of pinpricks stabbing the darkness. Around the trapdoor, a single delicate slice of light hung like a sheet of infinite thinness. As good as daylight for Chism's eyes. Not long later, the door flipped open, drowning them in brilliance.

"Dozen men with dozen bows await ye," called a man from above. "Attempt escape if ye dare."

Two buckets appeared from above, lowered by ropes with hooks at the end. When they touched ground, the men above jiggled the hooks free and raised the ropes. The trapdoor slammed. Darkness returned.

"What's in the buckets, Chism?" asked Lieutenant Serrill. The time to think hadn't been good for him; he already sounded dejected.

The first bucket contained liquid and a ladle. The odor was earthy, but not dirty. Chism lifted the ladle and sipped. "Water."

"What are you doing?" snapped Wot. "That could be laced with anything—arsenic, lead, nervelock, belladonna, mercury, human waste, anything."

From the far end of the sitting wall, where he crouched alone next to the latrine trough, Mave said in his rapid way of speaking, "Why would they take us prisoner and then—"

"Shut yourself!" barked the lieutenant.

Mave flinched and put his head down onto his crossed arms.

Infighting would help no one, so Chism changed the subject. "The other bucket has a loaf of bread and three apples." He tore the heavy, flat loaf and handed it out, then gave an apple to the lieutenant and one to Muehner. "Eat half of your apple then pass it on. I'll share with Mave." He kept the smallest piece of bread for himself.

Chism handed the last apple to Mave, and they all distracted themselves with eating.

Lieutenant Serrill took two bites, handed his apple to Gorman, and said, "Go ahead and finish it. I'm going to get some rest." He stood, hunching because of the low ceiling, and shuffled to the bramble wall. He stretched out alongside it and closed his eyes.

The rest of the Elites ate in silence, then spread out or leaned against one of the sitting walls to rest. Chism brushed aside the absurd impulse to post someone to keep watch. He got as comfortable as possible curled up in the empty space next to Mave and fell asleep trying to think of anything he could have done to prevent Kilven's death.

Screams like a tortured calf's awakened Chism. The wall of thorns had grown hands and attacked Lieutenant Serrill. When Chism's eyes blinked the sleep out, he realized the hands came from the next cell through gaps in the bramble wall. Near the lieutenant's legs, one hand stabbed repeatedly with some sort of homemade knife. The lieutenant squirmed his leg out of reach, but his arm had been pulled into the wall nearly up to the elbow.

The other Elites blinked and stared and squinted but did nothing.

Chism had to act, but he couldn't bring himself to touch Lieutenant Serrill.

"Grab him!" he ordered.

The Elites grabbed an arm here, a leg there. In the darkness, Wot latched onto Muehner instead of the lieutenant.

Chism yelled, "Pull!" and stepped back out of the way.

They yanked, pulling Lieutenant Serrill away from the wall, but an arm from the other side of the wall still held tight to his hand.

"They still have hold of his arm!" shouted Chism.

Wot shuffled around and manually located the hang-up. With a cruel look on his face, Wot grabbed the hand and bent the thumb back. Lieutenant Serrill came free and the hand disappeared back into the wall.

The other Elites fell backward in a pile, and Lieutenant Serrill's screams changed to moans.

"I shivved him up like goose," said a man on the other side of the wall.

"Feel this," said another. "I think it is beard."

"Filthy Wonderlanderman beard," said the first. "Worth broken thumb."

It wasn't beard. Just above his forehead, the lieutenant had a bleeding bald spot. That wasn't the worst of it. Extracting his arm from the bramble wall had been like pulling strings of fish hooks down the length of his arm.

Gorman pounded on the ceiling, ordering bandages and salve. Shadows moved above, but the trapdoor didn't budge.

Using two sticks he broke off the wall as pincers, Chism bent and did his best at picking the thorns from Lieutenant Serrill's arms. It wasn't quick, but time abounded. The officer's moans turned to sobs—the only sounds he made. Prisoners on the other side of the wall continued to laugh and taunt as the Elites used most of their water to rinse Lieutenant Serrill's wounds.

Chism threw his pincer sticks into the latrine and stretched his cramped fingers. "I've fished out all I can, Sir. Without a knife or tweezers the rest of the thorn tips are going to stay where they're at."

Lieutenant Serrill took a deep breath and said, "I take complete responsibility for all of this. I don't deserve to lead you." He shuffled on hand and knees to the corner furthest from the brambles and the latrine and curled up.

No one answered him. Chism suspected after Lieutenant Serrill had a chance to rest he'd feel differently.

The odor from the other end of the cell did nothing but grow worse as the day wore on. Even worse than the stench was the lack of activity. No Thirsty to sharpen or run forms with. No room to pace, no room to spar. No one else could even stand up straight. Chism tore a loose corner of goat pelt off his vest and sat against the wall, rubbing it between his thumb and forefinger even when the rough hair made his skin raw.

An hour or more passed in silence. Chism couldn't sit still for one more minute, much less the thousands of hours he had to look forward to.

"Who's up for a lesson?" he asked.

Again, no one answered.

"Come on. You pick the subject and the teacher."

"Take a day off, huh?" said Muehner. "We have all year."

"Unless Kilven survived and comes to rescue us," said Wot.

Gorman shook his head in the dark. "He didn't. They got about a dozen arrows in him."

After a time of silence, Muehner said, "Maybe the queen will ransom us."

"The Queen of *Hearts*?" said Wot with a bitter laugh. "What a contradiction of terms."

"Even if she wanted to she can't because—" Mave started in a rush, but Muehner cut him off.

"Shut yourself or I will, Mave."

Gorman said, "Have the Elites ever paid a ransom, Wot?"

"No," said Wot immediately. "Never."

Mave had been right with his explanation. The queen and the Elites couldn't set a precedent of paying ransoms. And after the destruction of half a city block and the deaths of who knew how many Domainers, the ransom would be hefty for half a dozen Elites.

"One year," said Wot. "Unless we find a way to get ourselves out we'll be sold."

Chism looked down at his bare feet. The dance he'd done early that morning on the wall would be impossible if he was missing his big toes.

Wot went on. "The big guy says they won't cut our toes off if we don't try to escape, but they will brand us."

"Will they torture us for information?" asked Chism.

"No," said Wot. "They don't care about information. When they invade Wonderland, their only strategy will be brute force. They even call themselves Indomitable."

With no hope of rescue, Chism quickly ruled out each possible escape idea on his short list. The only conclusion he came to was that dying soon might be better than being sold as a slave after a year of confinement. Physical torture would be better than waiting for the earth and wooden walls to slowly squeeze the life out of him. Already the cell felt smaller than it had that morning.

By trapping him physically the barbarians had doomed his mind to a torture worse than any they could have devised on purpose. If less than one day could do so much to Chism, by the end of a week he'd be raving mad.

Chism almost came out of his skin when a quiet voice from behind said, "I'll study with you." Mave had leaned close, but withdrew under the scrutiny.

Wot glared in Mave's direction, probably considering whether to tell Mave to shut himself.

"Over here," said Chism, and the two scooted up to the latrine trench. The spell of impending doom was broken, but he still felt lingering jitters. In his quietest audible whisper, he said, "What do you want to study?"

Mave shrugged and said in the same quiet tone, "Whatever you want to."

"Let's do strategy. I know how to fight, but never thought I'd be sub-commanding a squadron." Mave needed a boost of confidence.

Maybe Chism could help by showing that not everyone thought Mave was an idiot, even if he did act like one sometimes.

"I resumed you'd be teaching the lesson, Sir," said Mave.

"You mean presumed," said Chism. Usually 'Sir' was reserved for lieutenants, not sub-lieus. But Chism was a Knight, after all. It neither pleased nor bothered him. "If you don't care, then I pick strategy. If you know anything about it."

Mave smiled a sheepish grin and nodded his head.

"So, where do we start, Mave?"

"The only rule to strategy is win before you fight."

It came out so rapidly that Chism had to pause to process the words before replying. When he did, it sounded like nonsense. "How can you win if you don't fight?"

"Fighting is the execution of the win. The outcome was decided before you entered the fight. Otherwise, you choose a different battleguard."

"Battle*ground*," said Chism. "And you can't always pick where you fight."

Mave fidgeted with his leather belt as his eyes darted futilely in the dark. It was obvious he enjoyed talking about such subjects. "Then pick who you bring and how you attack."

Chism huffed at the simplistic explanation. "I'd rather go into a fight knowing I'm the best."

"There's always someone better, Sir. You may be more dangerous than a furious bandersnatch, but somewhere there's a soldier as good, better, or just plain lucky."

"Frumious."

"Huh?"

"An enraged bandersnatch is frumious, not furious," explained Chism.

"Yeah, frumious," said Mave.

"So, if uncertainty is a certainty, how can you possibly win before a fight starts?"

Mave smiled. Some of the strain on his face relaxed away and his voice got a little louder. "With tactics. The cohabitator to strategy."

"Collaborator?"

"Uh-huh. Like an Elite and his Fellow, strategy and tactics go hand in hand." Mave dropped his head and Chism heard him swallow.

Chism turned the conversation away from thoughts of Fellows. "That's not what they taught in the Academy. They said strategy is the overall plan and tactics are the steps you take to accomplish it."

"Those are definitions," said Mave, "but I'm telling you *how* to do it. Here's the key to tactics—use everything available to you."

"Isn't it better to use what you're best at? I use Thirsty when I can because my strength is swords, even though I can hold my own with a staff."

"Think broader," said Mave. "Geography. Weather. Your opponent's weaknesses."

Infrequent rapping, like fingernails tapping a wooden door, came from above.

"I see where you're going," said Chism. "But there has to be more to it than that."

The tapping quickened, as if a thousand birds pecked at the other side of their ceiling. Chism looked up and saw that the stark darts of daylight no longer singed the air. They were subdued and blurred.

Rain.

"If I apply the second rule to the first," Chism said to Mave, raising his voice to be heard over the downpour, "you have to gather everything you will need to win before you need it."

"Yeah, basically."

"How do you know what you'll need?"

"You need everything you need."

"Ugh," said Chism. "You sound like my brother." He slid over to escape a trickle of water.

"It's part of winning before you start. Gather what you need and use everything you need to win."

More rain found its way through cracks in drips and streams. A trickle of filthy water appeared in the trough. The stench became a tangible force invading the tiny cell. Chism and Mave scooted back.

"We'll talk more tomorrow," said Chism, covering his face with the filthy goatskin.

Mave nodded and looked behind him, suddenly remembering the animosity of the other Elites toward him. The relaxed, excited look disappeared, replaced by tight cheeks and bunched eyebrows. He sat against the wall at the edge of the trench and breathed through his hands.

The flow down the trough was a steady stream. A minute later the water was rushing and carrying unpleasant passengers from upstream to down, depositing them somewhere in the ground beyond the Elites' cell. It didn't take long for the water to start flowing clear.

Mave watched the water as if it were a river he had to figure out how to cross. In a voice almost too quiet for Chism to hear, he said, "It's a good time to make water and move bowels."

Rain was the only thing that would keep the trough close to a manageable level of repugnance. The Elites would only be helping themselves if they sent as much as possible downstream at times like this.

"Do your necessities now if you can," said Chism to the others. He loosened the rope around his sheepskin pants.

On the far end of the cell, three paces away, Gorman crouched and walked over. Even without a head he wouldn't be able to stand straight in the tallest corner. He lined up next to Chism, with Wot and Muehner soon following. When everyone else finished, Mave took his turn.

Lieutenant Serrill didn't move.

The rain didn't give Chism something to do, but at least it was something to distract him for a while. The stream in the trough was a bit of outside that passed magically through their tiny prison.

"Smells clean," said Mave, appearing next to Chism. "How's it look?"

Chism kept forgetting that the others couldn't see like he could. "Clean."

"Think it's portable?"

"You mean potable? Or are you planning on carrying it somewhere?"

"Yeah," said Mave. "Potable."

"Maybe," said Chism. "But I'm not thirsty enough to try it."

"Good enough for me," said Mave. "I haven't bathed in days." He stood, hunched as he was, and took off his furry tunic and loosened the leather belt that held up his thick leather pants.

On their first day traveling in the Domain, Mave had earned a private lecture from Lieutenant Serrill after the lieutenant made sure they were alone. Mave had dipped himself in a stream and come out looking like a rugged Wonderland noble instead of the filthy Maner he was supposed to be portraying. Vanity and hygiene ran deep in Mave, even in a dark cavern in the middle of enemy territory.

For some time, Mave stood naked on the edge, listening to the rain patter onto the timbers above them. Trying to work up the courage, or trying to decide if he'd be even dirtier when he came out? Chism couldn't tell.

From the next cell came a clear Wonderland voice. Chism leaned over to listen and heard it change to a slurred accent he didn't recognize. Then a completely different language, harsh and guttural. The men in that cell must be a collection from all over the world.

The second that the frequency and strength of the splatting slackened, into the water went Mave.

Brilliant. "You waited until it was as clean as possible but still running strong, didn't you?" asked Chism.

"Yeah," said Mave. "It'll rescind soon."

Recede, thought Chism.

The water continued to rush as Mave rinsed and scrubbed. As if planned, as soon as Mave stood to drip dry, the water level quickly dropped. By the time he stepped out and began putting his clothes on, it was barely more than a trickle.

"You'll be the most popular boy at the Pit ball," said Chism. With Mave's looks, it would have been true even if he was filthy.

Mave chuckled. "I'd go mad down here if I couldn't stay clean."

You won't be the only one to go mad down here, thought Chism. He'd never been completely assured of his own sanity, and figured it was only a matter of time for all of them.

Night fell early under the cloudy sky, and the Elites began to fit into a sleeping formation. Lieutenant Serrill uncurled and straightened into a line along the wall furthest from the latrine. The clean wall. The cell was just long and wide enough for them to sleep side by side and still keep a safety zone along the bramble wall to prevent more attacks. The configuration pushed one person right up to the edge of the latrine. By seniority and unspoken agreement, it was Mave.

Chism took the slot next to Mave and lay on his back, his hands tight against his sides. At any moment, Mave or Gorman could shift and touch him. He considered lying on his side to increase the distance on both sides, but that would leave his back exposed. Better to be able to defend himself if one of the men moved.

The Pit closed in as he lay there staring up at the beams of the ceiling. The others were practically on top of him. Uncontrollable shudders worked through Chism's limbs with every imagined touch. In such tight quarters, it was just a matter of time. Depending on his level of sleepiness, Chism was likely to do anything from jump up screaming to break an arm.

One of the men began to snore. Next to Chism, Gorman sat up, pulled his furry vest off, folded it like a pillow and rolled onto his side. He didn't touch Chism, but it had been a close call.

Something touched Chism's temple. He slapped it hard enough that it stung and he realized it was only a bead of sweat. Breaths came as fast as if he'd just finished his morning routine and he couldn't get it to slow down.

I can't do this.

Careful to stay in his slot, Chism sat up and turned his back to the wall. He brought his knees up like a shield and watched. If Mave or Gorman moved, he could spring out of the way.

At least he could see. He'd give up his night vision if it made the terror go away, but in the meantime, he'd stay vigilant. There was almost nothing available to him, but he'd take Mave's advice and use every asset he possessed.

So he watched.

5

Chism was awakened by a blinding pillar of sunlight. The other Elites, except Lieutenant Serrill, sat up, forearms pressed to foreheads to shield their eyes.

Two buckets came down, just as they had the day before. The hooks were shaken loose, and someone called, "Put hooks on yesterday buckets."

Muehner was closest. "Should I do it, Lieutenant?"

Lieutenant Serrill didn't answer. His eyes were open, even blinking, but he didn't speak.

"Do it," said Chism.

Muehner gave him a brief defiant look, and then followed the order.

After latching the second bucket, he stepped back out of the way, kicking the full water bucket over in the process. It flooded around Lieutenant Serrill. Without using his injured arm, the lieutenant sat up slowly and crawled to a dry spot, then lay down on his side.

"We need more water!" shouted Muehner. "The bucket spilled."

"Use piss trench," came the answer, followed by a chorus of laughs and the slam of the trapdoor.

"Muehner, Muehner, Muehner," said Wot. "You really maved that one up."

Instead of apologizing, Muehner laughed, as did Gorman.

Chism investigated the other bucket. A loaf of dark, heavy bread and three apples.

"Same food as yesterday," he said, tearing off part of the loaf. "Wot, make sure Lieutenant Serrill eats."

As long as Chism was reasonable and fair, they should accept his leadership. The key was to not give them any reason to say no until the habit was in place. Not that he wanted to lead; it was simply his duty until Lieutenant Serrill took over again. He divvied up the rest of the bread, keeping the smallest piece for himself.

Wot took the bread and felt his way to Lieutenant Serrill. "Eat some bread, Lieutenant." He was successful in getting food in, but only with constant prodding.

With the food gone, silence reigned. It was deeper and darker than the Pit itself, weighed down by the absence of Kilven. The thought of sitting in it for hours and days and longer made Chism's breathing speed up again.

"Lieutenant Serrill," said Chism. "With your permission, I'd like to do a short lesson."

No response. The man didn't even turn his head.

"If they keep us on this diet," said Chism, "we won't have energy for anything physical, so we should sharpen our minds."

Lieutenant Serrill waved one hand in Chism's direction. That was enough permission for him.

"The key to strategy is this," he announced. The other Elites looked up at him from their places against the wall. "Win before you fight."

He went on to explain the basics of strategy and tactics as Mave had explained them. They made objections similar to the ones Chism had made the day before. He kept it short, mostly because of his limited knowledge. Mave kept quiet.

Later that day, Chism asked Mave for another class. The gloom fell from the Elite's face immediately.

"Yes, Sir." He kept his voice low enough that the other men couldn't overhear. "What topic?"

"Pick up where we left off yesterday," said Chism.

"Oh. Good." Mave's eyes zipped around the darkness and he bit his lip as he mentally prepared the lesson. "What's the purpose of military strategy?"

"To win battles," said Chism.

"What purpose does winning battles obchieve?"

"Achieve," corrected Chism.

"What did I say?"

"Obchieve."

"Okay, so what's the purpose of winning battles?"

"Achieving objectives."

"Or obchieving, you could say. No matter. Think bigger."

"We fight battles to win a war."

Nodding rapidly, as if Chism wasn't getting the idea quickly enough, Mave said, "Strategy on battlefields is intended to hasten the end of war in favor of our objectives."

Chism processed the quick words, then nodded.

"So," asked Mave, "the goal of military strategy is political gain?"

Chism considered. Politics was far beyond his comprehension. And even farther beyond his interest.

Mave grew impatient. "The answer is yes. The goal of military strategy is political gain. You're a pawn. You may be the Red Knight, but you're still a pawn who does what the political powers wish. We all are."

Red Knight, thought Chism with frustration. *Vaylee's beard, even here I can't get away from it.*

"Pawns don't always lose to queens," said Chism.

"But they'll be sacrificed every time if it gives the queen an advantage."

"So that's the lesson?" asked Chism. "I'm insignificant?"

"Not *in*significant," said Mave, "but less significant than the objectives. You are smaller than Wonderland and smaller than the Circle and the Sword."

"Alright."

"I want you to think about why you are fighting, Sir. Not just to follow orders or win a battle. You are there so that the politics of the situation change in the right way."

"When I win battles," said Chism slowly, "the politicians I work for get their way."

"You got it," said Mave with a smile. "So always make sure you're on the right side."

"Everyone's always on the right side. Just ask them."

At nightfall, when the Elites began to take their spots for sleeping, Chism lay down next to the latrine trench. No rain that day meant standing waste, but a turd was unlikely to roll over and rest an arm on him in the middle of the night. Besides, Mave had taken enough from the squadron. Taking the worst spot was a small thing Chism could do to try to mend the group.

"What are you doing, Sir?" Mave asked when he discovered Chism in his spot.

"Take the next slot, Mave."

"I can't let you sleep there. You're in charge now. Plus, it's my fault we're here."

Wot jumped in. "Admitting it doesn't make it better, stupid."

"Mave," said Chism, "we all make mistakes. But we're a squadron. Brothers." *Maybe even friends?* wondered Chism. He didn't understand the concept well enough to know whether it applied or not. "There has to come a time of forgiveness, even of yourself."

"But Sir—"

"It's an order, Mave." That ended the discussion. "Just keep all of your body parts to yourself."

Only having to face one direction in order to protect himself,

Chism was able to stretch his cramped body. He still had to sleep lightly and keep one eye open, but it beat fending off attacks of worry all night as he huddled against a wall.

The next morning, the customary meal was lowered in the customary buckets. Gorman fed the lieutenant, who wouldn't talk or respond in any way. After giving everyone enough time to eat, Chism taught the three what he had learned about politics.

Later in the day, when Chism and Mave started their private lesson, Wot said, "Look. Stupid Mave has to have personal tutoring sessions so he can keep up with the rest of us."

"What do you expect?" said Gorman. "He's useless. A thirteen."

With eyes on the ground, Mave asked in a fast whisper, "How much longer are you going to take credence for my lessons?"

"Credit," said Chism. "I haven't taken any. I'm just teaching."

"What are they supposed to think?"

"About what?"

"You already have an aura of mystery and inevitability."

"Inevitability?" asked Chism.

"Inavoidability? Imperturbability?"

"Definitely not that last one."

Mave thought for a second. "No, invulnerability. That's it."

"What does that even mean?"

"You know, you can't be vulnerated."

"I know what *invulnerable* means," said Chism. "What does the whole *aura* thing mean?"

"You were the best swordsman at the Academy when you were twelve."

"I was fourteen. I just looked twelve."

"Okay, what about that duke and his family that you rescued? You killed over twenty Maners. Unarmed."

"Eight. I had a pair of throwing knives, and I didn't even fight them all at the same time."

"Oh. *Only* eight." Mave rolled his eyes, probably forgetting that

Chism could see everything. "Well, there's also the incidents with Duke Jaryn. Who tries to kill a duke and lives? Twice!"

"I didn't try; I threatened. There's a huge difference."

"You put a sword to his throat. Then you cross all of Wonderland alone, with a hole through your leg, and go in front of the Red Queen, deserving a beheading, and she makes you her Red Knight! And then you stroll into a parlor of nations and end a war?"

"The parlay of nations was all my brother. I'm still not really sure how that happened."

"Irregardless, everyone already thinks there's nothing you can't do, so why do you have to steal my credence? Credit."

Chism let out a muted sigh. If a job got done, why did it matter who ended up with the credit? It had only been a day since Mave had taught him that they were all pawns working for the same objective.

Then he remembered Mave had wanted a bath badly enough to take it in a rain-washed piss trench. Vanity seemed to drive Mave like the Circle and Sword drove Chism. That was probably something he should remember if he was going to be a leader, even though trying to keep track of all of his men's specific motivations and eccentricities sounded like torture. Hopefully Lieutenant Serrill would recover soon.

"Fine," said Chism. "Tomorrow I'll stand up and say, 'Mave's going to teach us about strategy.'"

"You can't do that."

"Why not? What would they say?"

Mave didn't answer. They had both heard the words enough to last the rest of the year. Chism didn't make him say it. "Do you want the squadron to exercise their brains and learn this stuff?"

Mave nodded.

"It's brilliant material, Mave, but if it comes from you, they'll see it as worthless. Wish it wasn't so all you want, but it is."

Mave nodded again.

Somehow, Chism didn't think his job of petting Mave's ego was done. "When you're wearing the Circle and Sword again and teaching classes at the Academy, *everyone* will know how brilliant you are."

For a moment, Mave's eyes grew wide and bright. They dimmed and dropped when he said, "I'll never wear the Circle and Sword again after what I did."

"If it makes you feel better, I doubt any of us will," said Chism.

"You'll be fine as heathers, Sir. You almost rescued us."

"You mean *fine as feathers*. If we somehow get out of the Pit, I'll probably be stripped along with you. *Almost rescued* means *didn't rescue*. I've never met the noble who prefers excuses over blame."

Chism knew how he himself felt about losing the Circle and Sword again—like there was no reason to even try getting out of the Pit. He wondered how much Mave felt it. But that was something too personal to ask.

6

"Let me guess," said Muehner when the buckets were lowered for the forty-second time. "Loaf of bread and three apples." His face was hidden behind his hands, and he had retreated to the furthest corner of the Pit. The light burned his eyes, he claimed. No, he usually used words like sear or incinerate. Or as Mave said, encinderate.

Routine was the only thing keeping Chism sane, but it seemed to bother the others as much as the darkness, the moist stench, the inability to stand up straight, the chilly nights, and Mave. To everyone except Chism, Mave was as bad as the fleas. They still didn't know the source of the training sessions.

Chism handed out the food. The biggest chunk of bread went to Gorman and smallest to himself. None of the men realized any discrepancy except maybe Gorman. He had to notice the size differential when he fed Lieutenant Serrill.

"You and me today, Mave."

They'd had to feed the lieutenant in pairs ever since Wot had accused Gorman of eating more than half of the lieutenant's apple. Chism was inclined to believe Wot, but without proof he couldn't do anything. Even if he did have proof, the only appropriate punishment would be to take food away from Gorman, and no one needed that. Before Lieutenant Serrill had checked out, he had been known for meting out appropriate punishments. He had once shackled together two of Chism's Academy classmates before they were even recruits because they wouldn't stop fighting. They spent days joined at the wrist. Dispensing appropriate punishments seemed like a good place for Chism to start trying to fill Lieutenant Serrill's shoes.

Wot said something and Chism looked over at him. He was crouched at a safe distance from the bramble wall gnawing on his bread and muttering under his breath. His days were spent staring like a cat at a wall of mouseholes, passing the shiv he'd broken off of the bramble wall from hand to hand. One day he had succeeded in snagging a goldglace fruit that rolled next to the wall on the far side. Another day he shivved a man's ankle when it was too close to the wall for a few seconds. Grayish, shaggy hair and a filthy face just added to Wot's madman demeanor.

Mave knelt next to Lieutenant Serrill and pulled him to a sitting position against the wall. Chism used his own sharpened bramble stick to cut a slice of apple. They had an unspoken agreement that Mave would touch the body and Chism would touch the food.

Chism held the slice up. "C'mon, Lieutenant, open up." Lieutenant Serrill's mouth opened in mirror image to Chism's, and Chism slid the slice in. After a bite of bread, they lifted the ladle for a sip of water, then repeated the process. Slice by slice and morsel by morsel, they coaxed the meal into Lieutenant Serrill's mouth. Later in the day, it would be their turn to help the lieutenant use the latrine.

Chism's small lump of bread and half apple filled his belly to a level of contentment as high as any meal he'd ever eaten. It seemed to be that way every day—scarce food simply tasted better. He allowed himself to luxuriate for a full half hour before summoning Mave to the corner.

"What's the lesson today, Mave?"

"Twixt the bandersnatch theory."

"Uh," said Chism, "I heard 'twixt the bandersnatch,' but I have no idea what you meant to say."

"No, that's what I meant. If the stories I heard about the Vorpal Knight and the bandersnatch are true, that's what he did. By sliding down that slope and placing himself between the woman and the beast, he declared, *I will win here or I will die. There are no other outceptible actcomes.*"

"Acceptable outcomes," said Chism. "But Tjaden didn't have any choice. It would have killed Lady Elora."

"No," said Mave. His speech gained momentum. "There were a hundred things he could have done—throw something, make noise, run for a bow, taunt the beast, cause an avalanche, instruct Elora on defense, fashion a rope so they would have an escape route ... even let her die."

"So the lesson is 'rescue girls in danger'?"

"It has nothing to do with girls," said Mave.

"But you can't be betwixt one thing," argued Chism. "Betwixt means between. There has to be a threat and something vulnerable, right?"

"No, 'twixt the bandersnatch' is just a catchy way to say it. It's the same as backing your army up against the cliff and thereby taking away the option to retreat. You're committing yourself and your men, and telling your enemy that you are there to conquest or die." Mave's eyebrows did a quick bounce. "Oh! It's the same thing you did both times with Duke Jaryn. You put your sword to his throat and said, 'I am here to die for this if I have to, but I will not accept any options other than death or victory. Or both.' You went twixt the bandersnatch."

Wot began inching closer, very feline in his slow movements, staring at the bramble wall.

"Who taught you all this?" asked Chism. The brilliant new lessons never ran out. "Did we have the same instructors at the Academy?"

Mave shrugged. "No one taught me. I just know it. And I bet if you look at all the Knights, most of them went twixt the bandersnatch to earn their Knighthood."

Closer still, Wot raised a finger to his lips. He flexed the fingers of one hand as if working life into it—getting ready to strike.

Mave said, "It makes sense. All of you Knights put everything on the line at one point. You proved that your lives are worth less than what you believed in."

"Let's see," said Chism, putting Mave's theory to the test. "I suppose *I* did. Tjaden walked right into the Jabberwock's lair, so that's obvious. Sir Gwillym—"

Wot pounced, jamming an arm through a hole in the bramble wall. Someone screamed on the far side of the wall, and Wot yanked his hand back, hooting like a kid who had just scored in an important game of kickround.

On the other side of the wall, the scream changed into a string of curses. Other Maner voices laughed and taunted. Chants of "Beardless" turned to "Chitless".

Chism and Mave moved even further from the brambles. No sense in taking chances.

Wot unclenched his fingers and revealed a clump of curly hair with two chits woven into it. He squinted down into his palm but didn't realize what he held until he used the fingers of his other hand to see.

"Chits!" He hugged them to his chest like treasure and bit his lower lip. His eyes were wild and bright.

"Let me feel em?" pleaded Gorman.

"No," said Wot. "They're mine."

Muehner spat and said, "Piss on their chits."

In the corner of the cell, Lieutenant Serrill sobbed quietly.

Chism looked at the bramble wall, and back at Wot. He still didn't know what the chits were all about. An idea came to him that might build some goodwill that could be called on in the future.

Chism scooted over to Wot and said, "I'll buy those."

"They're my prize. I got them. I got chits."

"Trade. For my apple tomorrow."

Wot's wild eyes looked from chits to Chism. "Your apple? All of it?"

"Half an apple," said Chism. "That's my ration."

"Half an apple," said Wot. "For two days in a row, not one. But I get to keep the hair and you just get the chits."

"That's a hard bargain," said Chism, pausing as if considering so that Wot would feel like he was getting a good deal. "I'll take it."

Wot thrust the chits forward. "No going back. You have to give me half an apple, two days in a row." He retreated to his lookout spot and watched the bramble wall. Stroking the hair, he rocked back and forth, muttering quietly to himself.

Bit by bit, the Pit was forcing Chism's men into different types of madness.

Chism had noticed someone crouching on the other side of the bramble wall during the lessons from time to time, but he never paid as close attention to the wall as Wot. Mave's lessons required all of the limited brain power Chism was able to muster.

Someone still lurked there. Likely someone looking to avenge lost treasure.

Chism scooted to the wall, but not too close.

"These your chits?"

A hand holding a sharpened stick appeared and scraped the air, but Chism was far enough away to be safe. It would be easy to grab the hand and break the wrist, but that was the opposite of his objective. All strategy was intended to hasten the end of war, and goodwill was one of his few assets.

The owner of the hand must have realized the danger of his position because he withdrew it.

"Tell me about chits," Chism said calmly, as if the other man hadn't just tried to stab him. He suspected they were as dear to the Domainers as the Circle and Sword were to him.

"Are you Red Knight?" The man's voice was surprisingly smooth, yet hard. Crisp, like an eggshell. Unique enough to momentarily distract Chism from the question it asked. If there was one thing he'd hoped he could escape in the Domain, it was the Red Knight nonsense.

"Who told you that?"

"I listen to you and your man."

"Overlisten, you mean," said Chism.

"You did not realize classes were not private?" The t's in his voice were sharp enough to break off and put in a pouch. "How does it feel to teach your enemy?"

"We're not enemies. We're prisoners."

"Booger that," said the Maner. "I am Indomitable. Soldier. Chits and beard and ne'er afeared."

Every lousy Domainer a soldier.

Chism's legs began to burn, so he switched from crouching to sitting. "So what is it about the chits?" The two in his hand were heavy. The small one silver, the bigger one gold.

"To many of us, chits are social standing. Represent patriotism." He paused. "We Aymatungula have word—depthswelkin. Encompasses all from underearth to firmament above. Chits are my religion and my life. I have traded over twelve years for those two chits."

Exactly like the Circle and Sword. Chism had spent enough time without the emblem to know how the other man felt. Like his skin had been stripped away in one piece. The only reason Chism carried on was because the Circle and Sword were imprinted on his soul like a tattoo. Even if he never wore the emblem again, it could never be expunged from his heart.

"How do you earn them?" asked Chism.

"Small chits earned for small contributions, such as day's work. Trade small chits for large chits and valuable metal chits."

Chism had traded his life so far, day by day for skills and opportunities that would allow him to serve the Circle and Sword. The idea was foreign and the word was unpronounceable, but he might have something in common with the barbarians.

The true measure of what the chits meant to the Maner would show in his answer to one question. "What would you do to get them back?"

"Anything," he answered without delay.

"Rations tomorrow?"

"Yes."

"Rations for a week?"

"Yes."

"Help me escape?"

"I will do anything possible," said the man. "Burn my beard, but that is not possible. Man who would betray chits to earn chits does not value them. It is powerful paradox."

"Would you give your little finger?"

"Yyyes," he said cautiously. "But I would ask why."

"Does it matter?"

"Only to assuage curiosity."

The only reason Chism asked was to gauge the importance and the man had already answered.

"Here's what I want," said Chism. "A neutral zone on both sides of this wall. No stealing, no shivving, no pulling hair. No touching. A complete truce."

"This is something I cannot deliver. I am only one man, so I can only guarantee safety to one man. Or I can guarantee safety to all of you *from* one man only: me. It is logical, yes?"

"What good would safety from only one of you be?"

"No good at all."

"So how can you guarantee safety for one man?"

"Is it not obvious?" asked the Maner. "I am one-sixth of my community. You are one-sixth of yours. Thought Red Knight would have more brains."

"You're not the only one to give me too much credit. How would you know it was me by the wall?"

"A totem, placed for us to see when you and only you are near spike wall."

"I don't know if I can guarantee your safety in return." Wot was most likely beyond obeying an officer who came between him and his obsession.

"That is not part of bargain. I only want chits."

"The agreement lasts as long as you and I are in these cells?"

"Yes."

"How much longer do you have?"

"Five months. I am next one out of cell."

It was a good bargain, but Chism would have to put a lot of faith in the honor of a barbarian. "How do I know you'll honor our agreement?"

"You do not," said the Maner. "I cannot even swear on chits because I do not have them. I would swear on beard, but I doubt it would mean aught to you."

Chism looked down at the bits of metal in his hand. "I'm not one to stand between a man and his religion. Hold your hand out."

The man did not hesitate to show his open palm, an impressive amount of trust considering what he'd been through ten minutes earlier. Wot was watching the scene closely, but the Maner's hand was shielded by Chism and the darkness. Chism dropped the two tokens into the hand, which rapidly retracted.

"I will never ever forget, Knight," said the Maner. "My debt is forever. And let it be said Red Knight's heart is as big as his beard."

It sounded like the man was overcome with emotion, but obviously he'd never seen Chism's chin. "Just Chism," he told the Maner.

"Zeemi."

"Can I ask you a question, Zeemi?"

"I have no other appointments. And I am in debt eternal."

"Who's Vaylee?"

"Vaylee is mother of the Indomitable and goddess of our warriors."

"A woman warrior?"

"No, she did not fight. Had twenty sons. From them, we Indomitable sprang."

"Did she have a beard?" asked Chism cautiously.

"Ha!"

The Elites, except for Lieutenant Serrill, flinched and stared at the wall.

"I've heard a bunch of Ma—Indomitables talk about her beard," said Chism.

"No beard. That is just crude expression."

"Hm."

"My turn for question," said Zeemi. "Is true you walked Phaylea for one week dressed as child?"

"A day."

"That was you who poisoned northeast well?"

Chism glanced over his shoulder to make sure no one else was close. He didn't need any more ridiculous rumors about him going around.

"No."

"You defeated Sevenchit."

"A what?"

"Sevenchit is title. Man at armory who you could have killed was very powerful, very important."

"The quartermaster?" asked Chism.

Zeemi laughed. "To call Sevenchit Overseer 'quartermaster' is like calling Suzerain 'soldier' or saying Panjandrum is 'magistrate'."

Chism knew he was revealing his vast lack of Domainer knowledge, but if he didn't have conversations like this, how could he learn? "That fight against the Sevenchit Overseer wasn't really fair."

"You let him live," said Zeemi. "Is much honor."

"It really wasn't much of a fight," said Chism.

"Well, there is also other rumor that blood bees extoxicate on your blood and not other way around."

Extoxicate? That sounded like a word Mave would make up.

Chism had heard of blood bees, but didn't really know anything about them. He simply answered, "No."

"There are some," said the Maner sincerely, "who speculate you are son of Vaylee, not merely super-great-grandson like rest of us."

In an even quieter voice, Chism said, "I never knew my mother, but I'm pretty sure it wasn't Vaylee."

"Burn my beard! You are saying it is possibility?"

Chism couldn't remember the last time he'd thought about his mother. There was no way to know how he should feel about her; no one in T'lai ever told him much because he never asked. She'd been married to his father, and as much as he hated to cast judgment based merely on association, it was hard to imagine her being a good person. Maybe that was unfair. He realized he was too close to the situation to see it through neutral eyes.

"They say," said Zeemi, "that Red Knight could steal all salt from sea and magma out of mountain."

"What does that even mean?"

"And they say you can win staring contest against fish."

"As advantageous as outstaring a fish sounds, I don't really see what it has to do with anything."

Before the Maner could reply, Mave crawled up and cleared his throat. "Are you going to chat with your new friend all day, or are we finishing our class?"

Friend? How absurd.

"So what about that totem, Zeemi?"

"Minute."

"Just a minute," said Chism over his shoulder.

On the other side of the bramble wall, some fabric tore. A length of silence, then some tapping.

Like a long skinny mouse, an object poked through the opening where Zeemi's hand had been. Chism took it and looked it over. It was Zeemi's old shiv, wrapped up and poked through a swath of rabbit fur.

"Lay that through hole in wall, and we leave you alone. Do not allow others use it, or we take it back. Do not misplace."

"Thanks," said Chism.

"Chits and beard," replied the Maner.

Chism scooted away from the wall.

"That was stupid," said Muehner. "He wouldn't have given chits back to you if the situation was reversed."

"You could have traded those for food," said Gorman.

Wot nodded. "You really maved that one."

"Leave him alone," snapped Mave. "They were his and he's lieutenant. It's his pejorative."

Chism wondered if they'd object to the claim of him being lieutenant or make fun of Mave's abuse of language first.

"What do you know, thirteen?" asked Gorman.

"Yeah, shut yourself, you stupid idiot," said Muehner.

"Yeah, you stupidiot," said Wot.

They laughed, and even though it had been days since such sounds had been heard, it was not refreshing.

Mave lowered his head and picked at something on his pants.

"Enough," said Chism, standing for the first time in a day or more. His body objected as though it were eighty-years old and he had to put a hand on the ceiling to steady himself. Example hadn't worked; it was time to resort to words. And if they couldn't see the look on his face, they could probably make out his outline. The effect of standing, which none of them did anymore, except Mave at bath time, might help accomplish the desired effect.

"Mave is still a member of Scaled Tiger Squadron. It's not your job or your *prerogative* to punish him."

"What about squadron justice?" snapped Wot.

The other two nodded.

"It's at the discretion of the squadron commander when and how that happens," said Chism. "That's me. And the Pit is no place for it. When we get out of here, we will worry about it."

It would most likely never be an issue. Chism was grateful for that. He had gone through squadron justice in Far West after the first Duke Jaryn incident and didn't relish the obligation to put Mave through it.

The three men glared in Mave's direction. Mave stared at the floor. They all stayed silent. Chism had no idea how it had happened, but these men, from five to twenty-five years his senior, still accepted his authority in a place where it could easily have disintegrated.

He went on. "Either be civil, or don't talk to Mave. Period. I'll dock rations of the next man to tell him to shut himself."

Chism considered telling them about the source of most of the classes, but it wasn't the time. He'd thrown enough at them for one day.

"Is that clear?"

Gorman and Wot had identical frustrated looks on their faces. Neither of them could see the other clearly, but Chism could. Eventually they both muttered, "Yes, Sir."

"Yessir," said Muehner. Under his breath he added, "Who wants to talk to that stupidiot anyway?" Gorman and Wot chuckled.

The strain of standing made Chism lightheaded, but he needed to drive home the point. Otherwise he'd end up fighting them about Mave every day.

"Let's settle this. Who here has the best mind for strategy?"

"You," said the three in unison.

"What do you say, Mave?"

Mave didn't look up and didn't answer.

"Be honest, Mave," said Chism. "Who's the best strategist here?"

"I am," said Mave.

The three laughed, and Muehner opened his mouth.

"Careful," said Chism, and Muehner closed it.

If Chism stayed on his feet any longer, he'd pass out. He lowered himself to a sitting position and took a few thankful breaths as blood returned to his head. Rain started slowly tapping on the timbers overhead.

"First," said Chism, "don't confuse the lack of using his brain with an inability to do so. Second, today's lesson is a competition. Come closer; I'd like to keep stray ears out." The approaching rain would help with that.

They scooted up, Mave on the latrine side, the others on the clean side.

"You have ten minutes," whispered Chism. "Come up with a plan for us to escape. You three, work together. Mave, you're on your own."

"Are you going to judge?" asked Wot.

"We won't need a judge," said Chism. "The winner will be obvious."

"You mean 'winners'," said Muehner.

"You're wasting time," said Chism.

Mave was already looking around the cell. It was an impossible test. That was one reason they hadn't attempted or even discussed escape. Chism also hadn't wanted to put his big toes at risk. Still, Chism couldn't wait to hear what Mave came up with. He tried to find a spot where water wasn't dripping down.

The three huddled and whispered and glared at Mave as if he would steal their ideas. It was as much action as Chism had seen from them in a week, but it didn't last long. With five minutes left, the three stopped discussing and stared smugly at Mave, who appeared to be daydreaming.

"Time's up," said Chism eventually. "You three first."

"He'll steal our ideas," said Gorman.

Chism stifled a laugh, but Muehner spoke up. "It's okay, we have more people. And the best plan."

"So come closer and go ahead," said Chism.

When everyone was close enough to be heard over the steady rainfall, Wot said, "First of all, there's no escape. It's a suicide mission. But if we have to do it, we'll go through the trapdoor."

Chism expected Mave to snicker or scorn, but he stayed quiet.

Wot went on. "We would need to break something off that wall thick enough to use as a staff or at least as a billy club. When they lower the buckets, we'll be ready. Two of us give the ropes a yank, trying to pull someone off balance and hopefully into the Pit so we can steal a weapon. At the same time, the other two will lift you up since you're the best fighter. You just have to hold off the guards while we lift the others out one at a time."

As Wot went on, all five of them turned their noses away from the running water. The first minutes of rainstorms were the foulest.

"The only hope is to subdue whatever kind of guards they have before they can raise an alarm. Then disguise ourselves again and sneak out of the city."

"Anything else?" Chism asked.

"I'll sink my teeth into the first one I can," said Gorman. "If I die, it'll be with a mouthful of meat."

Wot inched away. Muehner did the same and said, "I'm not sleeping next to you anymore."

"What do you estimate our chance of success?" asked Chism.

"Five percent," said Muehner.

"One percent," said Wot.

"Same odds as a goat at a bandersnatch gathering," said Gorman.

"What's wrong with their plan, Mave?"

"Well, they've figured out how to lose a fight before it starts."

"More specifically," said Chism.

"How long can you stay vertigo, Sir?"

"Vertical?" Chism had thought he'd hidden his shakiness a few minutes earlier. Maybe Mave was talking from personal experience. "Three minutes. Maybe four."

"How many fully rested, armed men can you fight off with only a bramble branch, all while trying to dodge arrows from the lookouts?"

"Shut—" started Wot, then said, "tell us your stupid plan, genius."

"One minute," said Chism. "How are Elites chosen, Wot?"

"They win local competitions and impress the Legates."

"What kind of competitions?"

"Staves usually. Sometimes other weapons."

"Exactly," said Chism. "All Elites are world-class swordsmen. It is a rare Elite that has the brain to match, but you are about to witness one. Go ahead, Mave."

"I agree with them," said Mave. "There is no escape."

Muehner barked a laugh. "That's the great mind among the ranks of idiots?"

"If I had to try," said Mave, "I'd start by getting bigger rations."

"Got some magic kernels stashed away?" asked Muehner.

Chism noticed Gorman looking in Lieutenant Serrill's direction and licking his lips. Whether Gorman was considering eating the lieutenant, or just eating his rations, Chism couldn't tell. He hoped it was the latter.

Mave continued. "My suggestion would be to leech Serrill's. Divide it up between us. If we try an escape, he'll just be a lodestone around our necks."

"Millstone," said Chism. He glanced over at Lieutenant Serrill, but the man made no sign of hearing anything.

"Yeah, millstone. But you're in charge, and I don't think you would let us eat his food." He leaned forward, lowered his voice even more, and pointed at the bramble wall. "We go through that."

"So you have an axe hidden somewhere?" asked Muehner.

"The metal grate in the latrine between us and them is rusty. I think we could break it little by little. It would have to be when the rain fills it, to cover the noise. When there's a big enough opening, we send Lieutenant Chism in to assassinate them in their sleep."

Wot grunted. "You think he's going to kill his new best friend in cold blood?"

Where was all the talk of friends coming from?

"He's going to use everything he needs to accomplish the mission," said Mave.

Muehner said, "So he kills them all and we're locked in a new cell with a bunch of dead bodies."

Wot eyed Gorman and said, "I'm not desperate enough to eat a man. Yet."

"Not just a new cell and dead bodies," said Mave. "Double rations."

"Triple," said Chism. "They eat better than we do. They're prisoners, not hostages. Remember the goldglace you found, Wot?"

"I'm starting to like this idea," said Gorman. He sat up taller and licked his lips more vigorously than before.

"Settle down," said Wot. "What about the bodies?"

"We could feed them to Gorman," said Muehner. Quiet chuckles eased even more of the tension. Mave hadn't had any part in the joke, but it opened the circle and made Chism feel like the five of them were becoming a group again.

Wot asked, "How does more food help us escape? We can't bribe the guards with food."

Mave looked at the far side of the cell where the latrine trench was filling with rainwater. He said, "We send the bodies down the poop chute."

"After we chop them up with your imaginary axe," said Wot.

"Their chits are metal," answered Mave. "We can sharpen them on the grates and use them as razors."

Wot put his hands up and scooted back out of the circle. "That's it. I'm not sleeping next to any of you."

"The guards will notice us the first time they send food down," said Muehner.

"Doubt it," Mave said. "We'll steal their clothes and keep our faces down. It's not like they count us. With their filthy clothes on our skinny backs, do you think there's any way they'll be able to extinguish us?"

"Distinguish," corrected Chism. "And Zeemi said he's the next one out of the cell and that won't happen for five months. So we shouldn't have to worry about any closer inspection."

"You never told us what good their food does for our escape," said Wot.

"We're starving on the current rations," said Mave. "We couldn't walk to the city gates in this condition. Once we have enough energy to do more than scoot around, we start digging."

"With your non-existent axe and tiny, razor-sharp chits," said Muehner.

"With bramble sticks and parts of that bucket that we accidentally broke."

"What bucket?" asked Gorman, looking around. "Oh. Yeah. *That* bucket."

Muehner pounded a fist weakly against the hard-packed dirt. "Twigs and fingernails won't go through rock-hard dirt very fast."

"That's why we'll dig around the grate at the end of the latrine." Mave's words came out faster than ever. "The metal on that end of the trench is too thick to break or bend, but around it is just dirt. If we dig far enough, we can make room to shimmer past. We don't even have to worry about where to send the dirt."

"How do we know there's not a bigger grate just past this one?" asked Wot.

"Remember the bodies?" asked Mave. "It will have been a couple weeks since they went down. If they get stuck, we'll know it, and we'll have to halter the plan."

"Alter," said Wot in the least cruel tone anyone had used toward Mave since their imprisonment. "And next time it rains, we just let it wash us all down the drain?"

"We go when it's dry so we don't drown," said Mave, without the sarcasm the comment merited. "And we send one person to investigate first, using ropes we fashion from the dead Domainers' clothes."

"Where do you think it leads?" asked Gorman.

"Somewhere big enough for a lot of water. Maybe even the sea."

"Maybe a giant lake of human waste," said Muehner.

"And body parts," added Wot.

No one challenged the plan or raised questions. After a short minute, Mave said, "It goes without saying that we make our run right after food comes. We eat ours and wrap theirs to take with us."

"Probability of success?" asked Chism.

Mave's eyes darted and his lips moved as he considered. "Two hundred times better than popping out of here like a lurkserpent. Maybe ten percent."

Considering the other options, those odds didn't sound horrible. Chism asked, "Probability of ransom or rescue?"

"Rescue, less than one percent. Ransom, maybe five. Unless one of you has very rich relatives."

They looked around at each other, but no one offered any hope.

"Let's try it, Lieutenant," said Gorman. It was the first time any of them besides Mave had called him that.

"I'm not crazy about those odds," said Chism. "Ten percent means that if we attempted the escape plan Mave laid out ten times, we die in nine of them. Close to the same odds if we wait. I'm not one to sit when I can act, but if we attempt this escape, that means leaving Lieutenant Serrill behind."

The others probably wouldn't mind. To one level or another, each of them resented Lieutenant Serrill for quitting, and they begrudged sharing food with him and helping him to the privy. Chism suspected that his comatose state was a natural extension of his propensity for fitting punishments and consequences. Deep down he didn't feel worthy to lead. Going into a stupor was his way of dealing with it. Maybe it could be classified as madness, but it was definitely a quirk, and Chism could relate.

Chism said, "If we survive a year, they separate us and sell us off as slaves."

"And possibly disfigure us," said Muehner.

"Where do each of you stand?" Not that Chism would abide by their choice, but it would help to know their opinion.

"Stay," said Mave.

Almost as fast, Gorman said, "Escape. The current rations will kill me before our year is up."

"I'm with Gorman," said Wot. "We're not maidens to sit back and wait for rescue. This is one of the most important moments in Wonderland's history, and we're rotting in a stinking dungeon. We don't even know what's happening between the Reds and Whites, much less if war with the Domain has already started."

In the darkness, everyone turned their head toward Muehner. "I wish the boy would have used that brain *before* getting us caught. He still has to face consequences if we ever get out of here, but I agree with him. Stay."

Two to two. Perfect. Chism's rashness was the source of most of the problems in his life. Maybe he was learning and maybe he was becoming timid, but he didn't want to rush into anything.

"We have some time to decide," Chism said. "That's our lesson for today. Tomorrow, Mave will teach us." Without having to re-teach everything, Chism wouldn't learn the lessons as well, but the other Elites would hear it straight.

Mave went toward the trough to bathe while the others scooted to a corner or wall. Wot took up his spot watching the bramble wall.

Chism approached Wot and said, "I want to try out this totem, but I'd feel safer with a lookout."

"Sure thing, Lieutenant," said Wot. "I'll keep an eye out. Both eyes out."

Chism placed the furry totem halfway through a gap in the thorns.

"Do not worry," said Zeemi. "We see it."

"You haven't forgotten that debt yet?"

It was a joke, but Zeemi answered with vehemence. "I will never forget, Knight. I swear it on chits." Metal clinked in the next cell.

The gratitude of a Domainer was worth as much as the respect of a donkey, as far as Chism was concerned. He just hoped to get some sleep out of the deal.

With plenty of worry, Chism lay down, risking his life and

sanity on the word of a Maner. He stayed on edge, ready to bolt away from the wall at the slightest threat. It still wasn't as bad as the threat of an arm brushing against him in the middle of the night since a shiv was more likely than the skin of an arm. Chism realized he had his very own style of madness, but unlike the other Elites, he'd brought his madness into the Pit with him instead of discovering it in the cramped darkness.

Eventually, he slept.

When he woke, very little light remained in the cell. Five hours? Six? Wot still crouched nearby, eyes scanning the wall.

"Have you been there the whole time?"

"Yessir. All safe and sure; no one tried to kill you or shiv you."

"Thank you, Wot. I didn't mean to sleep so long."

The darkness intensified quickly, and before long, the Elites took their accustomed places. Chism lay down past their heads, along the bramble wall.

"Spread out a little," said Chism. "I'm going to sleep over here."

"Want us to post a guard?" offered Gorman.

"No. Get some sleep. We have a big day of nothing planned tomorrow."

Chism lay in his safe zone, afraid he'd be awake for hours after the nap. Before long, sleep crept in at the edges of consciousness. It was a fine substitute for food and energy. The sleep was cold and fitful—even more so than normal after the rainstorm. The season was turning. He bent onto his side and pulled his knees up close, but without any covering besides his worn clothing, it was impossible to get warm and sleep came and went in uncertain doses. Just when he'd finally discovered some space, the weather schemed against him.

As usual, in the morning they wallowed where they lay until the trapdoor opened. Chism stretched then crawled to switch the bucket hooks. Muehner covered his face and curled up to hide from the light. Wot and Gorman scooted into the glow of the shaft. It wasn't direct sunlight, but they still bickered over it.

When Chism reached for the first bucket, a shadow crossed the stream of sunlight. Chism tried to duck out of the way, but he wasn't quick enough to avoid being struck by a heavy, soft bundle.

It startled more than hurt him, and he reached for it.

"Buckets, Wonderlandermen!" shouted someone from above.

Chism moved to swap the hooks as Gorman investigated the thick grey bundle. "Blankets!"

It was the most wonderful word Chism had ever heard.

"Wool," said Wot.

The old buckets went up and the door slammed, forcing the cell to fill with darkness.

After checking the food bucket, Chism called, "Gorman, come take a look at this."

Gorman was there in no time, exploring the food bucket with his hands. "One, two, three, four, five ..." Before Gorman reached six, there were tears in his voice that kept him from finishing. He stood, bent at the waist, and delivered a whole apple to each Elite.

Muehner grumbled, "I'd trade a month of apples for a cold chicken leg." He took a bite of the bread Chism handed him.

As soon as Chism got his fruit, Wot hurried over, licking his lips. "You said your apple, that's what you said. You said you'd give me your apple today and tomorrow. You didn't say half an apple, it was your apple. That was the deal." His eyes flickered from the apple to Chism's face fast as a butterfly's wings.

The deal had been half an apple for two days. If there was one thing Chism would always know, it was numbers.

Wot was probably lying. He had one of the best memories for small details of anyone Chism had ever known.

But for one day, Chism didn't care.

Not only would he sleep safe from incidental and deliberate touching, he would sleep warm. And in two days he would receive an entire apple every day as his ration. The king and queen in their Palassiren palace did not live half so well as Chism and his men.

7

Light flooded the cell for the one hundred thirty-third time. Or was it one hundred thirty-four? It should be a simple one to remember. 1-3-3 and 1-3-4 were so different in function and feel. So which was it? If Chism didn't figure it out right away, he knew it would be jumbled forever.

Muehner cringed away from the light, making tiny whimpering noises. Wot and Gorman clawed at each other, each stating it was their turn for sunlight. There was room for both of them, but they didn't see it. And Chism was too distraught over losing count to intervene.

Was the previous day one-three-two or one-three-three? Did the numbers have a peaked impression or a sense of bully? Triangular or unfair?

With monumental effort, Chism pushed himself up to his knees, then got one foot under him and used the bramble wall to pull himself to standing. Thorns tore the skin of his palm, but he held on to keep from tipping over.

Shielding his eyes, Chism shouted into the sunlight, "How long have we been down here? How many days?"

"Buckets!" was the only answer.

"A hundred thirty-three or a hundred thirty-four?" He shook his totem at the opening as if it would force them to answer.

"No buckets today, no food or water tomorrow!"

"Just tell me! How many?"

"Last chance."

"Tell me!"

Near his ankles, someone jiggered the hooks, but they weren't fast enough. A short length of rope fell into the cell and the door slammed, sending specks floating down into the tiny spears of light.

On day 130, Mave had said *cavity* once and *cavalcade* thrice. One and three, like one-three-zero. There was no doubt about that. If Chism could figure out how many days it had been since that lesson, he could go from there. "When did we do a lesson on cavalry?" Someone had to remember.

"Who cares?" moaned Gorman. "No food tomorrow."

"When was it?" demanded Chism.

"Two days ago," said Wot.

"It was three," said Muehner.

Around a mouthful of apple, Gorman said, "It might have been four."

"Four days ago was catapults," said Wot.

"No, it was total war," said Muehner.

"Total war was before sieges," said Gorman.

As they continued to argue, Chism slid over to Mave. "When was cavalry?"

"I don't remember," Mave answered. "And you know what? It doesn't matter."

"Don't say that!" snapped Chism. "Don't say that." Chism slid across the cold dirt to the bramble wall. "Zeemi! When did we do cavalry?"

Through the wall, Zeemi said, "Booger if I know."

Chism ran his fingers through his hair, trying to force the numbers to behave. His fingers came away with ... some number of hairs in them. How many? How many? How many! He couldn't count the days, he couldn't count the hairs. He'd lose all the numbers any minute now. If they weren't already lost.

"Lieutenant," said Mave. "You can't fall apart over this like Serrill did."

"Just tell me when we did cavalry," pleaded Chism.

"No!" shouted Mave. He dove toward the bramble wall. Chism's blanket was disappearing through the opening where he usually rested his totem.

Mave was too slow. The blanket eluded him like a snake into a burrow.

"Where were you on that one?" snapped Mave toward Wot. "You stare at the stupid wall all day, but when we need you once, where are you?"

"The lieutenant maved that one, not me. Why'd you do that, Lieutenant? Why'd you leave your blanket there?"

"Doesn't matter," said Chism. His head itched, so did his inner leg. Lice and fleas loved body heat during winter.

"Divide the bread, Lieutenant," said Gorman.

It must be his turn to pick the crumbs out of the bucket, thought Chism.

Chism picked up the bread and absentmindedly tore it. With the numbers not fitting into place, nothing seemed right. He couldn't even remember whose turn it was to feed Serrill. Lieutenant Serrill.

Muehner took two chunks of bread, saving Chism from having to ask.

"The bucket's mine," said Gorman as he followed Muehner to help Lieutenant Serrill to a sitting position.

The other Elites had given up on figuring out the day of the cavalry class. Chism felt like giving up too. There was nothing left worth holding onto.

Wot sat in the same spot as always. Scanning the wall, waiting for a chance to lash out. He hadn't been successful for sixty-one days. Or was it sixty-two?

He mumbled, as usual, and the words were repetitive enough for Chism to pick up on most of them. "Shouldn't have sold the chits, shouldn't have sold them. Need to get more, more chits, more shivving, more blankets back for the lieutenant. Any day now, any day now, any day now." His voice grew quieter but his lips continued to move. One hand held a thorned stick, the other moved constantly to whichever body part was being targeted by vermin at the moment.

The food in Chism's hand hardly appealed to him, but holding on to it would just torture the other men. He took a bite of the bread, hoping it would prompt a memory of how many times he'd eaten the heavy, gritty bread. If his degeneration continued, he probably wouldn't even be able to count the six pieces into which he had to break the bread every day.

Nothing. He tore the bread up into pinchable pieces and dropped them into the bucket. Gorman needed it more than anyone, but if Chism just gave it to him it would create problems with the others. Even with the extra rations today, there would be big problems with Gorman when the buckets didn't drop tomorrow.

Chism really didn't care. He leaned against a timber wall and stared at the space. The cell seemed smaller than ever. How had it held six men for a hundred and thirty-something days?

Don't fool yourself, he thought. *Five men and a boy.*

Mave appeared at his side, and Chism jumped. How had he not seen him approaching?

"Scratching only makes it worse," said Mave.

Chism pulled one hand from his hair and the other from his armpit. He folded them across his chest, and they rose and fell quickly with his breath. He couldn't speak; it would require too much air, and he wasn't getting enough as it was.

"Whoa, Lieutenant. You're breathing harder than a warhorse after a charge. You have to slow it down."

That made no sense. If he slowed his breathing, he'd get even less air. Faster. He had to get more air into his lungs. His eyes bugged as if even they could allow more air in.

"Chism." Mave reached out a hand as if he'd put in on Chism's shoulder.

"No," grunted Chism, trembling in fear. "Don't ..." Three more rapid breaths. "Don't touch me."

Like a man backing down from a snarling dog, Mave lowered his hand. The panic from the threat of his touch remained.

Pain pricked Chism's hands, and his fingers grew stiff and unresponsive. His toes curled and cramped. If the rest of his body contracted like that, it would be impossible to get any air. He breathed even faster.

I can't breathe.

Chism wanted to say the words out loud, but he didn't have enough air.

I'm going to die. Without the numbers, just like without air, Chism couldn't live.

What he saw made him wish he could do exactly that. Climbing out of the latrine trough, with a smile even wider than the cell, was the Cheshire Cat.

For the first time in the Pit, Chism sobbed—breathing and gasping and blubbering and unable to unclench his hands. The world and the cell closed in so tight he could barely see, could barely breathe. He made his lungs and throat work faster. More air. He gasped for more air.

But air didn't come. Only blackness in his eyes, which quickly penetrated his mind. Death wrapped him in its comfortable, smothering grip.

8

It wasn't death after all. Chism cursed fate and the Domain and the numbers for leaving him. Then he opened his eyes. The first thing he saw was the last thing he wanted to see: a pearly grin, sharp in most places. Sixty-one teeth. He knew it without even counting and blew out a breath of relief.

"How many teeth does a cat have?" asked Chism.

"He's lost it," muttered Wot. "We're all mad here, but not him. Not until today, anyhow. He wants to know how many teeth a cat has. Might as well ask how many quills in a porcupine's tail. Or on a porcupine's back. Yes, on its back."

"I don't know much about cats," said Mave. "How are you feeling?"

"Does sixty-one seem like too many?" asked Chism, attempting to sit up. His breaths came at a normal pace and Chism realized his body must have reset itself.

"Sixty-one seems purr-fect to me," said Cheshire, right next to Chism's ear. "Much better than the mere thirty that cats have." He was larger than a normal cat, especially in the head and face area. Thick stripes, alternating light and dark, ran like ladder rungs from his nose to his tail.

"Don't get up," said Mave. "You're still a little shaky."

There were sixty-one for sure. Even if Cheshire hadn't confirmed it, Chism would bet his totem on it. What threw him off was the symmetry of the smile. "Sixty-one isn't divisible by two or four or any other number. How can it be symmetrical?" Side to side symmetry made sense, but only on either the top or bottom. But it was impossible for 61 to be symmetrical in four quadrants.

The hope that he was back to normal disappeared. The laws of symmetry said that 61 was altogether impossible. Wrong numbers had filled the numerical vacuum and Chism was definitely worse off for it.

"Yep," said Muehner, "finally cracked. I'm sorry, men, but it's refreshing to see that even the best of us can't hold on forever."

"Hard to disagree with that," said Gorman. "Even though it took him twice as long as the rest of us."

"I'm not the best ..." began Chism, but he lost his thought. There were 61 for sure, but that simply was not possible. Chism was witnessing an impossibility. Maybe he had cracked for real. He'd seen it happen to his brother in the space of an instant.

"Why did you come here?" Chism asked.

"What kind of question is that?" replied Mave. "We had a mission, remember?"

In a barely audible voice, Cheshire said, "Yes, that's right. We all have our missions."

"What's *your* mission?" asked Chism, leaning closer to stare into Cheshire's face.

"To innervate Phaylea and report on the Domainers' preparation," said Mave.

"My mission is *you*," whispered Cheshire, still fixing Chism with his infuriating smile. His tufted ears twitched with what Chism could only interpret as glee.

Chism pushed himself up and leaned back against the wall. He put his hands on his head. "Can you get us out of here?"

"Maybe four months ago," said Mave. "We're too disseminated now."

Cheshire put his paws on the wall next to Chism and stretched upward. "I believe the word he is looking for is 'emaciated.'"

With eyes closed and head against the wall, Chism said, "Who cares anymore?"

The Cheshire Cat went on. "I likely have the ability to assist in an escape, but that goes far beyond my purview. Or preview, as your handsome young friend would say."

"I don't have any friends," insisted Chism.

"Don't say that," said Mave, kneeling directly in front of Chism. Maybe even close enough to hear Cheshire's whispers.

"If Gorman sees you," said Chism, "he'll eat you."

Mave looked over his shoulder, but Gorman had his face in the bucket. "You're scaring me, Sir."

"In that case," whispered Cheshire, "I'll make myself scarce. As usual it's been a pleasure." He lowered himself to the ground and padded toward the center of the Pit.

"Feel free to visit again," said Chism. "I suggest the day after we get out."

Just as the Cheshire Cat reached the spot under the trapdoor, it opened.

"Is it tomorrow already?" asked Chism. Was it possible he'd been unconscious overnight? Or longer?

No one bothered to answer.

Muehner raised his arms in front of his face and plowed backward into the corner. Wot and Gorman slid toward the sunlight as fast as a couple of shriveled up worms. Just before they reached the spot where Cheshire sat, the animal leapt into the air and caught the bottom rung of a ladder. He climbed as it descended, causing the ladder to sway in midair. Up the rungs he went as down the rungs came, resulting in no progress, but looking as graceful as a cat in a tree.

"Don't touch ladder until we get it down!" ordered a man from above.

"No one is touching," said a man with a familiar thunderous voice. "Maybe hold ladder like you wear fur, not feathers."

The ladder touched ground, and the Cheshire Cat padded up into a world unknown to Chism. His colors must be turned off, since Chism could see him, so to the men up top Cheshire would be invisible, unless he decided to show himself by turning his colors on.

"Red Knight," shouted the voice he recognized. Skytusk. "Climb."

Chism wondered if the time to be sold had arrived. It couldn't be a year already, could it? A year had ... 365 days, and he'd only been in the Pit for a hundred and thirty ... something.

"If Red Knight still lives, please to climb ladder," said Skytusk.

Using the timber of the wall to steady himself, Chism rose to his feet. Mave held out a hand, but Chism waved it away. By inches he shuffled one foot in front of the other toward the ladder. It came as no surprise, but he'd grown no taller. If anything, he had more space between his head and the ceiling than when he'd arrived.

For a minute he just held the ladder, catching his breath and summoning strength. His fingers and toes still tingled from his incident and he didn't trust them to function properly. The meal he'd skipped and the small portions he'd taken everyday didn't help either. However, if he was going up into the Domain as a representative of the Elites, Wonderland, and Queen Cuora he shouldn't look as fragile as dry apple peels.

Groaning with effort, Chism lifted one foot to the bottom rung. He took a few quick breaths and tried to pull the other foot up. His arms shook, and his first foot screamed in pain at the pressure being placed on it. Mere inches short of the rung, his strength gave out, and his foot fell back to the dirt. He rested his forehead on a rung and filled his lungs with air.

Three Elites—all of them except Muehner and Serrill—sat or crouched around him and the ladder.

"Let us help you, Sir," said someone.

"No," grunted Chism. They couldn't do it without touching him.

Again he drew from his very shallow reserves and lunged upward, moving more slowly than a weed growing in a field. One toe caught the edge of the rung, and he was able to shift his weight and slide it the rest of the way on.

Victory.

Now only about ten more to go.

"We do not have month to wait," said Skytusk from above. "Wrap around ladder. We pull you up."

Chism shook his head and made to raise his arm one rung, but the ladder launched upward and the rest of the world lurched downward. He bent his free arm around the side of the ladder and hugged it for all his life was worth.

From beyond the bramble wall, Zeemi called, "Farewell! I will never forget debt, my friend."

Chism lacked the ability to dispute the title. All his faculties were directed to not being sheared from the ladder by the violent light. His eyelids did almost nothing to reduce its intensity. It bathed his skin in searing, splendid warmth. The only thing in the Pit that had grown comfortable was the darkness, and even that one comfort was being stripped and left behind.

As soon as the feet of the ladder were set on firm soil, Chism slumped to the ground and lifted an arm to screen his eyes. The other Elites might be used to blindness, but Chism needed to see what awaited him. Through squinted and shielded eyes, he peered around. More than a dozen fur-clad guards—he'd count the rest when he could see properly—were gathered in the courtyard, but two figures stood out.

The first was cat-shaped with an oversized smile. Next to him was the unmistakable profile of a man wearing a large top hat and a coat with tails.

Chism's brother had come to the Domain.

9

"We would both thank you to not touch him, please," said Hatta.

Chism glared through a gap in his fingers and saw a guard reaching. The man pulled up short, but paused and looked at another man.

"Listen to him," said the familiar voice. Chism peeked and recognized Skytusk. He looked even bigger than when he'd stripped Chism and given him fur on the city walls 133 or 134 days before. His long, braided beard was full of chits.

The other guard backed off.

Hatta reached down to lay a linen veil across Chism's eyes. Then he tied it around the back of his head. Chism still had to squint, but he was able to lower his arm. Next, Hatta offered a waterskin to Chism's mouth. Chism kept his mouth closed, took the skin, thanked his brother, and raised it himself. He might not be able to fight, but he didn't have to let anyone treat him like a baby.

It was watered wine, and after nothing but apples and bread for over four months, Chism wanted to drain the waterskin. He forced himself to stop after two large swallows.

Hatta knelt next to him, setting his walking staff on the ground.

He brushed a clump of hair off Chism's right shoulder, then another off of the left. Without touching him, of course.

"If I didn't know you were my brother, I could mistake you for a starved kitten." He scraped more stringy black hairs from Chism's goatskin tunic. "But your hair doesn't seem to be attached as rightly as a kitten's would."

Domainers stood around, silently mocking, or, even worse, pitying Chism. The Red Knight, defender of the Circle and the Sword, champion of the Queen of Hearts—weak and stooped in front of them. Beaten, in their minds. He just knew it.

Chism had not come this far to crawl. The slog up the winter creek by Cactus's house came to mind. It seemed like years since he had fled Duke Jaryn and Far West Province. That had been hard—no, impossible. And he had beaten it, exhausted and blood-depleted and all. For more than an hour after his strength gave out he had drawn on sheer will.

It was that reserve that he needed to find now, even though starved and sanity-depleted there was no guarantee it still existed.

Chism reached out fingers that looked too bony to be his and wrapped them around Hatta's walking stick. It was as thick around as Chism's emaciated wrist. Like a man rising from the dead, he hid all emotion and strain from his face and stood, leaning on the staff.

Three soldiers, that he could see, put hands on hilts or hafts of weapons, their fingers working in readiness.

That's right.

Apparently some of them remembered him from the city wall. Others among the guard looked at their wary companions as if they were scared of a sick borogove.

Still they watched him, judging his queen, his people, and his Circle and Sword by one wasted boy. Chism wanted to kill them all. He might not be able to see the color red, but he knew what blood looked like. He would bathe them in it and leave no doubt about his color or his skill. The Blood Red Knight.

"You're not thinking like Mave," said Cheshire. "Better said, you're not thinking. Period. Like Mave."

The animal was right. Chism's energy would be better spent making sure that Mave didn't do anything stupid. He had the rest of his life for vengeance. More fate-granted time if his brother truly was there to ransom them.

The closest guard was skimming the scene, looking for the source of the sound. His eyes eventually settled on Hatta, who was nearest to the Cheshire Cat.

Chism abandoned the plan to fight, but he held tight to his fury. It would fuel that deep reserve if he ever had to draw on it again.

"Did you ransom all of us, Hatta?"

"If you mean the Elites," said Hatta, "then yes. If you mean anyone more, then sadly, no."

"Bring them up," Chism ordered the guards nearest the Pit.

Skytusk used his beard to motion toward the hole, and they lowered the ladder.

In a private tone, Chism said to Hatta, "How much was the ransom?"

"It was a bargain, really."

That was impossible. Not only were they Elites led by the Red Queen's personal Knight, they were responsible for a score of deaths and the destruction of half a dozen buildings. Chism's exaggerated reputation could only have raised the price.

"How much?"

"Not as much as it was worth to me," answered Hatta. "Hence, a bargain."

As Chism searched for the words to thank his brother, emotion rose into his throat and through the rest of his face, blocking everything but tears. At least the blindfold concealed his wet eyes. Too bad it couldn't hide the gut-deep blubbering.

Gorman was the first one after Chism to be raised. One moment, Chism wondered why one of the junior members of the squad was being lifted out. The next moment, he wondered how he'd missed the magnitude of the man's emaciation. Filthy skin hung everywhere in flaps, like thin wings. The skin under one arm completely covered the rung on which it rested. No muscle remained anywhere on him.

He fell to the ground as Chism had and was given a veil and the wineskin as the ladder was lowered again. Gorman drained the skin.

"Meat," he grunted.

"In good time," said Skytusk. "There is food prepared for you in wagon."

A good time for Gorman was immediately. He located the wagon, just behind a row of guards, and scooted to it on hands and knees. Using the wheel spokes as rungs, he scrambled up and into the back of the wagon and began rooting through the supplies.

"Light rations, Gorman, or you'll regret it," called Chism. The man made no sign of having heard.

Muehner wasn't next up, as Chism had hoped. They might have a hard time getting him out before dark.

The man on the ladder was Wot, and before the ladder even cleared the opening, he dove off. He botched the landing, tripped, and fell forward onto his hands. He wasted no time in getting his legs under him and stretching as tall as he could. Joints creaked and popped as he stood erect.

"Oh, the back hurts," said Wot, "but it is so good to stretch and stretch it. I'll stretch it for days then stretch it another day." He spun in a circle with his eyes closed tight and his arms high above his head. The bones of his elbows protruded like knobs on a cabinet. His leather pants had worn off above the knee and only stayed up because of a cinched leather cord. The furry tunic looked like an animal that had been scraped off a highway, even down to Wot's ribs showing through the mangy gaps.

One of the guards abandoned the ladder to make a barrier in front of the opening so that Wot didn't fall in. Another man stepped forward to help lower the ladder.

Hatta approached Skytusk and said, "Is bread so expensive in the Domain? Can I buy some for the prisoners in that Pit and that Pit and that Pit and c.?" He pointed at the line of trapdoors.

With a wide grin Skytusk said, "Those prisoners are not for ransom. They eat and live better than hostages."

"Do they eat as well as you?"

"Not by tenth," said the commander. "Pit cannot be a comfortable place, or all would want to live there."

"And how good, or not good as it were, would hostages eat?" asked Hatta.

"Food is untainted, but small in portion. Elites will share story of being hostage. All of your land will hear, and see, how horrible is life as hostage. People pay ransoms much faster and much bigger."

"I'd prefer to just leave each other alone instead of hassling with hostage-taking and ransom-paying and very expensive bread."

The commander guffawed and slapped Hatta on the back. "Life so simple would be life boring, Hatterman!"

Next out of the Pit was Mave, as undernourished as the others but far cleaner. If he had been pale when they'd gone in, he bordered on translucent when he was brought out. His eyes were much too big, and the bones of his face were prominent enough to scare children. Chism doubted he'd ever recover the handsomeness he'd taken into the Pit.

Mave stood carefully and stretched, one hand shielding his eyes at a time. When he crouched, a guard gave him a veil and a wineskin.

"Glad to see you thinking instead of acting, Mave," said Chism.

"Yes, Sir. Don't feel so much like acting whereabouts now." He still talked so fast it almost came out as a buzz.

"Is Muehner going to come up?"

"Doubt it."

Chism squatted next to the opening, thankful for a reason to be off his feet. "Muehner. Come on up."

He didn't reply.

"Muehner. We've been ransomed. Come grab the ladder."

"I can't. The sun is searing me."

"You're not even in the sunlight."

"See what I mean? The humors in my eyeballs will boil if I go out there."

"Cover yourself with blankets," said Chism. "We'll lead you to the wagon and you can stay covered until nightfall."

"Are you sure it's a real ransom? It might be a ruse to sell us."

"My brother's here. He paid the ransom." More ... feelings rose inside Chism, but he was able to push them back down this time.

Amidst sounds of cloth rustling toward the ladder, Muehner said, "Didn't know you had a brother, Sir."

Over four months together and they knew relatively little about each other. Chism simply replied, "I didn't know the sun could boil your eye humors."

When they finally pulled Muehner up and out, he was wrapped like a sloppy gift with the Elites' blankets. Not a speck of skin showed. Even the arm which he used to cling to the ladder was wrapped independently up to the armpit.

"Carry him to the wagon," Chism ordered the nearest guards. "Clear a spot in a corner, and don't let those blankets touch anything." As soon as they made camp, Chism would burn them, fleas, lice, and all.

Chism stood and shuffled to the commander. "We have a catatonic man down there."

"Won't be first time we remove body from Pit." He barked some quick orders, and men scrambled down the ladder, carrying a rigging of some sort. Other men set up a triangular frame above the opening and attached ropes to it.

"Veil his eyes before you bring him up," ordered Chism. Serrill couldn't be trusted to cover them.

When they hoisted the ropes, Serrill hung like a moth in a cocoon. His body was rigid and unmoving. When they laid him on his back, one arm and one leg remained held rigidly in the air.

"You want to take him?" asked Skytusk. "Or leave him here?"

Chism wondered if the commander was making a joke, but he was in no mood for it. "Load him in the wagon."

The Maners obeyed. Serrill's ransom would most likely be a waste of money; Chism doubted that any amount of sunlight or freedom would be enough to break through his stupor after so long.

He followed slowly as they carried Serrill to the wagon and gently laid him opposite the bundle that was Muehner. The lieutenant kept one armed raised, as if he was waiting for someone to shake hands.

Skytusk stood nearby, as did Hatta and Cheshire. Chism looked at both humans.

"Are we done here?"

"Aye," said the commander. "There are some few weapons in wagon, in case you meet brigands. As long as you display flag we attached, no honest people of Domain will bother you."

A tiny flag fluttered pathetically from a small stick on the front corner of the wagon. Chism didn't even care what color it was. He began to slowly climb the spokes into the wagon.

"Safe travel," said the commander. "I hope to meet on field of battle."

Chism paused and looked up at the man. Eight large chits peeked out of his braided beard. His eyes were pale and confident.

"Not half as much as I do," said Chism, sincerely.

"Vaylee's beard, boy. If you were Domainer, we would drink bloodhoney wine together on this day. Chits and beard and ne'er afeared."

Spit and shear and burn your beards.

Chism focused on not doing what Mave would've done at that moment.

It took Chism so long to mount the wagon that the chieftain ordered planks brought to boost him. Chism barely had enough energy to get angry, and certainly not enough to resist the aid. The other Elites were helped in and settled. Hatta sat alone on the bench. He held reins but did not use them. With a gentle word, he got the horses to start walking. Chism made a point to ignore the Domainers and all their stares. Vengeance could wait until Chism was a human being again.

All six Elites were crammed knee to jowl in the back of the wagon. Where there wasn't a man, there were supplies. Chism used them as a barrier between himself and his men. Overall, the tight quarters were a comfortable position to be in.

Grease glistened on Gorman's fingers and face, and a pile of chicken bones was scattered in his lap. His features contorted in pain. He clutched his stomach, moaned, and leaned forward.

Wot squatted behind him, peering out at the Maners and muttering under his breath. His face was just a skeleton with skin stretched tightly over it. With one hand he lifted a large chunk of dark yellow cheese to his mouth. With the other, he clutched a shiv he'd fashioned from the bramble wall. If the Maners weren't so cautious about catching the prisoners' fleas, Chism would have ordered him to stand down.

Muehner and Serrill lay still as corpses.

"Muehner," said Chism. "You under there?"

"Yes, Sir. Gorman's not eyeing me like a ham in burlap, is he?"

A small chuckle escaped Chism's throat before he could stop it. "No. I don't think Gorman is craving meat any longer. You want some food?"

"I can wait until it's safe to come out."

"Have a few bites," said Chism. "Get your lazy stomach back to work little by little." He wedged some cheese in between the blankets and into Muehner's hand. Without leaving the safety of blankets, the hand burrowed toward the head like a mole and deposited the morsel.

The wagon rocked as Gorman pushed himself up onto his knees and vomited over the side. Before Chism looked away, he noticed Domainers jumping out of the way.

"That's right," said Chism. "Show them to take us hostage."

Gorman wiped his mouth with one hand while the other reached into another food sack.

Mave leaned back against the sidewall near Chism. He tore a small loaf of bread and handed half to Chism.

"I have to thank you, Sir."

"No, you don't. Not after my malfunction this morning." Chism tore a small bit of crust and lifted it to his mouth.

"If you hadn't defriended me in the beginning, I would've ended up worse than Serrill."

"*Be*friended." Chism didn't understand what he'd done that made Mave think they were friends. "I didn't treat you any differently than I treated them."

"Exactly. You were the only one who reached out to everyone. You even kept Serrill alive."

"A hefty heap of good that did."

"Without due respect, Sir, you're blind."

"Maybe you noticed—we're all as blind as moles."

"I've been an Elite for about six months," said Mave. "If by some miracle I don't get extolled, I plan on spending the next nine and a half years trying to become half the Elite you are."

"Expelled, not extolled. They're pretty much opposites in this case."

"All I know," said Mave, looking with veiled eyes directly at Chism, "is I owe my sanity and my life to you. Someday I'll find a way to repay you."

"Enough sappy talk. Save it for your wife."

"I don't have one," said Mave. "Wanted to wait until I became an Elite before I worried about that." He looked away, out at the city. "Now I guess I'll never have to worry about it."

Maybe there was something Chism was supposed to say to comfort Mave, but he didn't know what it was, so he focused on ignoring the Domainers. Citizens had lined the winding streets of Phaylea like it was a parade. However, instead of the insults and rotten vegetables that Chism expected, they hurled salutes of "Hee!" and respect-filled shouts of "Red Knight" and "Sir Chism Wonderlanderman."

"What's wrong with these people?" Chism wondered aloud.

"They know greatness when they see it," said Mave.

Chism still had no idea what he'd done that was so special. If it weren't for Hatta, he'd still be underground, trying to scrap together the shreds of his sanity.

One old woman crowed, "Vaylee's own!" Chism hoped the comment wasn't directed at him, even though it followed him through the streets after that.

Chism decided he'd rather sweet-talk Mave than listen to Maner nonsense.

"Stop me if you've heard this," Chism said. "My own squadron took the Circle and Sword from me as squadron justice after the first Duke Jaryn incident. I was not an Elite, and barely part of the squadron until I could make it back to Palassiren to stand trial."

"And let me guess," said Mave. "It wasn't as bad as you thought it would be?"

Chism chewed the grainy bread slowly then swallowed. "Of course it was, Mave. Worse than dying. But I still went back voluntarily and stood trial."

"So you're telling me that everything will work out?"

"I doubt it. Would you throw me out of the wagon if I said you seriously maved it up twice?"

"You say what you want, and I'll learn what I can from it."

"Learn this—think before you act. I had to learn that, and nearly ended up dead in the process. If you can learn it, you'll be an Elite to rival the greats. If you can avoid a court-martial, you'll be a Knight someday. You'll go down in history."

"Who's getting sappy now?" asked Mave.

"I meant what I said about the scarcity of decent brains in Elite bodies," Chism told him.

"And I meant what I said about the scariness of leaders back in the Pit."

"Scarcity, not scariness. I said the word two seconds ago."

"Maybe I did that one on purpose," Mave said with a small smile. "You really had me worried. I thought you might go the way Serrill had." They rode in silence for a bit then Mave said, "But I meant what I said about allegiance. I owe you more than I can say."

"Tell you what," said Chism. "Making it out of the Domain without doing anything stupid would be a perfect start to repaying me."

Gorman twisted and heaved again, spattering the feet of the parade-goers.

"Slow down, huh," said Chism. "This food has to last us five days."

Dragging the back of one hand across his mouth, Gorman eyed Chism and eyed the nearest bag of food. His hand moved toward the sack.

Imagine that, thought Chism. *Me telling other soldiers to slow down and think.*

The hypocrisy was lost on Gorman, who folded the sack's opening, stretched out his legs between supplies and leaned back against his own sideboard.

Somehow the leader prerogative still hadn't disintegrated. But there was plenty of time between Phaylea and Palassiren yet.

10

Two hours after leaving Phaylea, the wagon entered an area forested with pinion junipers and greenstick trees. The city was blocked from view, as was the soon-to-be-setting sun.

Chism removed his veil and squinted until his eyes grew accustomed to twilight. The other Elites followed his lead.

"Muehner," he said. "The sun's going to be behind the trees for the rest of the evening."

"I think my chances are better under here. How's the moon look so far?"

"Not up yet."

"Let me know how full it is when you see it," said Muehner. "I don't trust it."

"What'd the moon ever do to you?" asked Wot.

"It's a sky imp that does the sun's dirty work while the sun sleeps."

Chism and Wot gave each other a questioning glance. But who were they to judge Muehner's variety of madness? Wot shrugged and went back to scanning the trees along the roadside. Chism climbed over the backrest of the wagon bench to sit next to Hatta.

He stretched his legs out in front of him and criss-crossed his fingers behind his head. The extra bread and a little dried fish in his belly had worked a miracle. Sun and fresh air didn't hurt either.

"Have the Elites taken to wearing animals instead of blue?" asked Hatta.

"These were our disguises for the mission," said Chism. "We had to look like Maners."

"This coat is new," said Hatta. "It's fox, but only in color." He glanced nervously back at Gorman's mucky orange sleeves, which were fox composition. Most likely in color too, if any color remained in them.

"What color are your pants?" asked Chism.

"Violet." Hatta smiled when he looked down at his pants. "Spring violet, not winter violet."

"And the hat is the same traveling hat. Purple, right?"

"Indubitably!"

"I can't believe you came all this way alone," said Chism. Hatta opened his mouth to argue, but Chism was ready for it. "Just you and the horses, that is."

"Targus assured me I'd be allowed to pay the ransoms and take the ransomed without any trouble."

"What about brigands? Rough roads? Bad directions? Wild animals?"

"Animals never give me trouble," said Hatta. "And I wasn't aware that the Domain had wrong roads or wild brigands."

"Every place has brigands," said Chism. "Who would ransom you if you were taken hostage en route to ransoming us?"

"Perhaps Cuora. She's the one who told me about you. She even sent some monies to help defray some of the cost of paying the ransom."

That surprised Chism, but it also explained how Hatta had been able to afford it. He did well for himself, but Chism still expected the ransom must have cost a small fortune.

"How are things between the Reds and Whites lately?"

"They don't seem to like each other," said Hatta. "Ever since Cuora and Markin took to being queen and king and the Whites left."

"I was there for that, remember? What's happened in the last six months?"

"Six months? Oh, very bad things. They are not any less unfriendly than they were more than six months ago."

"Huh?"

"What I mean to say is, they are on the brink of a state in which they will soon undertake aggression and prisoner taking, but they can't decide if they dislike the other more so or less so than they dislike the Western Domain."

From the wagon bed, Mave interjected, "You mean war, Hatter?"

Chism gave him a sharp look. His brother was obviously trying to avoid the word.

Hatta smiled and said, "Rum cake, plum cake, angel cake, tart."

"What are those?" asked Chism.

"Modes of cakery, of course."

"What do they have in common?" asked Chism, hoping that if he played along he could get back to details regarding the impending war.

"The tea party which was interrupted by this journey had each of those cakes present, but no others."

"Was Cheshire there with you? And Haigha?"

Hatta drummed his fingers on his chin and considered. "It's always so difficult to say where Cheshire is or isn't."

"And that's when you got the message from Cuora?"

"Not from Cuora, from a courier," said Hatta. "Well, from her, but not entirely *from* her."

"Did you go through Palassiren on your way here?" asked Chism. He was close to finding out more about the Reds and Whites again.

"No," said Hatta. "The experiences I've experienced there haven't been pleasant experiences, taken as a whole."

"What about the Provinces?" asked Mave, not noticing Chism's shaking head. "Did you see their armies? Where were they?"

"Oh, I'm sure I—what I mean to say is, I saw a pair of jubjub birds in a nest in Serpent Gap. But no serpents."

It was useless. With Mave there, Chism would never ease Hatta around to talking about military issues.

"This looks like as good a place as most and better than some to make a camp," said Hatta. He leaned forward over the footboard and patted the paler horse and made soothing sounds. The horses came to a gentle stop.

"Do you have tents?" asked Chism.

"Tents! A good idea of which I only just now gained possession." He smiled his full smile.

"Flint and steel?"

Hatta shook his head.

"Blankets or bedrolls?"

"Bedrolls, yes! And bread rolls too."

"What other supplies?"

"A box of nails. A towel, of course. Pink tunics. Blue trousers. A sack of sacks—you never know when you will need a sack. Hats and boots for the tops and bottoms of you. Some prosthetic beards, a tea set, a croquet set, set of bowls, and a barrel of nails. A small one."

"That's a lot of nails," said Wot, still scanning the trees.

"Pink tunics?" asked Chism. "When we went into the Pit, pink was a woman's color. I think."

Hatta shrugged. "I can't support Red or White, but I can support Red *and* White. Perhaps white and red stripes next time?"

"I'd wear a dress and bonnet if it meant getting out of this flea hovel," said Chism.

Mave stuck his head inside a dark sack made of courser fabric than the others. "Looks like the Maners sent a flint," he said. "There's a sling here, too. And a couple of knives."

"Good," said Chism. "Mave, get a fire going."

"Mind if I take a dip in the stream first?" asked Mave.

"A quick one," said Chism. "Muehner, it's pretty dusky. You ready to come out and get a bite?"

"What's the moon like?"

Hatta answered, "It's like a solid piece of mercury tonight. A liquidity of silver."

"Nuh uh," said Muehner. "I have exactly as much light in here as I want."

"You can't live in that flea tent for the rest of your life," said Chism. "What would it take to get you out?"

"An umbrella."

"Unfortunately I don't have a single umbrella," said Hatta, "but I have two if that will do."

"One for each hand," mused Muehner. "Even better."

"Make it one total," said Chism. "Keep a hand free for eating. Help gather firewood first. Gorman, you up to clearing a spot for bedrolls?"

"I'm more stuffed than a bird with a gut full of frogs, but I'll do what I can."

"Wot, firewood duty as well."

"You got it. Yessir. Find some firewood to make a fire. But watch out for the bright fire; it'll be bright, and we haven't seen fire, not for a fire of months." He carefully climbed to the ground and began scanning, still mumbling.

"Everyone watch out for snakes and scorpions and such," announced Chism. "Move just as slowly as you've been moving for the last few months, and they'll have plenty of time to avoid you."

Chism handed Hatta supplies from the wagon, and Hatta carried them to the appropriate areas. Between armloads, Chism caught his breath.

Muehner came out from his blankets while a residue of sunset still showed on the horizon. An oversized umbrella shielded every bit of his skin from the full moon.

The veil would have made the bright moon more bearable, but

Chism would never adjust to the light if he hid from it like Muehner.

In thrice the time it would take any other squadron to set up a full camp, the Elites had bedrolls placed and a small fire burning. They removed their furs and leathers and brushed as much dead hair and vermin off their bodies as possible, then dressed in the pink tunics and trousers Hatta had brought. Luckily, there was plenty of rope in the wagon, or the clothes would have slid off of them.

Each man—Muehner first, before the fire grew too bright—dropped his own Domain clothes and blanket into the fire. When the burnt hair stench cleared, they sat in a half circle, each man brushing shoulders with the next as they paced another meal into their mouths. Chism sat as one bookend, with a gap between him and Mave, Hatta sat next to Wot as the other bookend. Muehner kept the umbrella between himself and the fire. Every once in a while, he gave the moon a distrustful look.

Contentedness, a feeling Chism never expected from Scaled Tiger Squadron again, emanated from the huddle of skeletal men like the heat that radiated from the skeletal fire.

"I hope you're not too attached to those beards, men," said Chism. "Or the hair on your heads." The sooner he separated them from everything tied to the Domain, the better.

All four reached up to run fingers through the hair on their face. Three of them started scratching.

"If I had a razor, I'd take it off tonight," said Muehner. Gorman, Wot, and Mave grunted in agreement.

That was a good sign. "Next town we come to," said Chism. He finished the crust in his hand then rose to his feet. "I'm going to find some more firewood."

"I'll help," said Hatta, also standing. "If you meet any creatures of the nocturne, you'll need me to interpret."

"If I find a stick thicker than my thumb, I'll need help carrying it," said Chism playfully. Without the crushing weight of the Pit, levity came easy, even at the expense of their pathetic condition.

Compared to the bright fire, the full moon cast a very acceptable amount of silver light for Chism's eyes. The brothers wandered through scrubby juniper trees and other low bushes without talking. Here and there lunging cactopi spread their eight spiny arms wide. Chism gave those plants a wide berth and gave Hatta a warning whenever he saw one. His eyes adjusted to the brightness and the desire to squint was fading. He was also struck by an inexplicable desire to stay near Hatta. The desire went beyond the wish to warn him about the dangerous cactus. Never in his life could he remember preferring the company of another person when he had room to wander.

"Hatta," said Chism. He bent to pick up a thin stick, tried to break it in half and failed. He tucked it under one arm. "How much do you remember about Mother?" Ever since Zeemi had mentioned her, uncertainty had persisted in Chism's mind.

"She was kind. No matter what ... anyone did to her, she still treated everyone kindly. Even ... well, even everybody. Also, she loved the colors in spring. That last spring before she left, she would walk with me in the every morning and tell me the names of every flower." Hatta smiled. "What would you think of when you attempt to remember?"

"Nothing." She had died when Chism was born. Rather, Chism was born as she died. "Definitely not kindness. She shouldn't have let Father be like he was, and if he wouldn't change, she had no business staying with him. She's responsible—at least in part—for our suffering." It all came out in a rush, like it was Mave talking instead of Chism. It felt like something else Chism wanted to leave behind in the Domain.

"What?" Hatta stopped in his tracks and stared at Chism. "How can that be? She did entirely all she could to help us and herself."

"Why would somebody wonderful ever be with *him*?" Chism's

opinions might not be fair, but without knowing his mother personally, he couldn't prove they were wrong.

"That has nothing to do with anything or anything else," said Hatta. "Often she risked her life for me."

Of course Hatta would see her in the best possible light. There was no use in discussing it with him; he never saw truth, only goodness.

Hatta wasn't done. "How could even what *he* did ever be *her* fault?" Slowly and clearly, as if concentrating to be clear and succinct, Hatta said, "She loved us."

The feeling people called love never came to mind when Chism thought about his mother. Or anyone else for that matter. If love was what he felt for Hatta, then it was a perplexing feeling indeed —strong caring mixed with duty and frustration. He couldn't conceive of feeling that way for anyone but his brother. Why would he want to?

"Love is just caring too much about someone," said Chism.

Again Hatta was stunned. "Love is the every-est color in the world. It's being rescued at the entirely perfect time. Love is days you'll remember forever and ever and days you couldn't want to forget." He stared at Chism, apparently waiting for comprehension. "Love is what mother did for us, which was entirely everything she ever could."

The rescue was the only part of what Hatta said that Chism could understand in the slightest, but even that sounded mostly like duty.

Hatta took a step closer. "Why would you suddenly be concerned about her, brother?"

The reason was so ridiculous, Chism almost didn't tell him. "According to Zeemi, there are people who say I'm the son of Vaylee —even though I told him my mother was dead."

"Hmm," said Hatta. "Given those choices, I'd be more inclined to say she was Vaylee than ... that other option you mentioned."

"Hatta, Vaylee is some Maner deity legend. Besides, you were there. I ... she died when I was born."

Hatta stopped and looked at Chism, surprise obvious on his face. "No one ever said that. They said she went somewhere else. Somewhere better."

"That's a nice way to say she's dead," said Chism. He saw some wood to his right. When he turned to pick it up, he noticed a silhouette standing in the darkness, watching.

Vaylee's beard. "What are you doing, Mave?"

Mave didn't move, mouth partly open, eyes still and guilty.

"Visiting the privy. The bush, I mean."

If Chism made the conversation seem like a secret, Mave would probably make a bigger deal about it. So Chism said nothing. He left the sound of water on gravel behind as he followed Hatta deeper into the darkness. Bunch of nonsense anyway.

Ignore it, and it will go away.

Exhausting himself wasn't a difficult task, but the low fire didn't require much fuel. Chism started walking back, carrying only a small portion of the total haul. Together, the brothers gathered enough for at least another hour of fire.

They found the area around the fire empty.

Chism dropped the sticks, reached for Thirsty, found only air.

"Muehner? Wot?" He said it in a whisper and slid behind a bush, motioning for Hatta to do the same. If there were enemies nearby, there was little Chism could do. But he was as likely to give himself up easily as a battlesnake was to retreat.

Only the fire made noise. Not even wind disturbed the silence.

"Gorman?" His voice carried just past the ring of firelight, but it brought no answer in return.

"Mave?" There was no reason his men should be any further away than that question could reach.

"Lieutenant Chism?" Mave's loud voice came from the direction of the wagon. "We're over here."

His voice sounded unruffled enough, but Chism still took care as he led Hatta toward the wagon. It wasn't far, but a few thick trees obscured their view of it.

Chism stepped around a tree to see his men hunched in the back of the wagon, blankets draped over their shoulders to keep the chill off. Muehner had his umbrella *and* blanket for protection.

"You men sure are a sight. Trapped within touching distance for months and what do you do as soon as you have room to stretch?"

A voice came from Chism's right, closer to the wagon than he and Hatta stood. "Like birds, huddled together like birds." The voice came from low to the ground. It sounded earthy, like cracking clay.

The Elites in the wagon crouched closer to the floorboards. One or two of them rustled around to place items in their hands. Chism looked at the ground in front of his feet for a rock, a stick, or even a handful of dirt he could use as a weapon.

A short figure with a profile like a heavy monkey stepped into the clearing between Chism and the wagon. It moved unhurriedly, as if considering every step, and wore a confident smile on its wide lips. In one hand it dragged a snake thicker than Chism's arm and longer than he was tall. At one end, the snake had no head. At the other, a rattle as big as a spyglass.

The creature's skin resembled the snake's, but less scaly. It had the thick, impenetrable look of an elephant's skin. Around its armpits, groin, ankles, wrists, neck, and head were fine feathers, black as a crow's.

"Targus," said Hatta with wonder. "Earlier today we were talking about a Targus who isn't a targus."

The strange animal peered at Hatta over one shoulder. It had the heavy brow and lips of a monkey and was as wrinkled as Hatta's old tailor friend, who had received his nickname based on the resemblance.

If one ignored the enormous headless snake in its hand, the targus was overall quite gentle in appearance.

Its reputation told the opposite story.

In the wagon, Mave had slowly risen to his knees. He pulled an arm into the air above his head and brought it forward. A knife flew toward the targus, glinting moonlight as it spun end over end.

It was not the full-strength throw of a healthy Elite, but it crossed the distance before anyone could say a word. Without turning around, the targus hopped to the side like a squirrel with eyes in the back of its head.

By the time the knife harmlessly hit the ground, the targus had faced the Elites in the wagon and spit a stream of liquid that splattered into a mist on the side of the wagon. A breath later, all four men collapsed inside the wagon. Dead? Stunned? Poisoned? Chism wished he knew more about what the creature was capable of.

The targus turned to Chism and Hatta. Staring out of deep, black eyes, it lifted the snake to its mouth and tore a chunk of meat from the neck. Smears of blood framed its mouth. As the targus lowered the snake carcass, it spasmed, and the rattle sounded a warning.

Chism considered pushing Hatta in one direction and bolting in the other, but the second he moved, the targus would spit. Even if they managed to avoid the initial threat, they wouldn't get far. One thing Chism had heard about targuses was their speed; the other was their cruelty. Chism was still weighing other options when Hatta stepped past him into the clearing.

"Don't worry," said Hatta. "I'll most likely protect you."

Chism didn't know if Hatta was talking to him or the targus.

With his hat in hand, Hatta made a simple bow. "My understanding understood that targuses avoided groups of people."

"And the humans It doesn't avoid It eats if not avoiding the humans." Its voice was as dry as the snake's rattle and as creaky as old wood.

"I certainly hope not," said Hatta. "In this case."

"It could eat you all, could It."

"The size of your stomach hardly looks large enough for that."

"It has size enough for your dreams has It. It could use more and more sleep spit so they sleeps more and more, could It. Then, dreamfeast on dreams."

"You could let us sleep on the effects and sleep off the effects and go on our way," said Hatta. "I'm fond of my dreams, ratherly, and I don't think anyone would enjoy the taste of these men's dreams after what they may've been through."

"Soldiers they act, but appearance is not like the act of soldiers." The targus ripped more snake flesh with its teeth, chewing just twice before swallowing. It pointed a stubby finger at Hatta and said, "But you like algae are as gentle as algae are you."

Unable to fight, Chism was out of his element, so he stood still and observed. He had seen the fingers of a brawler who'd had his hand stomped in a bar fight. The day after the injury, the fingers looked similar to the targus's.

"Would you have a name, perchance?" asked Hatta.

"It is my name is It," said the targus.

"Pleased to meet you, It. I'm Hatta."

"It?" asked Chism.

"Yes," said Hatta. "It."

The targus make a clicking sound in his throat that sounded like *It*.

"Oh," said Chism. "A name."

"And how old would you be?" Hatta asked the targus. "Or how old would It be, if you prefer?"

"When It was your age, It's mother carried It. Still did It's mother when at your age was It."

"Why do you do all the things you do and eat all the things you eat?" asked Hatta.

The targus looked back and forth between the brothers. "We all must do what we all must."

"We are soldiers," interjected Chism. "Elites, from Wonderland. What *we* must do is return to Palassiren."

"Palassiren," said the animal. "It's uncle, Es, his body is there, is the body of Es, It's uncle in Palassiren."

Hatta said, "If you hadn't missed the knife, or vice versa, your body would be on the ground next to the snake's. How fortunate."

"Skill and speed are not fortune. They are speed and skill."

With round, barely bendable fingers, it scooped up the knife and lobbed it softly toward Chism. It landed in the gravel in front of him.

"The knife. Throw at me the knife."

Chism picked it up. The handle was antler, so it wasn't symmetrical, but the balance seemed expert enough. "You want me to throw this knife at you?"

"Yes, yes," said the targus.

"And you won't spit at us and eat our bodies and dreams?"

"No no."

Chism flipped the knife into the air, testing the weight. The handle outweighed the blade, so he gripped the blade carefully. He wasn't as good with throwing knives as his Fellow, Ander, but he was as proficient as the average Elite. Maybe the targus was underestimating him because of his weak appearance.

"Ready?"

"Yes, yes."

If the targus was going to give him a shot, Chism would take it. More than likely, it was their only hope of survival. He took aim, stepped toward the creature, and flung the knife. It struck just off his target—the center of It's body—with the point making impact over its heart. Half of the blade should have sunk into its chest. The knife fell to the ground, leaving no sign of impact.

"Amazing," said Chism. It really did have the skin of an elephant. "I've seen your uncle, Es." After Captain Darieus died, the Elites were given tours of his museum of animals. Of some animals, they all knew plenty. Of some, one or two knew—or assumed—a lot, and they each taught the group. Of a select few, nobody knew anything for sure. The targus was in the last group.

Underestimated did not begin to describe Chism's original assessment of the species.

"He was where was he?" asked the targus.

"In a museum of sorts."

The targus snapped a guttural sound. It sounded like a large bird clamping its beak, and it sounded like a curse. He tore another chunk from the snake and chewed noisily.

"A dirty, showy human museum of humans." It clicked angrily. "Showy. Dirty."

"I can get Es's body," said Chism.

The targus's face snapped toward Chism. "Telling truth are you truth telling?"

Chism nodded. "I know exactly where Es is."

As slowly as a prowling cat, the targus came forward. "Your dreams I will keep. Bring the body, and when you bring the body, your dreams I will no longer keep."

"What good are dreams?" asked Chism. "They can't prevent a war."

With an unbelieving look on his face, Hatta said, "Dreams can do anything, brother. In dreams, you can be or do whatever you want. One man can move the world."

The brothers faced each other.

"Dreams are nonsense," said Chism. "As imaginary as a rainbow."

"Yes!" Hatta nodded excitedly. "Dreams are exactly as exquisite as a rainbow. They are approximately the greatest thing in the entire world, rounding up, of course."

"Dreams do not feed children or stop invading armies."

"But they give starving children a reason to not give up. And they give soldiers a reason to protect their lands and family and family's lands."

"Both of you are right are you both. Neither can understand without understanding the either. It will help to them will It." The targus curved his huge lips and eyebrows in thought, then added, "If they want to bring dreams back, Es's body bring back will they want."

Without warning, It spat a short spray into each of their faces.

Hatta dropped immediately. Chism held his breath and wiped his face as he bolted into the brush. He made it three steps before his legs and brain gave out.

11

Sunlight touched Chism's closed eyelids, searing them like open flame on paper.

"Burn my beard," he said, and brought his hands up. His skin was cold from lying in the dirt without any covering, but the first rays of the day were too sharp to be comfortable or lucky. He knew he still had far to go before finding any luck.

Why am I lying in the dirt?

It took only a second to remember the targus. And the spitting. And that snake.

As far as Chism could tell, he was still alive. That was unexpected. Even better, he didn't think anything was gnawing on his toes.

Leaving his eyelids to do the best they could at their job, he used hands to examine the rest of his body. His pale dungeon-skin would have given way to the targus's teeth much easier than the snake's had.

His skin seemed to be intact. Yet for some reason, he had a hard time caring overmuch. The desire to return to Palassiren and regain the Circle and Sword had fled. If it didn't hurt so much, he would lay back and sleep again. If only he didn't have a squadron to run.

With a curse, Chism sat up. Cupping his hands around his eyes, he staggered to the wagon and dug around for a hat. He shoved the first one he found onto his head and pulled the brim as low as possible. If he squinted and cocked his head forward, the light was bearable.

His men lay where they'd fallen the night before.

"Muehner. Mave. Wot. Wake up."

They didn't flinch. Chism watched for a moment to make sure they still breathed. All of their chests rose and fell.

"Mave!" Chism didn't want to touch him, so he banged on the side of the wagon.

Mave lifted his head, didn't open his eyes. His head slumped again.

Chism stepped next to Muehner's head and yelled, "Muehner!" Practically the same response.

On the other side of the wagon, he stepped up to Gorman.

"Bacon! Cake!" No response. He gave up and went in search of Hatta.

His brother was in the spot where he'd fallen the night before. Unlike the Elites, his eyes were open, and he sat cross-legged, hands in his lap, staring at the ground in front of him. In the sixteen years or so of his life, Chism had never seen Hatta's face so devoid of life, as if someone had shuttered the light of his life.

"How do you feel?" asked Chism softly.

"If you meant, 'what do I feel,' I could answer more easily." For a long moment, there was no answer. Just as Chism was about to ask, Hatta said flatly, "Nothing, brother. I feel entirely nothing."

"It's probably just the aftereffects of the targus's poison. Let's move, just in case he intended us to sleep longer. If he comes back to feast on our bones and dreams, I'd rather be far away."

"Oh, I would think it would be too much too late for that. Dreams are as gone from my head as you are from the Pit."

"If you want your eyeballs and toes to be gone as well, then sit there. If you want to keep them, move."

Hatta looked up at him blankly. "Move?"

"Hitch up the horses. I'll gather the supplies we left lying around. The other Elites are sleeping in the wagon."

With a nod, Hatta stood. He walked toward the horses, passing within inches of his traveling hat.

"Hatta." Chism picked up the hat and placed it on his brother's head. "You don't want to forget your purple traveling hat."

"Yes, I suppose I wouldn't." He continued toward his task.

That worried Chism even more than his bland expression and lightless face. Purple never failed to earn a smile from Hatta.

As Chism patrolled the campsite, he kept his head low and angled away from the sun. There wasn't much to collect: flint and steel, a few blankets, and a small sack of food that had somehow survived nocturnal animals.

If there was any doubt about whether the targus had been there, the blood in the dirt and the tracks of something with small feet dragging a thick snake removed it. Too bad the darkness that hung over him and especially over Hatta hadn't trailed away like the tracks.

"How goes it?" asked Chism as he walked up to the wagon to place the supplies inside. The effort of lifting the items over the side rail barely winded him. A huge improvement from the day before, but an improvement that didn't change the way he felt in the slightest.

Hatta didn't answer. He stood next to the wagon's bench with something in his hand. Chism approached and heard the whisper of a snake rattle before he recognized the huge keepsake in Hatta's hand. The horses were still tied out where they'd been the night before.

"Have you been standing here this whole time?"

Hatta continued to shake the rattle and said with the faintest hint of his old half smile, "My dreams are in there."

Chism decided to hitch up the horses himself. If, in Hatta's brain, the rattle helped relieve the lingering effects of the sleep spit, Chism would give him a little more time.

"Listen," said Hatta, before Chism reached the first horse. He handed him the rattle.

It was the size of a small, skinny loaf of bread. Chism put it to his ear and shook it, only to humor his brother.

The swish wasn't loud, but it was unmistakably speaking to him. *Thirsty*, it said, *hanging at my hip*. Chism stopped shaking and stared at the rattle. The words and impressions stopped immediately. He shook again and held it next to his ear. *Honey and fresh bread and a home. Lucky rays of the sun. Ander at my side and a squadron of dark-clad Elites in the Circle and Sword at my back, following me like children follow a father—a good father.* It said, *Two half-kingdoms and a realm of united barbarians all in peace and living within their borders and their laws. No more children abused and afraid—*

"Did you hear it?" asked Hatta.

Chism's head snapped toward his brother. He nodded and looked at the rattle in his hand. "Those aren't your dreams in there, Hatta." There was no opening of any kind into the rattle, but somehow the targus had found a way to distill his dreams and cram them inside. "Those dreams are mine."

"That's impossible. There's colors in there. So many colors it's bound to burst open at any moment! And animals that don't have to worry about being safe, and they're gentle to each other and everyone's even gentler to them. I hear the smiles of a million faces. The Jabberwock was in there, Chism. And his mate. And they didn't have to kill anybody because nobody ever killed them first. New patterns for my hats. And buttons. All the buttons ever invented, every shape and hue. Let me listen again."

Hatta had started out smiling, but by the time he finished speaking, all joy had left his face. He breathed fast and licked his lips.

"We need to get on the road," said Chism. "When we're moving, I'll give it back."

Hatta looked like a child who'd lost his only toy. He walked toward the horses, despondent. Chism followed to speed up the process. Instead of talking gently to the horses and using his odd talent, Hatta untied the rope and walked toward the wagon. The animals' ears moved in all directions, and they chuffed nervously as they followed. Chism kept an eye on his brother as he went through the steps to hitch the horses.

When both brothers were up on the bench, Hatta picked up the reins and snapped them. The horses looked back, obviously confused. He flicked the reins again, and with an angry whinny the horses began to walk.

Hatta held out his hand toward Chism. It passed into the shadow of a cloud.

Chism handed over the rattle and watched the slightest smile return to Hatta's face as he shook it next to his ear. Chism climbed into the back of the wagon and used a walking stick to arrange the Elites more comfortably than he'd found them. There was no way to place them all without any overlap, and it made him shudder to think about touching someone else for so long, even when asleep, but there was only so much room in the back of the wagon. Personally, he'd rather be dragged behind the wagon by his eyelids than tangled up with another person. Using clean blankets, Chism covered their sensitive eyes and skin from the sun. Then he climbed up to the bench and did nothing as the clouds deepened and darkened.

For miles they rode. The only sound between them came from the huge rattle. Chism heard nothing out of the ordinary when Hatta shook it. After shaking a while with one arm, he switched to the other. Then back again a few minutes later.

"How are your hats selling?" asked Chism. Not that he wanted conversation, but he was concerned about his brother.

"Shh," said Hatta.

"You hungry?"

Hatta waved a hand in Chism's direction without looking over.

"What color is your hair?"

Hatta didn't acknowledge the question.

Whatever, thought Chism. *Suits me just fine.* He dug a pair of apples out of a sack and enjoyed them and his own foul mood in silence.

Clouds finished filling the sky as the Elites slept and his brother rattled away. The desire to do nothing was outweighed by Chism's aversion to sitting still, so he climbed over the side of the wagon and eased himself down. The ground was as unstable as he expected and his legs even more so. He stumbled before catching himself. But he did not fall. That fact should have brought a proud smile to his lips, but the muscles in his face had too little memory of that, and there was no well inside of him from which he could draw the will to remind them.

Just walk, he told himself. *No reason to be cute or fancy.*

As the wagon passed him, Chism snagged the water barrel tied to the rear corner of the bed. He used the wagon's momentum to keep his pace up.

After what felt like ten miles but was likely less than one, a blanket started moving. Mave poked his head out, keeping his eyes shielded. The movement dislodged the blanket covering Muehner, his blanket-mate.

"What the sugar!" said Muehner. His umbrella snapped open, and he scrambled to curl up under it.

"Where'd the moon and dark go?" asked Mave. "Whatever happened, it didn't feel like sleep."

"Hatta," called Chism, but his brother didn't respond. "Hatta!"

He just kept shaking the rattle.

Muehner reached forward and jostled Hatta's shoulder. Hatta turned around, wearing an annoyed expression.

"Stop the horses," said Chism, annoyed at his brother's annoyance. "The men need to stretch and I need to sit."

With his free hand, Hatta yanked on the reigns, and the horses stopped so suddenly that Mave ended up in Muehner's lap.

"Get off, stupid," said Muehner.

Mave hurried off as if he was afraid he'd get beaten. They took different paths down, and Chism took an altogether different one up—a slow path in which he had to stare at his scrawny wrists much longer than he wanted to.

No one spoke until Mave and Muehner had climbed up and the wagon was on its way. Chism tossed each one an apple. Neither offered thanks or anything that approached a smile. Muehner bit into his as if it had offended him somehow, and Mave nibbled his apologetically.

"What's the lackwit doing?" grumbled Muehner, motioning toward Hatta.

"Do you remember the targus?" asked Chism.

Muehner grunted something that sounded affirmative.

"It left us all sleeping and left the rattle of that snake behind."

"Biggest snake I've ever seen," said Mave.

"Shut yourself," said Muehner. "You don't get to talk anymore."

"Are you lieutenant now?" asked Chism.

Muehner glared, but he didn't open his mouth.

After a moment of consideration, Chism said, "Sorry, Hatta, but it's not fair to keep that to yourself."

Hatta continued to rattle dreams into his ear until Chism held out his hand. When he placed the rattle in Chism's hand, Hatta's shoulders sagged, and his gaze fell to his lap. Chism wanted to spite Muehner by bypassing his seniority, but he realized it would be a poor strategic move.

Muehner sneered at the rattle before raising it to his ear. The shaky swish lit up his face like a candle in a dark room. Not a complete transformation, but more smile than they'd seen on Muehner's face in months. After a few seconds of listening, Muehner pulled the rattle around in front of his face and stared at it, trying to make sense of it. He went back to shaking in a matter of seconds.

Mave looked puzzled. He was close enough to hear the rattle, but it obviously made no sense to him.

"Give him a few minutes. Then we'll pass it around," said Chism. Mave shrugged and averted his eyes. Hatta glanced over his shoulder every few seconds, but his face fell forward each time he saw someone else using the rattle.

Part of Chism hoped for a challenge when he demanded the rattle from Muchner a short while later. Maybe a scuffle would clear the muck from his mood. Muehner challenged him with a look, but nothing else except the glare he fixed on Mave.

As hesitant as a girl tying a gold-tipped ribbon in her hair for the first time, Mave blushed and rattled. The pace increased immediately, and his pale face seemed to glow with a shadow of handsome that Chism hadn't thought he'd ever see again. One hand became two, although the quality of the rattle didn't improve. As Mave shook, he began to pry at the layers of the rattle with his fingers like an otter clawing a clam.

"I need that," Mave hissed. "I have to get it out!" He turned to the side rail of the wagon and slammed the rattle against it.

"No!" shouted Hatta. He dove over Muehner and tackled Mave against the back of the wagon. "Don't break my dreams!"

Chism couldn't remember the last time he was too stunned to act, but there he sat, frozen in disbelief.

Muehner grunted a malevolent chuckle, but he did nothing to help Mave extricate himself. When Hatta emerged, cradling the rattle like a baby, Mave pulled his hat down and licked a cut at the corner of his mouth. Blood also rose to the surface in a scratch across his cheek.

"What was in there?" asked Chism.

Mave's chin dipped. He turned away and stared at the dust cloud left by the wagon wheels.

That's fair, thought Chism. *I wouldn't say either.*

The scuffle had awakened the other Elites. After finding hats for them, Chism had to talk Hatta out of the rattle again. Wot stopped muttering for the duration of his rattling, and Gorman licked his lips repeatedly to catch the drool that dripped from the corners of his mouth as he shook it.

Serrill continued to lie like a pile of rocks. The arm that was raised the day before was now clenched so tightly in front of his chest none of the men could straighten it.

"See if you can pry his fingers," said Chism.

Mave and Wot working together were able to force two open at a time.

"Muehner," said Chism, "take the rattle from Gorman and slide it into Serrill's hand."

They did as he said, leaving Serrill gripping it so tightly that his knuckles blanched even paler than the rest of his skin

"Grab his wrist and give it a shake," said Chism.

They couldn't extend the arm, but there was enough give in his tonic muscles to produce a sound that Chism could hear. The sound grew smoother and more natural.

Mave looked up and said, "He's relaxing the arm!" A hint of surprise showed on Mave's face, but the happy emotions Chism thought he should see were absent. From everyone.

As the Elites shook their former lieutenant's untensing arm, Serrill's eyebrows moved slightly together. His eyes glanced to various corners of the clouds overhead. He blinked. That was almost as surprising as Hatta's violent outburst. Tears formed in both eyes and trickled down to get lost in shaggy hair. His expressionless mouth made determining the reason for the tears impossible. Based on the experience of the others, they had to be tears of joy.

"That's enough," said Chism after another minute. He knew he should thank them, but didn't feel like it. "The targus made us all feel like something left on the floor of a tavern for a week. I hope it takes less time than that for it to fade. In the meantime, we have this. We'll pass it around."

All five conscious men moved slightly toward the rattle. A hand here, a leaning torso there.

"Hatta first. We're in his debt. Then me, Wot, Muehner, Gorman, and Mave."

Wot muttered, "Mave's last because he mav—"

"Because he's junior," finished Chism. "Everyone will spend five one-hundredths of the time they have the rattle helping Serrill shake it."

Hatta snatched the rattle from Mave and brought it up to his ear so fast he hit himself hard enough that he winced. His eyes went blank, and his desperate smile returned.

"Does the idiot have a timepiece?" asked Muehner. His scowl was quickly creasing permanent lines into the loose skin on his face as he glowered at Hatta.

"I'll do the counting. We'll tie a scarf on a spoke and I'll keep track. Start with a hundred turns per man. And Muehner," Chism waited until he had Muehner's full attention. "I don't care if you feel like someone ripped out your insides and replaced them with soft dung—the next time you call him anything but Hatta, I will crack your skull."

Hatta didn't seem to notice the labels or care, but it wasn't right.

Muehner mumbled something and looked away.

They stopped the wagon briefly to tie a shred of cloth to one wheel. The Elites in the back rooted for food and stared vacantly at the passing landscape.

I can finally forget about everything and just count, Chism thought with anticipation. He rested his chin in his hand and looked down at the wheel. *One. Two. Three. Four.*

There was definitely something wrong. The mindless task of counting didn't give him the comfort it always had before. It was neutral—better than dealing with quibbling Elites, but not a joy like it should be.

Just a matter of time until it wears off.

"One hundred," he said, some time later. "One hundred!" he repeated and reached for the rattle. Hatta didn't take notice until Chism had his hand on it. He kept his eyes on the rattle as Chism handed it back to Wot.

"What about your turns, Si—" asked Muehner, biting off the title.

"I'll pass for now." He hadn't figured out how to assist Serrill without touching him. The rattle interested him, but apparently not to the extent that it did the others. Especially Hatta. Not enough to make him touch Serrill for a prolonged time. Or any time at all. And Chism wasn't about to rig up ropes and stand over the catatonic man like a puppeteer.

When Wot began shaking, Hatta turned and stared ahead at the road, not seeing the horses or anything else.

Chism took his hat off and looked it over. It was pale. His guess was light green or sky blue.

"What color is this hat?" he asked.

"Yellow," said Hatta. He didn't turn his head. He didn't smile. How long had it been since Hatta had said "yellow" without smiling?

Chism turned his attention to the wheel and counting Wot's turns. One by one, the Elites took their turns, then helped Serrill with his and started over. The only thing resembling banter was Wot's dark mumbling from the far corner of the wagon.

In the early afternoon, they stopped near a creek to rest and water the horses. Chism asked for Wot's help, and they estimated the size of the wheel and how many turns per mile. Chism hoped having more numbers in his head would help break the spell sooner.

As they climbed in and took their places again, Chism announced, "Starting tomorrow, everyone walks part of the way. Half mile the first day, more each following day. Exercise will help us shake this."

The men were too depressed to even grumble.

As the sun approached the horizon, a town came into view. Chism wanted nothing to do with Domainers, so he looked for a spot to turn off. They settled in a sandy area behind a large dune.

"I'm going to town for supplies," said Chism. "Hatta, would you like to go?"

He shook his head and handed Chism a purse.

"Any volunteers?" They all stared at the dirt. "Mave, looks like you're it." It was a piss-boy job, and Mave was the best man for it. Plus, if there was one person he needed to keep an eye on, it was Mave. Hopefully the rest of them could survive an hour or two without an adult to supervise them.

He gave orders to set up camp and lift Serrill out of the wagon to prevent bedsores. The Elites were only concerned with how to share the rattle without being able to count turns. In the end, Chism stuffed it into his pouch. That was an acceptable compromise, and they set to work.

Chism checked the purse and saw Domainer coins. He told Mave to bring the flag from the corner of the wagon and they started walking to town. Chatty Mave didn't say a single word. They found the supplies they needed, ignored comments by the locals, and returned to camp.

Camp consisted of a weak fire and a pile of blankets that hadn't even been laid out in bedrolls, but Chism didn't say anything because Serrill lay on a blanket within the circle of the firelight. One knee was bent into the air, but the rest of him lay flat.

After setting up a watch schedule, Chism said, "We'll all feel better in the morning. There's a razor with the supplies. Shave your heads when you shave your beards. We need to shed as much vermin as possible." He looked at Gorman and considered telling him to shave his arms and chest as well. But Chism didn't even feel like taking the effort to give the order, so it wouldn't be fair to expect Gorman to follow it. He left his men sitting silently around the fire and laid out a bedroll.

Hours later, just as the faintest light of morning began to force darkness out of the eastern horizon, Chism felt a tug on his bedroll. It was Mave, waking him for his hours at watch. Chism grunted and climbed out of bed. He ate bread as he checked on the others. If what they were doing was anything like what Chism had done, it couldn't be called sleeping. Apparently, sleeping without dreams was just going to a dark place for a while.

He felt as much like doing nothing as he had the day before. But with strength returning, he had no reason to not get back to his morning routine. A staff would have to do in the place of Thirsty.

Thirsty. His most trusted friend. What he'd longed for more than anything.

Peering inward, Chism realized he didn't care if he ever held Thirsty again. Somehow in his intense lack of emotions, the lack itself was painful.

Why should a man who never cared about having friends be so undermined by the loss of one? Everything had changed since the targus but really the biggest lack Chism could put a name to was the loss of Thirsty. The abandonment of the one who'd been most loyal. It wasn't the physical separation—they'd been apart for months. It was the lack of connection. With every bond of friendship severed, Chism felt alive in definition only. His heart beat and his chest drew breaths, but his core had been gutted, left empty and dead.

Chism decided to not dwell on such thoughts. They would just make everything he was suffering more real.

He chose a branch on the ground and started working simple forms. His muscles and lungs gave out long before his routine ended. He knelt to catch his breath and rest, and then started again. By the time the sun rose, his hands were blistered and he could barely lift his arms.

The satisfaction he expected didn't come. However, the nothing he felt was preferable to the nothing of doing nothing. Without hope he waited for the sun to crest. Predictably the first rays felt as normal as any other rays.

"Wake up," Chism said as he walked man to man, prodding their piles of blankets with his boot. None of them had taken the effort to lay them out into bedrolls. Nobody obeyed the wake up order, so he went back again, nudging with more firmness. "You can sleep in the wagon."

A third round was necessary, and he stayed with each man until he was on his feet. Camp was easy enough to break, and they resumed the journey after helping Serrill take care of the necessities. They could feed him on the road. The rattle rotation picked up where it had left off.

As much as they wanted to avoid people, the only suitable road passed directly through a town. Chism took a break from carving the handle of his staff and watched his men closely. They didn't need any more trouble. Hatta started straight ahead. Muehner, who still wore a veil, scowled at anyone who would look at him. Wot shifted his gaze twice every second and mumbled. Mave cared only for the rattle. Gorman didn't seem to notice anything except breakfast's cold sausages, which he ate as if he was being forced to.

Rain began to fall as soon as they entered the town. Heavy drops stung their faces and bare arms. It couldn't dampen their spirits further, but it did prevent them from improving. It lasted only an hour, much longer than it took to pass through the town, but the men's moods did not improve when the clouds began to clear. When Chism ordered them to walk, one at a time beside the wagon, they did so without speaking.

Chism continued to whittle a branch into a rough sword shape as he stared at the wheel and counted. During watering breaks, he used the improvised sword to build up strength and remind his muscles of their former skill.

Late in the afternoon, Chism called an end to Mave's one hundred wheel turns. Each man took his five turns helping Serrill, and as Mave crawled up to the front to hand the rattle to Hatta, he settled on the rail of the wagon bed and leaned close to Chism.

In a whisper like he'd done at the beginning of the Pit, Mave said, "I'll take your turns helping Serrill. There's no reason for you to pass the rattle."

Chism shook his head.

"Have you considered wearing gloves or wrapping his wrist in a blanket?"

Chism nodded. A brief touch with a barrier would be bearable, but never for such an extended time.

"If you change your mind ..." Mave said, and he let the offer hang. He took a wide berth around Muehner to get back to his spot.

"Thanks, Mave," Chism forced out. He had wondered if Mave's words about loyalty had been just talk.

If anything, their moods diminished day by day. Chism had to supervise every step of the minimal effort required to make and break camp and care for the animals. Every minute he wasn't acting like their father, Chism practiced with his wooden sword. Strength and stamina returned slowly.

On the fourth day, Muehner and Gorman refused Chism's order to hitch the horses. They claimed seniority trumped the rotation that had been set up.

"We are one day from Wonderland," said Chism. "I'll bring you up on charges if you don't obey."

"Empty threats," said Muehner. "Our Elite days are done."

Wot and Gorman nodded agreement.

"If you want to eat, you work," said Chism. Perfect. One more thing for him to supervise. One more thing to get in the way of his swordplay. "Actually, Mave, you're in charge of supervising the food." Maybe a responsibility would help him get better.

"Perfect idea," said Gorman. "Let him mave up the most important thing we have."

Grumbling, Muehner and Gorman hitched the animals and led them to the road.

Chism stared at the road ahead of them. Hatta sat next to him. A man with nothing left in his life except madness—and not the happy madness that made life bearable for him and everyone around him. But there was no way the dark mood could keep up forever.

A small deer appeared at the side of the road. Hatta continued to stare straight ahead.

"Look," said Chism.

Hatta's eyes slid over to the deer, then back without lingering.

A wagon wheel thunked into a pothole, and the animal darted away.

Hatta was as bad off as the Elites. Judging by the amount he spoke, a witness would think him mute. Chism added deer to the list of animals Hatta had ignored—vultures, borogoves, groundhogs, various snakes and rats, a scalidink, coyotes, peccaries, even a fat black lizard with bright markings that Chism couldn't even name. That didn't even count the animals Hatta could have spotted that Chism had certainly missed.

More creaking of wheels and crunching of gravel filled the two hundred and thirty turns of the wheel after the deer.

When Hatta spoke, it nearly caused Chism to forget his count. "You'll be glad to hear that you missed a targus." His voice was flat, and his eyes still rested lazily on the road ahead.

Before Chism could ask what he meant, a trilling voice sounded from beside him on the bench. "I do my best to avoid animals who are often so … unpredictable."

"Cheshire," said Chism, doing his best to make it sound like a curse.

"Hello to you as well," said Cheshire, fading into Chism's view.

"No," said Chism. "Everything else I can handle, but I can't deal with you."

The Cheshire Cat gave Chism an extra-wide grin, then turned to face Hatta and turned his colors back on, growing fainter and fainter until he was entirely out of view.

"Do try to keep your hat high and your smile wide, Hatta."

Chism gritted his teeth and began counting the turns out loud. "Seventy-one. Seventy-two. Seventy-three."

Hatta looked at his lap, like a child being scolded by a parent.

"Up, not down," urged Cheshire in his infuriatingly upbeat tone. "Forward, not backward."

"Eighty-two, Eighty-three, Eighty-four."

His brother adjusted his hat to sit a little taller on his head. No one spoke for another fourteen turns of the wheel.

"You might feel blind to it now," said the Cheshire Cat as Chism counted, "but never forget that the world is full of colors and kindness."

"One hundred. Shoo!" shouted Chism and swiped his hand across the bench where he'd last heard Cheshire's voice. His hand brushed away only air in the attempt. He scanned the seat for any sign of the creature—footprints in the specs of dirt of the floorboard, a shadow, a stray hair.

When Hatta's eyes settled on something above the footrest, Chism flung a foot out. This time he connected, and something flew from his foot. It brought no joy, but it also brought no guilt.

From the ground as the wagon passed, the voice came. "Stay together, brothers." A moment passed in silence. Then, Cheshire's voice came from the side of the wagon bed next to Mave. "Stay together at least until the targus gives you back your splendidness."

Chism pulled his boot off and heaved it.

"Hey," said Mave mildly as he stared at the boot where it had fallen to the bottom of the wagon. He pulled his hat lower then massaged the shoulder where the boot had hit him. "What was that for?"

"Oh," said Chism. "Your turns are up."

Hatta climbed into the back to assist Serrill for five turns, then took his seat while the others did theirs. Serrill responded as he had the first time. Just as he had the first time, when the rattle was removed he went as unresponsive as before.

"Why do you hate him?" asked Hatta.

"Cheshire?"

Hatta nodded.

Because he represents every annoying part of you but lacks the blood connection. Because his view of the world is flowers and funniness. Because I can never hope to feel the thousandth part of his cheerfulness. Because he knows me and even though he is nothing that I am, he doesn't hate me like I hate him.

Chism bit his tongue. None of his thoughts would be healthy for his brother's mood. A small part of him wanted to give Cheshire a break. After all, a few cheerful sentences from the creature had done more for Hatta's melancholy than Chism has accomplished in four days.

Chism finally settled on, "Some people were never meant to be friends."

"Like you and me," stated Hatta.

Chism nodded. "It's a good thing we're brothers."

"He said we would find our splendid again." Hatta still didn't smile, but Chism heard the slightest hint of hope—a timbre unheard since the targus.

"He's as mad as a hatter," said Chism. Words he'd normally never say to his brother just kept coming out.

"Thanks be for that, or else—" before Hatta could finish, someone passed the rattle up, and Chism was as forgotten as yesterday's breakfast.

As he started counting again, Chism glanced ahead on the road and spotted Eastend, a small Maner city. Timber walls, moat, and filthy beggars outside the gates. It was a new city, perhaps fifteen years old, but it had been constructed with better defenses than most Wonderland cities.

"Take a good look, men. That's the last Domain city any of us will ever see, fortune willing."

Only Mave and Wot looked.

The road led into the city, but Chism wanted nothing to do with it. They had plenty of supplies to make it back to Wonderland. Chism ordered Muehner off the wagon to blaze a trail. Grassland lay ahead of them for a couple of miles, but the last thing they needed was a horse to break a leg from wandering into an unseen rill or a wagon wheel to crack against a boulder.

Their pace slowed, but every turn brought them closer to the Provinces, which was nearly as good as the Interior. After one hundred turns, Gorman took Muehner's place and Muehner took the rattle. Then Mave replaced Gorman. Chism blazed trail while Serrill and Hatta took their turns.

Each plodding horse step moved them closer to a string of trees. If Chism was correct, their goal lay just on the far side. An hour before nightfall, they arrived at a clearing alongside the Vlitta River. It should have been the most welcome water Chism had ever seen, but to his eyes, it only represented more weeks of drudgery.

For the benefit of his men, Chism pointed to the far side of the river and said, "Home."

They shrugged, grunted, and generally let him know that they cared as little as he did. They knew what the word meant, but the feeling behind it no longer existed. Chism was beginning to lose hope that it would ever come back. If only he wasn't acting lieutenant. Then he wouldn't have to worry about them.

"This side of the river would do for a camp if we weren't Elites. It may be dark before we find it, but we need a place to ford her so we can sleep on Wonderland soil tonight."

Chism sent Wot and Mave upstream while he and Hatta went downstream and the others stayed with the cart. Each pair would walk a half mile, then return. If neither had encountered a suitable spot to cross, they would pick a direction and slowly lead the wagon along the river's edge until they did find something.

The river was narrow and deep the length of their half mile. Elevation change would make pulling the wagon that route impossible. They walked back to the wagon in silence.

From the edge of trees surrounding the clearing where they'd left the wagon, they saw nothing but trampled ground.

"Skewer and serve my liver!" Chism wanted to cut, bash, or otherwise destroy something. But even swinging his practice sword through tall grass would make an unwise amount of noise.

Hatta stepped up next to him and said, "I seem to recall a wagon formerly being drawn into and left in this clearing. What could have happened?"

"Capture? Desertion? Quicksand? Mave?" Chism's mood did not foster vigilance; the others could have washed down the river right next to them as he and Hatta made their way back up.

It was too much to hope for, but Chism took a senseless risk and walked into the clearing. If an ambush awaited, so be it.

"Took you long enough," said Mave from the far side of the clearing. "Me and Wot found a natural ford a hundred paces up." He turned his back, and as he walked upstream, he added, "They're probably acrossed already."

Don't hope for too much, thought Chism. It was becoming dark as he and Hatta caught Mave up.

12

It wasn't exactly a hundred paces. A hundred and thirty by Chism's count, even allowing for his shorter-than-average stride. When they reached the ford, the wagon was midstream. The water tickled the bellies of the horses, but only stray drops reached the underbelly of the wagon.

Three quarters of the way. The horses came out of the water and drew the wagon up intact onto the sandy shore.

No one cheered or even smiled. Chism hastened his step until he stood on the opposite shore, dripping from the armpits down. Eyes closed, he blew out all of the Domain air possible and opened his lungs to the air of Wonderland.

Unsatisfaction. He would have told Mave that wasn't a word, but it fit the moment.

Chism walked back across the river. On the other shore he unlaced his trousers, dropped them, and left the Domain exactly what it deserved.

And still he felt unsatisfied.

13

The Elites plus one made camp in Wonderland. When they woke the following morning, they awoke with the same gloom they'd grown used to. A few hours of walking brought the city of Knobbes into view.

As they traveled through farms which had stood fallow for over a decade, they passed the occasional abandoned structure. More frequently, foundations of structures. Soon after the Domain had pushed their border up to the Vlitta and built Eastend, they'd begun raiding into Farr West Province. If not for Sir Hunbold, the Domain would have extended dozens of miles further. But because of his efforts, the borders of nations were defined. Even so, farms were left behind as hundreds of families fled into the city or farther into the Interior.

A grown-over road approached the city, and smaller, barely discernable roads and paths crisscrossed the prairies surrounding the city. Even in their neglected condition, the paths were better than forging through prairie and abandoned farm land.

The city gate in the west wall of Knobbes was drawn as tight as the staves of a bucket. There was no reason to open it; no one ever approached from the west.

"I can't go into the city," said Chism.

"Choke that," said Muehner. "Elites are safe. There's a truce."

"Choke the truce," snapped Chism. "Elites might be safe, but I'm not safe. Heard of Duke Jaryn? He still thinks I tried to kill him. Twice."

"You're an Elite," said Muehner. "Acting lieutenant and the Red Knight. He wouldn't dare."

"What's stopping him?" asked Chism.

"Queen Palida and the other Provinces."

Chism couldn't count on that. "Even if he was scared of repercussions from them, I can think of a hundred and four ways for him to arrange an accident."

Without looking at anyone, Mave added, "No one would say boo to a duke who decided to publicly execute the most hated man in the Province. Even if there were stanchions or consequences for him afterward, it wouldn't do Lieutenant Chism any good."

"Sanctions," said Chism.

"The hate in that man," said Hatta, staring into the grass in front of the wagon. "It turned his skin the ugliest shade of red I've ever seen. Except for, maybe, the fresh color of blood."

"I'll go back into the Pit before I wear this ridiculous pink tunic back to Palassiren," said Muehner. "We Reds may not be their favorite people, but I'd wager the rest of us get in and out alive."

Chism rubbed his eyes. "If what Hatta told us is even close to the truth, we might find more trouble in there than you think."

"Him?" said Muehner with a sneer. "He's not the most reliable source."

Gorman, who was already beginning to soften around the bony processes of his body, said, "We need other supplies too. Like, well, such as ..." He exhaled sharply. "Food. We need more food."

Chism looked at Mave. "I thought you were supervising that."

"He's been walking every day," said Mave. "Everyone has."

"Fine," said Chism. As far as he knew, Gorman hadn't vomited since the first day. He had as much muscle to replace as the rest of them combined. "We don't have enough coin to send someone in to buy supplies. We'll have to appeal to the Whites. Hatta, what color were you wearing when you ransomed us?"

Hatta shrugged. He didn't even make eye contact.

"Who remembers what color he was wearing?"

"I didn't see anything that day," said Muehner. "Except the inside of blankets."

"There was chicken that day," said Gorman. "And vomit. More vomit than chicken, I think. How does that work?"

"Everything looked white," said Mave. "I barely looked at the ground in front of my face."

"Feet," said Chism. Then, remembering how hard standing had been, he decided it might not have been a mistake after all. "Wot, you look at everything within your field of vision a hundred times a minute. What color was my brother wearing when we came out of the Pit?"

"What color? What color was he wearing? He was wearing a hat. It was purple, but the hat had a … a turtle pattern even though the, even though it was purple. And he was wearing boots, but he was wearing the same boots just now, yes the same boots. He was wearing a hat and a boots, and he had a tunic and trousers. And the tunic he was wearing, it was green."

"Green," said Mave. "That's it."

"A normal green?" asked Chism. "Natural or fake?"

"What do you mean?" asked Mave.

"Is it a color that stands out? All of you can wear pink, but I'm going to wear his tunic, and I don't want to walk into Knobbes looking as bright as a caterpillar."

"How'd you know caterpillars were green?" asked Mave.

"Think for one second who my brother is, Mave," said Chism. "Actually, don't even think about that. Focus on getting us into the city and out again."

"The green wasn't bad," said Mave. "A little mossy in color with some glimmer shimmer to it, but some dirt from the side of the road should hide that."

The tunic be oversized, but that would only help him play the part of a child. Again, Chism thought back to Mave's words: *Use everything available to you.*

As the wagon wended through the prairie's paths around the north side of the city, Chism climbed into the back of the wagon, took off his shirt, and dug into Hatta's bag. Mave raised an eyebrow and keened his head to get a look at Chism's back. Chism rotated so only the plains animals could see the large scar in the shape of a 13. Its existence and origin weren't common knowledge. He found the shirt and put it on, then climbed down from the wagon and crawled through various dirt patches.

"How's this?" he asked Mave, catching up with the wagon.

"Should do," said Mave. "The shaved head makes you look like a kid. So does the dirt you still haven't washed all the way off your face. Better pull some of that hatred from your eyes, though. You go in there looking so intrepid, and you'll be challenged for sure. Try trepid instead."

"Is that even a word?" asked Chism.

Mave shrugged. "You knew what I meant, didn't you?"

Chism ignored Mave's advice about the angry face. When the time came, he'd cower. He moved Muehner to the front bench and took a spot in the back of the wagon.

The east side of Knobbes came into view as they wrapped their way around. Chism waited for it to resemble the city he'd visited with Scaled Tiger Squadron less than a year ago, but even when they reached the road and got a clear view of it, he could barely see the similarities. The walls of the city proper stood tall and stalwart, but the forecity, the portion outside the gates, had grown considerably. Low buildings seemed to spill from the stone walls, large and sturdy close to the city but lower and more flimsy at the fringes. A low, insignificant wooden wall contained the forecity in a half-mile semicircle. Near the outskirts of the sprawling newer city, many houses and buildings were mere frames or walls only.

Scowling as usual, Muehner said, "Last time I was here, all this was nothing but fields."

"If you think it went up fast," said Chism, "wait until the Maners get here. It'll go down faster than dry grass in a fire."

Eventually, the path they followed approached the main road into Knobbes. Groups of people moved away from the city, some afoot, some ahorse, and some a-wagon, like the Elites. Nearly everyone on the road was loaded with possessions. They were leaving and not coming back. The people of Far West Province knew invasion was coming soon.

The Elites turned west onto the road, traveling against the flow of people. Not a person passed without obviously noticing their ridiculous tunics. The only option to avoid stares was to remove the tunics, but a group of scrawny, pale, shirtless men would draw even more attention. At least their faces were clean-shaven or they'd still look like Maners.

"You're drawing too much attention," Chism said to the men who rode in the back of the wagon with him. "I'll watch and find you. Muehner."

"Yeah?"

"You're in charge. Mave."

"Yessir?"

"Think."

Traffic on the road tightened like sand at the neck of an hourglass as a farmer and his sons passed a short string of merchant wagons, all headed away from the city. The Elites' wagon had to pull to a stop to allow them all to pass. Chism slid out of the wagon in the jumble of the two groups and began walking away from the city.

It wasn't long until a sizeable group of mismatched travelers approached headed toward Knobbes. Three men on horses wearing swords accompanied a caravan of five wagons. All together a couple dozen people were spread out through the caravan. It would be an easy group to blend in with.

Chism stepped to the side of the road and bent over to dump an imaginary pebble from his boot. After the majority of the caravan had passed, he melded into the rear of the group, walking toward the city again. Their pace wasn't fast, but even this much walking pushed the limits of his endurance. He was glad he hadn't spent the last five days lounging on the bench next to his brother.

He spotted the Elites a quarter mile ahead and realized that Hatta still drove the team that pulled the wagon. Even if Chism had rehearsed a story, Hatta couldn't lie convincingly. Maybe he would keep his head down and stay as silent as he had for the last week. Still, there was no excuse for not forming a better plan with the Elites. He'd had nearly a week to do it, and all he'd come up with was *I'll watch you and find you*?

There was nothing to be done about it, though. The Elites were approaching the gate into the forecity. Chism couldn't tell if any guards watched the entrance. If any did, it wasn't more than a couple. Traffic passing through the gate slowed again as parties squeezed past each other. The delay allowed the groups Chism walked with to close the gap to fifty paces. Chism stayed near the edge of the group in order to see the Elites' wagon.

No one stopped the Elites or searched them at the gate, but plenty of onlookers pointed, laughed, and called out. Chism was glad to see them continue past the two ornamental guards. The Whites who could help outfit and provision them would be in the city proper.

Even from his distance, Chism could see Muehner glaring at everyone who met his eyes. Wot's lips moved, and his eyes flicked across faces and scenery faster than wind.

Numerous side streets—more like wide trails worn into the ground—crossed the highway leading into the city itself. The buildings of the forecity were new, but hastily constructed and for the most part, abandoned. Nobody wanted to be stuck on the outside of the city walls when the Maners came.

The Elites turned onto a side street before reaching the city gates. A nearby corralled area was their destination.

Chism came to a stop in front of a fruit vendor and browsed the food as he kept a surreptitious eye on his squadron. A tall shopkeeper with thick black mustache came out from behind the display table and stood close enough for Chism to smell the sweat that showed under his armpits. When staring down at Chism didn't work, the man folded his arms, leaned forward, and cleared his throat.

The goal was to avoid attention. Chism didn't look the part of the Red Knight, but if people looked close enough, they might recognize the face that had graced a thousand couriers' posters a year ago. He ducked his eyes and moved away from the stand.

Muehner was talking to a man outside of the corral. Within a minute, they both nodded, and the man swung the gate wide. Two young men came forward and led the horses into a corner of the corral.

The Elites and Hatta climbed down from the wagon, looking like five old cripples and an idiot servant. Next to normal healthy people they looked as frail as straw men but less flexible. Their heads were shaved, except for Hatta, but hats hid most of their pale scalps. Whatever effect the pink had was purely bonus outlandishness. Hunched together and glaring around as if they were afraid of catching a disease from the other citizens, they walked back to the main highway.

At a slow pace and with his head down, Chism watched the progress of his squadron. A group of cackling ladies stepped in front of him. One of them said, "Not as skinny as this one," and reached for him.

Chism jumped back out of her reach, but they formed a wall in front of him, grabbing and fussing.

When he made it away from the women, the Elites were gone.

Suddenly the street was packed with people, carts, horses, and mules.

Without thinking, Chism bolted up the back of the nearest wagon. He spotted his men not far up the road on the other side of a wagon full of grain. Chism sighed in relief. If they were captured or even separated, his lack of planning could turn into disaster. His men were less than a block away from the city gates where Chism had almost been trapped by the portcullises on his last visit.

As Chism watched, six men wearing hooded cloaks stepped out of shadows, alleys, and the crowd itself to surround the Elites and escort them into a two-story pine building. It was as easy as ushering helpless chicks into a henhouse.

"What are you doing, boy?" shouted a man from the front of the wagon.

Chism barely heard him. "What just happened?" They were gone. The men in hoods had pulled off a perfectly choreographed exit from a stage and taken his men along with them.

"Hey!" shouted the man. "You want a ride, hire a cabriolet."

Chism stepped into the street. The wagon wasn't moving fast enough for him anyway.

By the time he was close enough to see the spot where his men had disappeared, only an invisible bubble of empty space existed in front of the building—a barn or stables of some sort, judging by the size of the doors. That explained how they got inside so fast, but it left a thousand other questions. Whatever had happened, no one in the street wanted anything to do with it.

Chism stopped short of the abduction site and leaned against the beam of a structure still under construction. He was careful to make it seem as if he looked at anything except the face of the building where his men were. As long as he kept his distance, he should be safe.

His men should have been unrecognizable as Elites with their scrawny faces and strange clothing. The snatchers had definitely been working together, members of a well-practiced group of soldiers or guards or mercenaries. But they hadn't been wearing uniforms. Even though they'd all been hooded, Chism hadn't noticed them until they'd accosted the Elites. If they were bandits or strong-arms, it was a well-organized group of them.

"Dash it all," he muttered. "Another rescue. There's no way." He barely had enough in him to get back to Palassiren.

But Hatta was in there. There was no way of knowing how long he'd last or what his captors would do if Hatta started acting like himself. Without his flair, without any friends, and without the rattle, who knew what Hatta would do?

Chism reached into his pouch and pulled out the rattle. If he couldn't rescue them, maybe he could sneak it in to the prisoners.

He rolled it between his hands as he considered options. The dry, chitinous layers of rattle scraped back and forth. Chism hadn't used it since the first day.

Serrill, he thought. *How am I going to get him and the wagon out of here?*

One rescue at a time.

What am I thinking? I'll end up in another Pit if I try anything. That or in a noose.

He put the rattle next to his ear and gave a little shake. It was smooth and sussurant, with an undeniable dreamlike quality. In the scrape of rattle layers he heard a scenario so clearly he had to blink to make sure he wasn't somehow seeing it with his eyes.

He heard it with his ears and his eyes and his heart. It was him, using the skill he practiced every free minute of every day, to the benefit of his men and his brother and downfall of his enemies. It was not a single mission but a life-string of missions in which his talents proved proficient for each task. He infiltrated, he fought, he commanded, he protected, he strategized. He was like a father to his men. There were no negotiations, no crowds of admirers, and no rulers patting him on the head. There were situations he needed that simply needed him.

Quit thinking like a targus and get after it.

The building to the south, a brickmaker of some sort, butted up against the stable. The door was closed, but it was too early to tell if lights burned inside. An alley to the south of that looked like a good place to start. Chism slipped the rattle into his pouch and put his head down as he crossed into the shadowy alley. Another hour would bring near darkness to the city, though it arrived in his soul as soon as the rattle stopped. But the decision had been made.

After getting his men out and home, he would have to take a serious look at continuing his service as an Elite. Duty for the sense of accomplishment it brought was one thing, but duty just for duty's sake wasn't giving him anything. Eventually, his lack of caring would lead to shoddy Elite work, and that wouldn't do anybody any good. As soon as he got back to Palassiren, he had to resign.

First, the rescue.

Chism examined the side of the brickmaker's shop. No windows looked out into the alley. A lucky break. Structures from the next street over abutted the back of the stable and the shop. No back entrance. Or exit, for that matter.

A creaking from the roof, soft footsteps, sent Chism hurrying back to the alley entrance. They had to belong to some sort of lookout.

He didn't stop at the alley entrance. Across the street was a larger alley. People passing on the highway provided cover for him as he crossed and crouched in shadows to watch from a distance. The back of the shop's roof wasn't visible from his vantage point, but the alley was.

A ladder appeared from above, and a man descended. His face remained in the deepening alley shadows. Chism could see only dark, curly hair down to the shoulders protruding from his hood. The man paced the alley slowly. Somehow he knew Chism had been there.

No food, no friends, no fervor. Even going to his own wagon for food would be seen as stealing. Any member of the squadron could seek help from the White Elites—except for Chism. Whether the reward still stood or not, bringing him in would bring prestige if nothing else. The thought of surrender crossed his mind. If it brought men who could rescue his men, it was worth considering.

The man in the alley climbed back up and out of Chism's view. The ladder remained. An invitation Chism was reluctant to accept.

By the time night fell fully an hour later, Chism had concocted a plan. Climb the ladder. What he did after that depended on who and what he found.

The possibility of a trap occurred to him. So did the certainty of his lack of options.

Traffic on the street still moved, but at a reduced density. Chism walked up the street toward the city proper for a block, but he didn't see anything on the far side of the stable that would help him. He doubled back and slid out of moonlight and into the alley.

A drawn sword blade waited for him in the alley. Chism could only see a hooded outline.

14

Chism stared into the cowl, but it would take time for his eyes to adjust.

"Snails and snot," said the hooded man. "You look like a cat kept you as a chew toy for a year."

The voice had the forced huskiness of a disguise, but beneath that it had a familiar sound. That worried Chism. Everyone he'd ever talked to in Far West wanted him dead.

He reached for his belt and found nothing. The old habit still ruled him.

"You won't find anything there because I sent it to Palassiren." The man took a step forward, and the face under the cowl became clear.

"Ander. You filthy beast."

Ander smiled even more widely and dropped his blade. "Chism, you slivered liver. I can't say how good it is to see you."

"What's with the black hair?" The last time he'd seen Ander—actually, every time he'd seen Ander—the man had sported a shaggy white mane.

"Disguise and all that. What were you thinking, walking right into this city? Did you leave your wits in the Domain?"

"We didn't exactly receive regular briefings on the goings-on of Wonderland in the Pit."

"Well, things are tenser than a sack full of strange cats between the Reds and the Whites." He motioned for Chism to follow him down the alley. "Boils on their bottoms, but the nobles can't see who the real enemy is."

"So if you're here, then my part of the squadron was taken captive by the rest of the squadron?" He should have suspected the captors of being Elites based on the sheer efficiency of the operation.

"More or less," said Ander. "A few are watching for you somewhere else."

As they climbed the ladder, Chism said, "I like the dark hair. If you'd consider leaving it like that, you might be able to attract a lady for once."

"Thank you anyway, but I'd rather look like myself than an older version of you."

"Let me guess, you're planning to pose as my grandfather until we get back to the Interior."

"Father should suffice. *If* I decide to take you with me."

Banter was routine. It performed a function, but it lacked its usual enjoyment for Chism.

At the far side of the shop's roof, a window into the upper floor of the stable was wedged open. Not as quietly as he would have liked, Chism walked to the window and skulked inside. Voices rose from the stable floor.

"... our bad luck that it was Serrill who went cracked and not Chism." It was Jenre, an Elite of five years. "I don't trust him."

A couple men murmured assent, but Chism couldn't make out individual voices until Mave spoke up. "If it weren't for Chism, none of us would have survived sane."

"Shut yourself!" shouted Muehner. "That might be true, but if it weren't for you maving everything up twice, we never would have been captured!"

The dull sound of fist on flesh brought Chism to the edge of the loft. Mave's face was hidden behind his arms, and Muehner had a fist raised to strike again.

"Who's in charge here?" demanded Chism.

The Elites below took half a step away from Muehner and looked at him. Muehner looked at his fist, blushed, and lowered it. "I am," he said.

"Wrong," said Chism. "I am."

The top of a ladder showed over the edge of the loft. Chism climbed down slowly but steadily. It was not the time to show how much effort a single ladder required. He needed to save his strength because it could very well come to blows when he told Muehner that he wasn't worthy to be the Elite's piss boy, much less their leader. No amount of hardship justified using his fists to discipline.

A new gap appeared in the midst of the Elites and Fellows. Chism took his place at the center and glanced around the circle. Twelve Elites and Fellows, including Chism. And Hatta. With Kilven dead, it left three men waiting for them somewhere out of the city.

The scathing words he'd planned to say to Muehner pushed at his tongue and tried to clench his fingers into fists. However, demeaning Muehner was the worst way to keep his loyalty or anyone else's—if there was even a chance of that.

Scaled Tiger Squadron, minus four. Half of them finally out of one dark nightmare and into a different kind of darkness. Battered, nearly cracked in some cases and definitely cracked in others.

"Like me or hate me, I'm your lieutenant for two more weeks." *Then I'll be no one's leader and no one's squadmate. Then I'll be nobody.* "We'll have order, and we'll have respect."

When he looked into the men's faces, they nodded reluctantly.

He couldn't punish Muehner too harshly, but he couldn't let him off. What punishment would Serrill come up with? The key was the fist he used on Mave.

"Muehner, since you love to use your fists so much, I'll let you do it some more. Once we get on the road tomorrow, your hands are going into the tightest-fitting pouches we can find. You can use your fists for *everything* for two days."

Chism didn't look at Muehner for acceptance. If he left room for doubt or challenge, Muehner was likely to take it.

"As far as squadron justice for Mave," said Chism, "you just gave it, Muehner. Anything else he gets can come in Palassiren."

Chism circled the opening and stopped in front of Hatta, who sat on a hay bale.

"We have a long way to go. At least we're not wearing fur or pink anymore." In a loud whisper he asked Hatta, "They're not wearing pink, right?"

A few of the Elites chuckled. None of the ones who'd been in the Pit cracked a smile. Chism showed one he didn't feel.

"Eat, drink, sleep," he said. "When the city gates open, we'll be some of the first through them."

The men cheered quietly. Most nodded at least. Alendro and Vassar told him they were glad to have him back. Jenre quickly apologized for what he'd said.

Chism looked around at his squadron. Somehow, he hadn't maved it up too badly yet.

15

The Elites left the city in shifts the next morning. With scores of people leaving and dozens entering the city, it was a simple matter. For once, they encountered no complications. Muehner and the other former captives, with the rattle, recovered Serrill and the wagon. Chism and Ander led another wagon, and the other Fellows and Elites a third and fourth.

They reunited two miles down the road. The healthy Elites had found the three missing soldiers. With the loss of Kilven and addition of Hatta, they formed a respectable sixteen-man caravan. Textile merchants, for those who asked. And while nine guards, six merchants, and one catatonic man was excessive for three and a half wagons of dresses, tunics, and trousers, it wasn't entirely unbelievable. Especially considering the fact that they were traveling from the Provinces to the Interior. In such times, a group could never be too careful.

The cover was probably a bigger production than they needed, but as Chism had suspected, they couldn't just stroll through White Provinces looking like a squadron of Red Elites.

Muehner grumbled when Chism appointed Alendro acting sub-lieutenant. Chism wanted to appoint Muehner eventually, but not after what he'd witnessed in the barn between Muehner and Mave. Muehner most likely would have complained no matter who was appointed—even himself. Alendro sat at the head of the company and acted as their leader in public. A boy in command would have drawn too much attention.

In reality, a boy in charge of a squadron of Elites and Fellows up to twenty-five years his senior was even more implausible, but somehow it had become the truth. Besides, not only was Alendro next in line in seniority, but he had a really nice cloak. The only reason Alendro hadn't infiltrated Phaylea was because his beard was patchy.

Chism and Alendro decided not to take the most direct path back to Palassiren. The "merchants" had come through Serpent's Gap less than a month earlier. It wouldn't be wise to go back the same way with the same merchandise. They chose the route Chism had taken when he fled from Duke Jaryn.

If it were just me and Hatta, Chism thought, *we could spend some time visiting Leis and Buckhairs and their family.* And back in the Interior, Hatta would probably be interested in spending some time in Shey's Orchard. Maybe they'd come back after Chism reported to Queen Cuora and King Markin. A life with no adventure didn't sound any worse than life as an Elite, just much easier.

They covered over fifteen miles the first day—a respectable amount for a convoy of that size. Small towns, farms, and homesteads dotted the landscape along the road. They wouldn't last any longer than the forecity of Knobbes once the invasion started. Days if they were lucky. Hours, more realistically.

The Elites and Fellows went to work as soon as Chism called a stop for the day, except for the Pitters—Muehner, Gorman, Wot, Mave, and, of course, Serrill. Chism was disinclined to force them to work.

As acting lieutenant, Chism didn't pound any stakes or gather any wood. He did work out a sentry schedule, plan a rotating care schedule for Serrill, patrol the area to plan their defense in case of attack, question the Fellow acting as quartermaster, and inspect the finished camp. It wasn't as tight as an Elite camp should be, but that was by design. A caravan of merchants wouldn't set up camp in a military fashion. The asymmetry made it difficult to inspect, but what was there in Chism's life that wasn't difficult?

The dinner stew was warm. It was almost good enough to be Chism's first enjoyable experience in seven days. Almost.

Sixteen men made a wide circle around the campfire. The night was not cold enough for them to require its warmth. The Pitters sat shoulder to shoulder again, with Serrill lying on the ground at the end of the line. Wot's mouth was moving, though he wasn't making any noise. Gorman took biscuit after biscuit from his pockets and nibbled them absently. The main difference between Hatta and Serrill was that the former stood vertical and the latter lay horizontal. Serrill had arms held straight out as if he was reaching for something. Muehner's Fellow, Cavvan, was asking questions about the Pit and receiving short, sharp answers. All day, the Pitters had ranged from silent to cantankerous to rambling when other members of the squadron had tried to pry bits of information out of them.

When Chism stood and began to pace the inner fire ring, the men grew silent.

"We spent over a hundred and thirty days in an underground cell. One minute of sunlight each day. A fist of bread and half an apple to eat. During the winter, they generously gave us each a whole apple. Fleas. A trench of open sewage. And a wall made out of brambles that separated us from Domainer criminals who wanted to hurt us as badly as we wanted to escape."

Even though Chism's face felt as hard as his heart, the Elites met his eyes as he paced around the fire.

"I doubt the others want to talk about it. I know I don't. Most likely, we'll all do our best to forget. It wasn't as bad as you'd think. It wasn't as bad as you'd imagine. It was worse. Short of adding torture, they designed the experience to be as miserable as possible so that Wonderlanders will ransom each other as quickly as possible."

Behind him, someone spat. Chism glanced back and saw it was Muehner.

"I agree, Muehner. I hate the Maners more than I hate—" Chism stopped. He had almost said *my father*. His father was one despicable person made worse by alcohol. The Domain was an entire society whose existence was based on gain through the maltreatment of others.

"I hate them more than I've ever hated anything." He couldn't bring himself to feel it as strongly as he should, but he knew the hatred burned under the surface somewhere. He only hoped that if he was ever in a position to do anything about it, the hatred would be there still, as hot as a forge fire. If it did fade, all he had to do was call back the experience of being pulled out of the Pit, as weak as a half-drowned cat, for the entire Domain to see.

"Enough about the Pit," said Chism. "We escaped it, but not unscathed. Our first night of freedom, a targus came into our camp and poisoned us with his spit. If my observations serve, we all feel as if everything that matters to us is locked away in a cage inside our chest. If there's a key to the cage, none of us have it."

Chism considered whether he'd shared too much. The secrets were not all his to tell. And what would possess him to share even if they were?

But you couldn't put honey back in the comb.

"I'm excusing the Pitters and Hatta from camp duties. There are enough of you to pick up the slack. We already tried to shake off this funk by working, and it had no effect. You'd spend more effort prodding us than you would just doing the work yourselves anyway."

The murmurs he expected didn't come.

"That includes sentry duty. I can't trust any of them to care about anything enough to want to protect it."

Why am I any different? There are nine men here who could lead better than me right now.

He did two silent trips around the fire, wondering if the men had picked up on the hypocrisy that he had just noticed.

"The Pitters will each walk one mile tomorrow. Every second day, we'll add a quarter mile." He had lost hope that exercise would help them climb out of their funk, but they needed to continue regaining their strength.

Chism took a breath. The word "hypocrite" was pounding so loudly in his head he couldn't make sense of what else he should say. Suddenly he knew what he had to do, and no feelings came to oppose his decision, so he plunged forward.

"One last thing. Being a hypocrite doesn't serve any of us, and it doesn't serve the Circle and the Sword." He stopped pacing and stood in front of Alendro. "I'm stepping down. Alendro, the squadron is yours."

Chism sat on the ground next to Hatta. He felt neither better nor worse, so what did any of it matter anyway? Tendering his resignation to Queen Cuora would be no different.

16

"Guts and gizzards, boy, but I still say it was a mistake." Ander had told him the same thing every day for two weeks, using different and ever-more-imaginative expletives. Ander walked on one side of Chism, Mave on the other.

"Nothing I can do about it now," said Chism. "We're here."

Palassiren was only a meadow away. The road that cut through the meadow was as busy as Chism had ever seen it. The flow of refugees out of Far West Province had thinned considerably, but even this far away fleeing people could be found.

Could it be the hordes of war already? The sellers and suppliers and seekers of glory that surrounded wartimes?

Possibly. Chism didn't really care. By the end of the day he would have nothing to do with armies. The sense of accomplishment and relief he should feel as part of a surviving squadron was hundreds of miles away—somewhere back in the Domain, being chewed on like a headless rattlesnake.

Far in the distance, past the city wall and past the inner city wall, Chism saw the Circle and Sword statue in front of the military grounds. It may as well have been a block of granite for all the emotion it stirred in him so he looked away.

Alendro, wearing his well-tailored cloak, rode the tallest horse of the group.

"What color is that cloak?" asked Chism.

"Blue," said Ander. "I think it's called royal blue."

"That's a good name for a color," said Chism. "Like it was named after that cloak."

"Stop acting like you know anything about what you're talking about, color maven. And stop changing the subject. You led the squadron until things got easy."

"Alendro got us home," said Chism.

Ander exhaled sharply, sending his black hair poofing out. "Alendro kept in force what you set out the first night."

"What does it matter?" asked Chism.

Mave perked up a little. "You deserve a medal or something. If you weren't a Knight already, they should make you one."

"What for?" asked Chism. The mission was anything but a success.

"We could have killed each other in the Pit, or all gone mad. Well, madder than we already are." Mave looked slightly confused. "Why else would you do all that if there was nothing for you to gain?"

"Keep your medals, Mave," said Chism. "And your titles, Ander. We made it back. Who cares who leads? Besides, the nobles aren't going to see anything successful in our mission. We lost a man—two if you count Serrill—and the information we lost them for is five months old."

"Heroes," said Mave in a pouty voice. "If they welcome us as anything less, it will be a tragedy and a cheat." He put his head back to its now-customary position, looking down at the dirt.

Chism felt bad for pushing Mave back into despondency, but it was best for him to have accurate expectations. Three days earlier, Chism had told Ander that if Mave was still an Elite at the end of the week, Chism would dye his hair white to offset Ander's black. When it grew back enough to dye, anyway.

Before they were close enough to the walls to be recognized, Chism took the rattle from Wot. It was a strange enough sight to the rest of the squadron, but Chism didn't want the whole city to see an Elite playing with it.

None of the Elites wore the Circle and the Sword or even the blue uniforms of soldiers. It had been too dangerous to take them into the Provinces, and there had been no quartermasters' depots on their route back. On any other occasion, the soldiers on the wall would have shouted "Elites!" as they approached. People in the city would pause to cheer as they made their way toward the Academy or palaces.

When Alendro rode within a stone's throw of the wall, one of the guards finally shouted, "Scaled Tiger Squadron! Elites!"

"Scaled Tiger!" shouted more guards on the walls. "Circle and Sword!"

Unlike every other time he'd heard that cry, Chism's heart failed to swell and soar—the final confirmation that he had no business being an Elite.

The cheers only survived a block or so into the city. Without uniforms the Elites blended in, just sixteen men, thirteen horses, and four more wagons clogging the streets. Chism climbed aboard the last wagon and sat next to Hatta. Since Hatta wasn't taking his turns with the rattle, he'd actually pay attention to what Chism said.

Mave followed and walked alongside their wagon. He'd stayed close to Chism since Muehner had assaulted him in Knobbes

In a voice loud enough only for Hatta's ears, Chism said, "We are on our way to see Cuora. Is that going to be a problem for you?"

Hatta shrugged.

"Is it going to be a problem for her?"

Hatta said something too low to hear and shrugged again.

What more could Chism do?

The main street into the city led in a direct line to the inner city and the palaces.

"Climb up here, Mave," said Chism, sliding over to make room. Mave joined him on the bench.

"I always wondered if the builders of Palassiren made a mistake when they built this road straight up to the inner city," said Chism. "If the outer gate falls, the invading army has an easy time reaching the inner gates."

"If the outer gate falls, invaders will have an easy time reaching the inner gates no matter how they would have laid it out." Mave's words were flat but speedy. "What you want is for the enemy to have a *slow* time reaching the inner city."

"But if the enemy has to wind through a city full of houses and shops, won't they just cause more loss of life and property?"

"The property is lost once the outer gates fall," said Mave. "Looters will loot; that's what they do. But a slow approach to the inner gates give us time to finish the invacuation of the outer city. That saves lives. There's also the possibility that the enemy forces will arrive at the inner wall in small waves instead of one large group. A good enemy commander would overcome that, of course."

"Evacuate all these people into the inner city?" asked Chism. "Where would they all fit?"

"Why do you think they built all those huge plazas? For speeches and parades?"

"Actually ... " said Chism.

"There are also caves leading into the mountains. I don't know how deep, but I'd bet silver to copper they're there. The only question is whether they lead all the way through the mountain to the other side."

The inner city came into view, and Hatta looked up from the street. It was completely separated from the outer city by its own crenellated wall, which wrapped around it like the letter C. Just beyond the gates was a huge open square. The palaces were lined up symmetrically beyond the plaza, with the military district to the right and mansions and upper class shops to the left.

They passed through the inner city gates with a few more cries of, "Scaled Tiger!" None of the wagons were searched, and only cursory glances were given to the men. Hatta received even less than his share.

Chism leaned close to Mave and in a whisper asked, "What color is my brother wearing?"

"Brown. Some grey."

It appeared that Hatta was as ready to give up his flamboyance as Chism was to give up the Circle and the Sword. Maybe the two of them could go back to Hatta's house and disappear. Chism would just have to designate an area where the Cheshire Cat was not permitted. For Cheshire's safety, of course.

Not long after the wagon passed the gates, Hatta set the reins on the floorboards and climbed over the rail. Chism handed the reins to Mave and told him to stay with Scaled Tiger, then followed Hatta.

"Where are you going?" asked Chism.

Hatta stopped walking and pointed at the Circle and Sword statue.

Sobs gently shook Hatta's body. He covered his face with both hands. The true hero, the rescuer was more miserable than any of them. And Chism had no way to combat it.

"Can I find you there when we finish?" asked Chism.

Behind his hands, Hatta nodded.

"Do you promise?"

He nodded again.

"It will probably take hours."

Again.

"Can I bring you some food or anything?"

Hatta shook his head. At least he was comprehending instead of blindly nodding.

"Here," said Chism, pulling the rattle from his pouch. "I'll come back as soon as I can."

The parting should have been a time for Scaled Tiger to call out a hero's cheer for their rescuer. None of them even watched him walk away.

Chism turned back to the guard house and approached the first soldier he recognized, an older man with heavy-lidded eyes. "Do you know me?"

"I know who you are, Sir Chism," said the man with a two-handed salute.

"That man, walking toward the Circle and Sword monument," Chism motioned with his head, "is my brother, and he's rather unstable lately. I'd consider it a great favor if you could keep an eye on him. Let me know where he goes if he wanders off."

"Of course, Sir. It would be my pleasure."

"Thank you," said Chism. "It may be hours until I return."

"Then you have my eyes for hours, Sir."

Chism caught up with the Elites as they dismounted and formed up. Since he'd given up leadership, his place in the squad was second to last in seniority. He and Mave entered the palace and judging chamber side by side. The Fellows waited in the foyer. Lieutenant Serrill waited in the wagon. Chism would have brought him in, but that wasn't his decision anymore.

The Red King—King Markin, Commander of the armies and the Elites—sat his throne when the Elites entered and lined up. Cuora, the Queen of Hearts, sat at his side. She was as unbeautiful and stern as ever. The thick black strands of hair that circled her head like a jumble of sticks just gave her a more severe look.

At least there was no sign of Brune. Hopefully the queen had tired of her Knave and dismissed or decapitated him. That just might be enough to make Chism smile.

The Elites lined up as properly as they could in traveling clothes. Someone with no knowledge of the squadron could pick out the five Pitters by their downcast faces and shoddy postures.

"I apologize for our lack of uniforms," said Alendro, flourishing his superb cloak and bowing. "We received notice to appear immediately."

"Bother your uniforms," said the queen. "Red Knight, step forward."

So much for blending in and fading away. "Your Majesty," said Chism, stepping forward and bowing.

"What happened?"

Chism glanced apologetically at Alendro who didn't seem to mind the breach of seniority then stated the facts of the mission quickly. The slightest dawdling over any detail would result in interruption by the queen, and he was not in any mood to deal with that. He included Mave's rash actions but left out the horrors of the Pit and the encounter with the targus. No reason to tell the whole world about his personal issues.

ALENDRO, MUEHNER, CHISM, & MAVE

He summed up the trip home by saying, "I passed command to Elite Alendro for the trip home due to myself and the other Pitters being unfit to command. Acting Lieutenant Alendro did a superb job in a mangled situation."

When he finished speaking, Queen Cuora said, "Pitters? More like *Pitifuls*. Do any of the other four Pitifuls wish to add anything?"

Of course they didn't. None of them cared enough about anything to waste the energy to speak.

But Mave surprised him. "Your Majesty, Sir Chism underrated his leadership role. He rescued us from the Maner prison then—"

Queen Cuora cut him off with a wave of her scepter.

Understated, thought Chism. *Not underrated.*

"Where is your former lieutenant?" the queen demanded of Alendro.

"In the wagon, Your Majesty."

"Go retrieve the man," ordered the queen. Two guards rushed out. "While we wait for Lieutenant Serrill, a trial."

King Markin's brow furrowed in concern. "Who is to be tried?"

"Elite Mave. Twice this could have been avoided for the price of some common sense."

The king cleared his throat. "I believe that is an Elite matter."

The queen spoke in manner-of-fact tones. "He single-handedly instigated an international incident."

The king shrugged and waved one hand as if delivering him up. On one side of the courtroom stood the executioner wearing his iron mask. In the back row of Elites stood Mave, concern as absent from his face as kindness was absent from the queen's.

Chism had been wrong. This could end up much worse than dismissal.

17

"Elite Mave," said Cuora. "Step forward."

Mave joined Chism in front of the Elites.

The queen stared into his face. Her own face, plain in regards to beauty but exceptional in regards to competence, remained unchanged. Wild black hair did nothing to detract from that image. If anything, it made her look as terrible as a thunderstorm. Her dark eyes stared as if they could peel away Mave's layers to determine his guilt.

"Marky, he's proven Elite unfitness, no?"

"No—I mean, yes," said King Markin.

"We start by stripping the Circle and the Sword," said Cuora quickly as if it were a foregone conclusion.

It was, of course. Chism had had no doubt of that.

"Now, the question of further sentencing. Prison? Stripes? Beheading?"

Chism spoke quickly, attempting to say as much as possible before being interrupted. "My lady, I'd like to speak for Mave. He bore up better in the Pit than any of us, and has been a model member of—"

"I won't hear it, Knight," snapped the queen. "There is no one here speaking against his character, so it won't do to have you speaking for it. We must have fairness, after all."

Perhaps Chism's words gave King Markin's tongue courage. "It does not appear Elite Mave's—"

"Former Elite Mave," interjected the queen.

"—Former Elite Mave's actions were malicious. Negligent, yes. Impulsive. Brash and irresponsible. Let us not forget he spent four months in the Pit. I recommend lenience."

Four months, eleven days. Or so.

Queen Cuora glared into Mave again. Twice her eyes met Chism's, as if he actually had vouched for Mave's character. Mave didn't help his own case by staring at the floor half a pace in front of the throne.

"Time served in the Domain's bedpan," declared Queen Cuora. "Dismissed."

Chism watched, unable to do anything and unable to care, as the greatest tactical mind in the kingdom shuffled from the throne room.

The two guards came in seconds later, carrying Serrill on a stretcher. The man was in no condition to be punished, so the blame would surely roll down to Chism, who had been acting lieutenant for most of the mission. Cuora would never be content with confining blame to Mave, the most junior member of the squadron, and Serrill, a man who was as active as a piece of fruit.

The same punishment Mave had received would suit Chism perfectly. Scaled Tiger Squadron would need three new members soon.

"Lay him there." She used her scepter with an intricate heart assembly at the top to point to the floor next to Chism.

They did as she ordered. Serrill's arms and legs were relaxed for once, but his neck was tensed and flexed, lifting his head off of the floor. By coincidence, his open eyes were pointed in the queen's general direction.

Bringing him here as evidence was uncalled for. If she was

going to dismiss Chism, she didn't need to rub salt in his wounds at the same time. At least his wounds were as numb as his joys. He just wished she'd hurry and do what she was going to do.

"Lieutenant Serrill," said the queen. "Describe the outcome of your mission."

He didn't so much as blink under her stare.

"Describe Sub-lieu Chism's actions and routine while imprisoned." Again she looked at Serrill as if expecting an answer. When none came, she rose from her throne and came to stand in front of the gap between Chism and Lieutenant Serrill.

"Sub-lieu Chism," she said. "My Red Knight. Youngest sub-lieu in the history of the Elites. You've earned some very high expectations. You've already described the mission satisfactorily. Now describe your routine while imprisoned."

He did so. The days were monotonous and his orders and actions were snugly repetitive. Classes helped exercise the minds, but the men were unfit to do anything with what they'd learned.

"You see," said Cuora, placing her scepter against Serrill's foot, "this is a man unfit for leadership." As if pointing out something to a child, she rested the scepter on Chism's chest. "This is a man of an entirely different sort."

Chism took a small step back. For some reason, even the touch of the scepter was uncomfortable.

"If this man's account can be believed," she reached and tapped Chism's chest, "then this man"—she tapped Serrill's foot—"would not be here in such fine condition."

Sarcasm. Perfect.

"Guard," said the queen, signaling a man who had been standing nearby holding a fancy wood box. "The pins."

The man opened the box and formally placed a pin in each of the Pitiful's hands. Muehner, Wot, and Gorman scowled at theirs then shoved them into a pocket. Serrill's medal was handed to Alendro with instructions Chism didn't pay attention to. Chism was the last to get his. A standard, square commendation medal with a gold wing against a white background. The freedom medal for former prisoners. As if Chism wanted to be reminded of the Pit every time he wore his uniform. He did the same thing the other Pitters had done.

"Acting Lieutenant Alendro," said Queen Cuora. "Thank you for bringing our boys safely home. Based on many circumstances, including the death of a Fellow and removal of three Elites from the squadron," she glanced at Mave, Serrill, and Chism, "I believe it is King Markin's plan to disband Scaled Tiger Squadron. Await further notice regarding reassignment or reorganization. Take the surviving squad members who still possess the power of speech to Armorer Mully so they can pass on what they remember of the Domain's preparations, and be prepared for further debriefings at a later date. You and your men are dismissed."

She hadn't even had the decency to explicitly dismiss Chism. Even Mave had earned that.

Whatever. He began to file out at the tail end of his former squadron.

"Where are you going, Knight?"

"You said we were dismissed." Chism's voice came out snappish, but he didn't care.

The Elites continued to make their way to the door, but at an obviously slower pace. They were as curious about the queen's intentions as Chism was indifferent.

"I dismissed Scaled Tiger Squadron. You are no longer one of them."

So being stripped of the Circle and the Sword was not severe enough punishment. Who cared? Who really cared? He just hoped Hatta didn't sit out by the statue for days while Chism rotted in another cell. Hopefully the soldier Chism had asked to watch Hatta would at least remind him to eat.

Chism retraced his steps and stood next to his former lieutenant, who still gazed with empty eyes at the throne Cuora had vacated. Chism stared at the wall behind Cuora as the last Elite filed out.

Not bothering to temper his tone, he said, "I've been through more than I can say. Cut me loose and have done with it! Whatever punishment you have planned, don't play around like a dog with a kitten."

"Cut you loose? Ha! I'd sooner cut Marky loose." She smiled at her husband as if she'd made a joke, then turned back to Chism. "I'm promoting you to lieutenant."

"No," said Chism.

The smile froze on the queen's face, no longer natural or joking. "It sounded like you just said 'no.'"

"That was the word I said," said Chism. "I'm tendering my resignation from the Elites."

"Because one man turned into a drooling fool? Because one mission went bad? Because Alendro looks better riding at the head of a squadron?"

She'd saved him from the headman's block after the incident with Duke Jaryn, something she did for very few. He owed her some sort of explanation.

"It's because I feel nothing more for the Circle and the Sword than I do for that white floor tile you're standing on. After what happened, I don't trust the men who went through it, and I don't trust myself."

"Pshaw! It's not important who *you* trust, it's who *I* trust."

"I'm resigning."

"I won't allow it. You accepted a ten-year commitment to the Elites. I don't think you have it in you to desert. I could save your neck if you did, but I am telling you right now that I will not do it."

The threat mattered not at all. Yet, while the passion for the Circle and the Sword was gone, duty remained. Still, not enough to give in. Chism and the queen stared at each other. Neither moved, and it was Queen Cuora who spoke first.

"I know more than what you've told me, Knight. Emissaries from the Domain came after they'd captured you. They told us about your near rescue as well as other mischief you created for them. Those barbarians have an odd respect for you, almost a reverence. It was quite creepy, really. They told me how miserable life would be for you in the Pit and that each day in captivity would drag you deeper into madness. After you escaped, Alendro and other Scaled Tigers sent notes ahead describing your skill in keeping your men sane."

Chism chuckled at the absurdity. "Sane? Muehner still thinks a single ray of sunlight will melt him. Wot rambles like a madman. He would have gouged Gorman's eyes out for ninety seconds of sunlight. Gorman nearly ate Mave. And you can see how well Serrill turned out. Then there's me. I had such a panic on our last day of imprisonment that I passed out because I couldn't remember if we'd been there 133 or 134 days. When the blackness drowned me, I thought I had died. Over one digit. Is that sane? Is that someone you want to trust with the lives of fifteen men?"

"So, a mission went awry. Welcome to the army. I honestly don't care if you all came home sad and that you can't stop thinking about all the bad things in your life. When the roses in my gardens grow white I don't carry them around and pout. And I certainly don't accept white roses." The queen leaned forward, tented her fingers, and said deliberately, "I paint the roses red. So here is what you will do: put on your Circle and Sword and go paint your roses."

Red. "I don't even know what that words means," snapped Chism. He hated it when people tried using colors to explain things. The queen was probably aggravating him on purpose.

"You know the meaning of the meaning, Knight. Stop being fragile and go to work."

"But why would you allow a mad person to—"

"Save your whining," said the Red Queen. "Who among us isn't a little mad?"

Chism was far from done. It went beyond a mere lack of ambition. It wasn't fair to other soldiers. "Most Elites hate me. Scaled

Tiger only followed me because I gave them no choice. They hated every day of it."

"When have you ever cared whether they love or hate you?"

"Never," said Chism. There had to be some way to get out of this mess.

"War is mere months away," said the queen. "We don't have time for their feelings. Or yours. And if the Maners who delivered the ransom demands were any indication, we need you more than anyone. Tell him, Marky."

The king nodded. "I'd love to hear details of the mission at a later date because when they talked about the Red Knight it was definitely with awe and admiration."

Chism ground his teeth. That nonsense accomplished nothing other than creating impossible standards for him to live up to. He decided to try a different tactic to prove no one would follow him. "If I decide to accept the lieutenant post, who would be in my squadron?"

"You will assemble your own squadron," said the queen. "Pick anyone you like."

"Regulars? This day just keeps getting better."

"Regulars, Elites, recruits. It's up to you. Any man you pick will be made an Elite by virtue of you selecting and training him."

"That will really be a bone in the craw of the other Elites."

"You're right," said Queen Cuora. "They don't hate you as much as you think, but they'll likely resent every man in your squadron after this."

Perfect. More duty. As Mave had taught in the Pit, the Red Knight was nothing more than a glorified pawn. He was only allowed to have opinions and desires by the leave of a queen and king.

Queen Cuora huffed out a frustrated breath. Sarcasm was thick in her voice as she said, "I know we're dear friends, and I'd *love* to spend the day chitchatting, but there are some other, very minor, demands on my time. So choose: squadron head or headsman?"

If he was stuck, he decided to be stuck in good company. "I pick anyone I want."

"Of course."

"And I train them how I want. That means I pick and choose which parts of the Academy they go through."

The queen curled one lip in a smile full of mischievousness. "I like where you're going. As the Red Knight, you will report to me, not through the normal chain of command."

"The first one I want is Mave."

"Please," said Cuora. "Can't you think of a less obvious way to fail?"

"You said anyone I wanted."

"Is it vanity?" She raised an eyebrow and studied him. "Will you prove you can succeed no matter how unfairly the deck is stacked?"

"I suspect Mave is off somewhere doing something impressively stupid even as we speak. I want a pardon for whatever it is." There was a small chance Mave would merely be looking for a bath. A very small chance.

"Fine, a pardon, but once you take him back under your wing you will be responsible for his actions."

"Of course. I'm his lieutenant."

She waved a dismissive hand. "I'm tiring of this. Go build your squadron, but do not waste time. I know you don't like being confined to my side, but if I need you, you still belong to me."

"I won't waste time," said Chism, "but I won't rush either. If I'm to build a squadron, I'll do it right."

"I'm anxious to see what name you earn." With a barely noticeable smirk she added, "Perhaps consider Red Squadron."

"I'd sooner name it White Squadron. At least that's a color I can see."

"Anything is better than Leighton's squadron." The Queen rolled her eyes. "What's that horrid name, Marky?"

The king recited, "Afflictive Bipeds Colonizing Deadhouses; Enemies Flee Girlishly Having Information Justifying Keeping Legion Miles Nigh Or Provoke Quotidian Risk Squadron."

Most people called them ABC Squadron.

"Speaking of the Whites," said Chism. "Are we friendly with them now?"

"Yes and no," said the queen.

"What does that mean?"

"It's not related to war issues," said the queen. "You wouldn't understand. But you personally should avoid the Provinces for at least the next two hundred years or so."

That suited Chism just fine. "I have to warn you: the men from the Pit—the Pitifuls, as you so accurately called us—will never be the same. Something's been taken from us, and it looks like it's never coming back. I doubt any of us will ever be useful soldiers again. Including myself. The ones I brought back will need to be watched closely just to make sure they eat regularly and get out of their beds on occasion."

"Except for Mave," objected the queen, "for whom you will have the privilege of caring."

"Except for Mave," agreed Chism.

"Why would you pick him if he's so damaged?"

"He has a lot of things in his head that I need."

"He's worthless, but if he gives you confidence, so be it." After a moment she said, "It is good to have you back, Knight."

If he didn't know her better, and himself as well, he'd think they actually were becoming friends. He wasn't about to lie, however, and say he felt anything at all.

"I'd stay and chitchat, but I have a squadron to build. Your Majesty," he made a short bow then turned to King Markin and saluted with both hands. "Sir."

As he walked out, he wondered what it would take to get kicked out of the Elites without being beheaded or thrown in prison.

The only Elite waiting in the entrance room of the palace was Ander. Falling into step beside Chism, he asked, "What now?"

"Lemons," said Chism. "We need to find some lemons."

18

Chism found Hatta curled up in the curve of the Circle, shaking the rattle and smiling. Ander had gone off in search of Mave.

"I'm finished," said Chism. He held out his hand, but Hatta ignored it. Chism gently took hold of the rattle and Hatta eventually let go.

Hatta stood but didn't look up. "So where's S?"

"Huh?" asked Chism.

"S."

It sounded familiar, but that wasn't uncommon for Hatta's nonsense. "I don't know what you're talking about."

"It's uncle."

It's uncle? "Oh. Es, the targus corpse?"

"Of course."

"And you want to do what with it? I mean Es."

Hatta's eyes danced nervously, staying too low to meet Chism's. "Don't you remember what It said? 'Bring back It's uncle and trade for dreams the uncle It will.' Or somesuch and somesort."

The words were vaguely familiar. "There's no way to be sure that's what It meant. Nearly everything It said was nonsense."

"Nonsense is a language I speak," said Hatta. He stepped side to side in a nervous pace.

"Not reliably enough to go off on some snark hunt. I have a new mission, Hatta."

"But, my dreams," said Hatta. "How will I do without them?"

"Even if I wanted to," said Chism, "I can't walk into the museum and carry the thing out."

"But you're the Red Knight. You could entirely ask Cuora."

"Cuora, *Queen* Cuora, only ten minutes ago set me to a task that will take me to the corners of the kingdoms."

"I went farther for you, brother, and it cost me my dreams," said Hatta, sitting back down. "It cost me everything I have."

Chism sat next to him on the lip of the Circle, leaving a gap. His brother's argument was impossible to argue with. If it wasn't for Hatta, Chism and his men—his former men—would still be rotting, body and mind in the Domain's armpit. But, time was already short, and Hatta wanted to chase down a creature that would most likely enjoy eating their knuckles one by one while they were still living.

"We'll never find It again, Hatta. We can't walk back into the Domain. Even if we did, he can't give you your dreams back. It's not like he's holding them hostage or something."

More tears formed in Hatta's eyes, began to push their way over his lower eyelids. "What do you hear in the rattle?"

"It doesn't matter," said Chism quickly. "Listen, Hatta, It poisoned us. Broke us. If we go back, he'll take the carcass and eat us both."

"Don't let him! You can make him do it." Hatta ground his teeth and said, "Kill him if he won't give us our dreams back."

Chism was certain the malicious expression had never crossed his brother's face before. But it was there now, and it almost scared some emotion into Chism. Almost.

"Are you listening to yourself, Hatta? This isn't like you."

Tears began to flow in earnest, accompanied by a slobbery

mouth and catches of breath when Hatta said, "Of course I'm not who I am! How can I ever will be without my dreams?"

Chism stood and ran his hand across his shaved head. Duty pulled him two ways at once, but there was no desire or will to go either direction. In fact, compared to the mountain of emotion Hatta had pulled from somewhere, Chism's passion was a pebble. There was a chance the queen would find out about the detour, and when she did she just might change her mind about—

"I'll give it a shot," said Chism. "If we get captured in the Domain, it will be into the Pit for both of us. No one to ransom us, either."

Between shudders, Hatta wiped his eyes and breathed in and out. "What does it matter? Can't be worse than the pit I'm in now." He stood and faced Chism. "So where is Es?"

19

Before starting some harebrained attempt to spring the targus carcass from the museum, Chism waited at the meeting place for Ander and Mave. He debated asking Mave for advice on recovering Es. If Mave did help, the plan would most likely go off without a problem and Cuora would never find out.

If Chism asked Cuora, she might just hand over the creature. If he was caught attempting to steal it without asking, she might realize how unstable he was and reconsider her decision to make him lead. However, if he was caught trying to steal the creature *after* being told he couldn't have it, *that* would have maximum impact.

Just when Chism began to wonder how much trouble Mave had made, Ander and he walked up.

"How bad was it?" asked Chism.

Ander shook his head, rolled his eyes, and exhaled. "Do you remember the Circle and Sword banner that used to hang in the auditorium?"

"The one that was about ten paces long?" asked Chism, then caught the rest of what Ander had said. "Wait, what do you mean *used to* hang?"

"Exactly," said Ander. "It's now resting about this high." Ander bent and held his hand a few inches off the ground.

"Could have been worse," said Chism.

"Oh, it is worse," said Ander. "I don't know how long he'd been holding it, but it's going to take some work to get the stench out of that banner. I must have missed the asparagus at breakfast this morning."

Chism looked at Mave. "Please tell me you didn't."

Mave shrugged. "Sorry. I had a pretty rough fifteen minutes of not being an Elite. At least I've been pardoned."

"Good," said Chism. "I'd hate a little thing like prison to keep you from another date with a targus."

"Teats and teeth," said Ander. "What are you talking about?"

Hatta spoke up. "We're going to find the targus that stole our dreams and trade them for its cousin. Or the body of its cousin, at least."

Ander looked at Chism. "Please tell me you're not serious about sneaking through hostile territory to get to even more hostile territory so that we can find a creature no sane person wants to be in the same kingdom with."

"I can tell you that life will never be boring in my squadron," said Chism. "Unless we get dropped into the Pit again."

"That's reassuring," said Ander. "Sounds like you've got your mind set on becoming Lunatic Squadron."

"That rings nicely in my ears," said Chism. "It's accurate, if nothing else." They started walking.

"And I suppose Mave's coming along?" said Ander.

Chism nodded. "Of course. He's the only other Elite in the squadron so far."

"Is he bringing a Fellow?"

"He doesn't have a Fellow or time to pick one."

"Wife?" asked Ander, his voice growing more pleading.

"Same answer," said Chism, "substitute wife for Fellow."

"Overseer? Mother? Governess?"

Chism raised an eyebrow.

Ander sighed. "And Hatta?"

"Coming along too," said Chism.

"Of course," said Ander. "Because the universe hates me. No offense, Hatta."

"Not offended," said Hatta. "I wouldn't want your job for all the buttons in Bolton."

"Mave," said Chism, "you're with me. Until further notice." He turned to Ander and Hatta. "You two start gathering supplies."

"Cheshire said you and I should stick together," objected Hatta.

"Inside the inner city should be close enough," said Chism. The day he started obeying Cheshire was the day he put on a purple hat and moved in with Hatta. "Grab my blues, Ander. I'm already itching to ditch whatever color this is. Get as much money as Mully will give you. After you get it, have him give you credit for the wagon and whatever else we still have in it. We'll be picking up a few men along the way."

"You mean soldiers?" asked Ander. "Or puppies who aren't even housebroken?" He glanced in Mave's direction.

"You think you have your hands full now," said Chism, "wait until you see how much you hate your life in a few weeks."

"Remind me why I ever agreed to be your Fellow again," said Ander.

"You have no one to blame but yourself for the second time around. You knew what you were getting into and who you were getting in with. Enough talk. I'll meet you in the barracks."

"Wait," said Ander. "What's our story when we go back into the Provinces? Do I need to buy ten thousand thimbles so we can act like merchants?"

Chism considered for a moment then said, "We're a family. Three brothers and a father."

"You're giving me permission to thrash anyone who steps out of line?" Ander's face took on a devilish grin.

"I'm giving you permission to try," said Chism. "One more thing: no pink clothes."

Ander chuckled. "I think I just found a way to get even with you for turning me into a nanny. If these two went along with me, you'd never even know."

"I'll dress you in welts if I catch you dressing me in pink. Dad."

They went their separate ways.

"Sir," said Mave as soon as they were alone. "Thank you for giving me back the Circle and Sword."

"I was only doing myself favors," said Chism.

"What do you mean?"

"I mean I chose you for selfish reasons. It will take some work to look after you, but you'll pay it back to the squadron a hundred times over."

"We'll be the greatest of all time. People will sing songs about us."

"I don't care what they say about us. I was talking about staying alive. We get that mind of yours used to thinking before that body of yours starts acting, and we'll be a force to be reckoned with."

"Yes, Sir," said Mave. "I was loyal before, but now, I don't even have words to describe it."

"Words are like leaves on a tree—noisy and bright one day, faded and brittle the next." Chism sped up, anxious to get to Cuora and hopefully convince her the he was the wrong person to put trust in.

Queen Cuora proved disappointingly accommodating in Chism's request for the targus carcass and a dozen lemons. He suspected she knew that he was determined to present a front of being mad. A servant was dispatched and the queen called for paper and pen which appeared immediately. She wrote out a letter vouching for Chism and expressing gratitude to anyone who aided him. The servant returned within minutes carrying a burlap-wrapped package half as tall as a man. And lemons.

Once again, Chism was dismissed.

By the time he arrived at Mully, the other Scaled Tigers had already given their reports and left.

"I've been holding something for you, Sir Chism." Mully disappeared into a small closet in the warehouse. When he came out, he was carrying something more precious to Chism than anything else in the armory.

Thirsty, sheathed and lonely.

Chism stared at his best friend. There was a reason he hadn't come straight to the armorer. He feared what he might not feel.

Mully pushed the sword forward. Chism accepted it, then closed his eyes and slowly slid the blade free of the scabbard.

Thirsty didn't make a sound. No purring, no humming. No crying for blood. Chism opened his eyes. The sword in his hand was definitely Thirsty—slightly curved blade, two-handed hilt, small quillons above the hilt to protect his hands. But something had happened while Chism was away. The targus. Not only had it stolen his dreams, it had stolen the life from his best friend.

With one hand on the hilt and the other flat against the cold steel, Chism silently asked, *Why, when I have nothing else, when I need you like never before, why have you abandoned me?*

Chism closed his eyes and listened more intently. He rested the flat of the blade against one cheek and concentrated. Thirsty remained as silent and hard as any hunk of metal. His most steadfast friend might as well have been dead.

"Do you have a report, Sir?" asked Mully.

Chism looked up from his lifeless friend. Former friend. "What?"

Mully sat at a desk, holding a pen, ready to make notations in a book. "War preparations? The Domain?"

"Oh." Chism slowly slid Thirsty into its scabbard. A dead piece of metal. As dead as doornails. "Yes."

There was nothing to be done about Thirsty, so Chism dug into his memory for the information he'd gathered in Phaylea. He felt confident in his report, not just the numbers but also how close each item was to the completion line in the warehouse.

"I know I'm young," he said at the end of his report, "but that surpassed any war preparations I could have imagined."

"Taking into consideration the age of the information and what we've heard from other spies ..." Mully furrowed his brow and scribbled in his ledger. "Four or five more months. Maximum."

Chism swore under his breath. His men would never be ready by then, even if he chose men already attending the Academy. It appeared they would either have to wait for the next war or show up very late to this one. Why bother with any of it?

It was bad enough he had to do things. Knowing his efforts would count for nothing made it even worse.

20

Four men drove six horses and three hundred thimbles and one burlap-wrapped carcass over a hundred miles in four days. Five horses would have been enough, but Chism wouldn't travel hundreds of miles with an odd number if he could avoid it. There was enough drudgery in his life that he would avoid *that* aggravation wherever possible.

A steady stream of refugees from the Provinces passed them heading toward the center of the kingdom. It made Chism wonder if the Maners would find any resistance at all when they finally invaded.

The first day of travel Chism had allowed Hatta and Mave to share the rattle. By their midday stop it became clear that wouldn't work. Hatta would not respond when the rattle was in his hand, and he couldn't focus on anything when the rattle was in Mave's. Mave was irritable before and after his turns, which meant he was irritable almost all of the time. They had no wheel to count, so Chism counted the horses' steps to track the turns. Hatta and Mave cared for nothing in life except the relief the rattle gave them.

Chism cut them back to a half hour in the morning and a half hour in the evening. It didn't improve their moods, but it did make them more utilitarian on the trail and around camp when things needed doing.

The other Pitifuls were out of luck. Hatta had found the rattle to begin with, so the Elites had no real claim to it. They all owed Hatta anyway, for ransoming them. Chism didn't know what the Elite leadership planned for the other Pitifuls, but he left specific instructions for people to look after them.

An hour after darkness had settled on the fourth day, Chism led his party off the Telavir Spoke toward Shey's Orchard. With plenty of moon and a slow pace, the road was easy. Chism reined his horse gently until Hatta's mare caught him up. Mave slowed his mount as well, staying by Chism's side.

"How long were you in Shey's Orchard?" Chism asked.

"Just the right amount of time," said Hatta.

"How many days? Months?"

Hatta considered for a moment. "Four months? No, five. Or perhaps seven. Either it was one of those numbers or a different one."

"Is there anyone you want to visit while we're here?" asked Chism. It was their last chance for Hatta to see friends before they went off on their snark hunt. The worst outcome involved a targus dragging their corpses around like the headless rattler. The best Chism could hope for involved a fruitless search for It and a lifetime without dreams for him and his brother, not to mention the other Pitifuls.

"Not particularly," said Hatta. He stared at the back of the mare's head just as he had for four days.

"Hatta," said Chism. "I worked with a boy, a young man, named Steffen when I passed through Shey's Orchard."

Hatta's lip curled in an unpleasant expression.

"How much do you remember about him?" asked Chism.

"As little as possible," said Hatta.

"Anything more specific?"

"Brown hair," said Hatta. "He's short. Taller than you. Shorter than someone my height. Strong as a grizzly bear and twice as mean. He had scars aplenty and civility alacking. A glance from him is more caustic than a barrel of lye."

"Did you ever see him act malicious?"

Hatta shook his head. "I never saw him act kind either."

"Anything else?"

"After Brune left, Steffen was entirely the person in Shey's Orchard I wanted most to not spend time with."

"What was it about him that offended you?"

"He was too soldiery," said Hatta without considering.

"He acted like me?" asked Chism.

Hatta nodded. "Not when you are acting like a brother or a friend or a commander, but when you act like a soldier. Like that time when you bolted and I was conscripted by the White army."

Good, thought Chism. *The kind of man I'm looking for.*

The outskirts of Shey's Orchard began to pass on either side. Farmland, farm animals, farmhouses. Lights burned in the buildings, but no one was on the road.

"If you change your mind about visiting old friends," said Chism to his brother, "we've got half a day tomorrow."

Hatta made a neutral noise.

Pitching his voice a little higher, Chism said, "113 Squadron, rest up tomorrow morning. I need to round up a few things while we're here."

"What are you after?" asked Ander.

"Lemons," said Chism.

Hatta spoke up. "Yes. That is how I would describe the taste Steffen gives me. Lemon. Steffen is a lemon."

Before Chism could tell them Steffen was the second thing on his list, Ander chuckled and said, "I don't think another ten years of lemons will get your hair to white."

True to the pledge he'd given Ander, Chism was trying to dye his hair, but black to white turned out to be more difficult than he expected. All he'd managed so far was a color Hatta described as overcooked chestnut shells. But Mave was an Elite, and Chism had promised that if Mave wore the Circle and Sword, Chism would dye his hair. If it helped to disguise himself in the Provinces and Domain, so much the better.

"You need to apply something to yours before we get to the Domain," Chism told Ander. "It barely has any black tint left in it."

"The price of a beautiful mane," said Ander. He reached back, pulled a hairbrush out of a saddlebag, and ran it through his hair. "I can't even cross into a kingdom where everyone wants to kill me without being recognized." He changed hands with the brush and started on his mare's mane. "It's a blessing and a curse, isn't it, girl?"

One of the first buildings they came to when they reached Shey's Orchard proper was the Dusty Tunic, a two-story inn. The group came to a stop in front of the attached stable and stretched and groaned. Every time Ander bent, a different joint creaked.

"Four days on a horse and you're popping like a pine fire," said Chism. "Do we need to leave you here and collect you on our way back?"

"Don't mind me," said Ander. "It's just my body reminding you that I have more experience than the rest of you combined."

"You have more experience than most squadrons combined," said Chism. "Try not to let any of your parts snap off while I go get a stable boy."

"Treat him with respect. He'll probably be older than you."

The door to the inn opened smoothly and Chism walked in, flanked by Hatta and Mave. The crowd in the dayroom was large enough that they barely noticed another three coming in. Only two tables out of the twelve in the room were empty. Even though it was busy, and probably had been since threat of invasion began to spread, the room was clean. The chairs at the empty tables were in good repair and organized neatly and symmetrically.

Chism liked the innkeep before the man even walked into the room.

"Welcome to the Dus—" The sturdy man froze midstride, one hand wiping the other with a cloth, and smiled like the town fool. "Hatta! Of all the people I didn't expect to walk into my inn." The innkeep remembered his legs and hurried to wrap arms around Hatta.

Hatta lifted his arms, but it didn't look like a real hug. His half smile was back, forced and small.

"How have you been, my friend?" The innkeep stepped back and looked at Hatta, who wouldn't meet his eyes.

"How have I been? Oh, that's an unpleasant question to answer. I'd much rather tell who I've been, which is someone besides myself and of my thirty-one skills, being someone who isn't me isn't one of them." His brow furrowed, and he added, "I don't think I even have thirty-one anymore. I seem to have misplaced many of them recently."

"What's happened? If you've come to stay, I hope it's something friends can help with."

"I don't think friends can do anything," stated Chism.

The innkeep looked at Chism and Mave. "I beg pardon for ignoring the two of you. As I was saying, welcome to the Dusty Tunic. Do you have horses?"

Chism nodded. "Six. One of my men is outside with them."

"Tidris!" called the innkeep toward the kitchens. "See to the horses."

A young man acknowledged from the back room.

If Chism was feeling like himself, he'd have the stable boy carry a cane out for his old Fellow. But he wasn't, so he didn't.

"You'll forgive the poor memory," said the innkeep, "but I don't recall your name even though I do remember the face from last summer."

"Chism. And that's Mave."

"Innkeep Tellef." He glanced down at the Circle and Sword on their uniforms. "Forgive the question as well, but aren't you young for Elites?"

Chism merely nodded, but Mave couldn't stay quiet. "He's not just an Elite, he's a lieutenant and the Red Knight."

Tellef's eyes grew even wider. "And here I thought Hatta was the grandest hero of the party."

Mave would go on if Chism let him so he said, "Business seems brisk, Innkeep."

"Aye." Suddenly Tellef looked exhausted. "It's this affair with the Domain."

"Isn't that good for business?" asked Chism.

"Yes and no," said Tellef. "Refugees don't carry much coin and there's only so much trade in services I can take."

"Some of us have coin!" said a full-bearded man from the table.

From the same table, his companion said, "And some of us are thirsty."

"Please have a seat while I tend to my other guests. I'll ask the missus to see what food she can find that won't require a long wait."

Chism thanked Tellef, who took a step away, then backtracked and placed a hand on Hatta's shoulder.

"I hope we have a chance to talk tonight or tomorrow. We've all heard how you ended the war at Kirohz, but I'd love to hear the details from you."

Hatta made the non-committal grunt Chism was getting used to.

Ander came in, and little bits of conversation came with him, but as was their custom, the other three concentrated on the table in front of them. Tellef eventually returned with food. He took a seat and asked for news from the kingdom. Ander answered most of his questions, even the ones directed at Hatta or Chism.

Yet another reason he's good to have along, thought Chism.

As soon as their dinners were eaten, Chism claimed exhaustion, and Tellef showed them to their rooms. Mave bunked with Chism, and Ander with Hatta. Not only was Mave inseparable from Chism, but it was the best way for Chism and Ander to supervise the two unpredictable members of the group.

It had only been a matter of months since Chism had been chaperoned by Ander for the same reasons.

Before the first wedge of sun appeared between the faraway mountains, Chism and Thirsty had found a secluded plot of ground not far from the inn. As was their custom, they were stretching in preparation for practicing sword forms. Mave was in the clearing as well, as had become his custom since the first few days after Knobbes. Mave had never attempted conversation, and that suited Chism. He hadn't ordered Mave to join him or even invited him to, but neither had he forbidden it.

Mave always stayed out of his way, mimicking the motions and improving in his swordplay. Chism got practice blocking out everything that wasn't pertinent to his activities.

There was very little room in Chism for superstition. His one indulgence was catching the first lucky ray of the sun every day. If a member of his squadron wanted to share it, Chism wouldn't be selfish. Before Tjaden had set off to fight the Jabberwock, Chism had given the ray to him and the adventure couldn't have turned out much better for Tjaden. In contrast, during the days leading up to capture in Phaylea, Chism hadn't been able to capture any lucky rays and that couldn't have gone much worse. More often than not since leaving Palassiren he had caught it, but had yet to feel the slightest twinge of luck along with it.

Enough endurance had returned for Chism to perform a proper routine, but his control was still lacking. A few minutes into the morning routine, a beam of sunlight glinted on Chism and Thirsty. It was going to be a good day. Half of the routine was defensive stances. By the time he reached the twentieth repetition of each action, Thirsty went where it was supposed to but trembled wildly as evidence of his fatigue.

Steam rose off of Chism's and Mave's sweating faces as they walked back to the inn in silence. After eating breakfast and dressing in their blues, Chism's small group followed him through town.

Nearly everyone they passed in the street greeted Hatta by name. Even though he'd only spent months there, it was clear the people of Shey's Orchard claimed Hatta the hero as one of their own.

"Hatta!" Another townsman waved Hatta down and caught up with them. "We heard you were in town and had to come say hello." A very pretty young lady with a gold-tipped ribbon in her hair walked along beside a man Chism recognized as the mirror maker. "What's the matter, Hatta? You don't appear to be feeling yourself."

"Yes, I'm not," said Hatta. "Usually I'm more myself than anyone else, but for a good while now no one has been feeling like me."

"I'm sorry to hear that," he said. "You remember Lily."

Hatta nodded.

"Any word from Lady Elora?" asked Lily.

Chism shook his head. "I don't think she was in Palassiren when we were there. I'm Chism; I was in Tjaden's Academy class. This is Ander, and that's Mave."

The last introduction was what Lily had been waiting for. The look she shared with Mave was much longer and deeper than the one she'd bestowed on the others. It had been a long time since Chism had seen a girl that matched Mave in attractiveness. With a shock, Chism realized that Mave's good looks were back, just like that. Either Chism had missed the transformation entirely, or Lily was having a powerful and sudden effect on Mave. The five days of beard on Mave only accentuated his good looks.

A girl like Lily would easily be the most beautiful in a town like this, and most likely in the nearest four towns as well. Her sister Lady Elora, was pretty, scars and all, but next to Lily she would seem ordinary. Underneath Lily's beauty, there was something that made Chism nervous. She was all sweetness and manners on the surface, but something ... wicked dwelt a little deeper that Chism couldn't pinpoint.

Could it be jealousy? Mave had been Chism's disciple and companion since the Pit and suddenly his world seemed to be composed of this girl. Perhaps deep down Chism resented Mave's recovery. As sure as sugar, Chism would never meet a girl who could have this kind of effect on him. If *love* was the cure for the targus, Chism was doomed. He shrugged off the strange hunch and took a half-step backward out of their way.

Mave strode forward and performed a bow that Chism hadn't even realized Mave knew how to do. Despair was gone from his face, which shone with a healthy luster that none of the other Pitifuls had managed. He nodded a formal bow to Aker as well.

He said, "It does not surprise me to know that a fine woman such as Lady Elora should come from such a distinguishable family."

Distinguished, thought Chism.

"Thank you," said Aker. "If the talk I hear around the house has anything to do with it, Lora won't be the only one who ends up married to a Knight."

After a short stunned look, Lily blushed. Chism may have too; being the only Knight present made him slightly uncomfortable. He caught a glimmer of a sharp edge in Lily's eye, but didn't know what it meant.

"I'm going to be a Knight someday," said Mave.

Lily bit one lip and glanced hopefully at Chism for confirmation. Chism wanted Mave's transformation to remain in place, so he nodded quickly.

With a flirty smile, Lily asked, "What Knight will you be, Sir Mave?"

Mave's eyes did the dance they did when he was thinking quickly. "I can't be the First Knight; that was Sir Darieus. Top Knight and Best Knight are accurate but not descriptive enough. My superior intellect is my strength, so something to do with brains or intelligence, but that also denotes superiorness."

Lily devoured every word, but her father seemed a little skeptical. "You mean something like the Red Knight? A title that shows you are the champion of an entire kingdom?"

Lily and Aker both looked down at Chism's pins, then at Mave's chest, which had none. Queen Cuora had refused to give Mave the escapee pin and the officials in charge of Pins claimed they had no Elite pins and wouldn't be able to come up with one because of war preparations. It sounded doubtful to Chism. Maybe he should have fought for Mave and demanded a pin. It would have saved the awkward situation he found himself in now.

How did I get pulled into all this? thought Chism. Trying to get himself out of the discussion, he said, "Mave's being accurate, Mirrorer Aker. He will be one of the greats."

That didn't convince him. "How old are you?"

"Nineteen," said Mave, his expression beginning to sour.

"Oh, don't let me get you down," said Aker. "I know nothing of high politics or the things of Knights. I've met Red Knights and Vorpal Knights younger than you, I suppose."

"The Elder Knight," said Lily. "That has some promise. Or possibly The Superior Knight. The Real Knight, or Knight of the Realm."

That was enough to restore Mave's hope.

Chism entertained the possibility of taking Lily with them. The plan had been to gather what they needed and be on the road after lunch, but Chism couldn't just ignore the only antidote anyone had found for the targus' poison.

She didn't have to go all the way into the Domain; Far West was close and safe. But, there were far too many problems with that. She would be a worse distraction than the rattle.

Chism was still far from understanding the extent of what the targus had done to him. Since when did he care about the tender feelings of other people? Why did suffering lead him to be concerned about fluff such as feelings? It didn't really matter. It was what it was, and Mave had a chance at healing here.

"Perhaps you'd like to call on Lily later this evening?" Chism said. "If, Mirrorer Aker wouldn't mind, that is."

"That would be acceptable," said Aker. "Provided they have a chaperone."

Chism couldn't do it. He was nearly as young as Lily, and his higher military standing would vex Mave all night. "I think Ander would not object to chaperoning."

Ander shot a brief look at Chism, then shrugged acceptance. Mave and Lily nodded giddily.

After short farewells, the group continued. Eleven more townspeople attempted to stop Hatta for a chat before they reached the far end of town. Apparently, a man in whatever garish colors Hatta was wearing, walking with three Elites, drew as much attention as a parade. Hatta tipped his hat to everyone and gave them his forced half-smile. To the people who tried to engage in conversation, he said the same thing: "Terribly happy to be seeing you and terribly sorry to be hurrying off, but my brother has some terribly pressing matters."

Between the third and fourth time Hatta sidestepped, Chism urged him to stay and chat, hoping that some spark of what Mave had found with Lily would come out in Hatta as he spent time with old friends. But Hatta made the same neutral sound and continued walking.

The orangeberry bushes and lemon trees they had to walk through to reach Grower Mikel's house brought back stronger memories of Chism's journey the previous summer than any other landmark thus far. Even if he'd been blindfolded, Chism would recognize that pleasant, tangy scent. He knew the memories would be even stronger at the destination he had planned after Shey's Orchard.

"Mikel?" shouted Chism when they reached the small brick house. "Lira?"

Lira came around the side of the house, holding a rake that was missing four prongs. Her pleased smile reminded him of Tellef's from the night before, but this smile was for him, not Hatta. A year of new age showed on her face, but her dark eyes held even more kindness and concern than he remembered. She leaned the rake against the house as she walked past and dusted off her hands on her apron.

"Chism," she said, reaching out for him. He dodged backward, and she immediately realized her blunder. Pulling her arms back, she said, "I'm sorry. It's so easy to forget and so wonderful to see you." She wiped a happy tear from one eye. Before he had decided to use her real name the year before, he'd given her the nickname Doty because of her propensity to dote on and care for people.

"You too." He knew it should feel wonderful, so the lie was not far off.

"Look at you in your Elite blues," she said, as proud as a mother would be. "Just like my Tjaden. Of course, Mikel suspected you had grand secrets you weren't sharing with us, even before he saw you at that battle."

"He's not just an—" started Mave, but Chism silenced him with half a shake of his head. First of all, there was nothing to be gained by reciting Chism's titles. Second, it was bad form to tell a mother that someone was advancing faster than her very successful and famous son.

"I'm sorry I had to hide it," said Chism. "Also, I never told you that Ander, my Fellow here, and I were in training with Tjaden and Ollie. Oh, this is Mave. And you know my brother, Hatta."

Mave and Hatta just bobbed their heads, but Ander bowed like he was at court and said, "I'm honored to meet the mother of the Vorpal Knight. Your son is a shining example to soldiers everywhere."

Lira's face beamed as though someone had sparked a lantern behind her eyes.

"Is Grower Mikel in the groves somewhere?" Chism asked before more small talk could be made.

"No," said Lira. "He's delivering some fruit to Stevva."

"Merchants don't come for it these days?"

She shook her head. "Not as often as they used to. I'm not sure why, but more people means less coin around. There's only so much we can trade locally, and we hate to see it rot and fall. Even with Mikel traveling two weeks out of three, we can't sell the fourth part of what we grow."

The war was months off, yet people all over the kingdom were affected in their own way. In Chism's Academy classes he'd been taught that coin tended to collect in cities during times of war, which hurt people in small villages. He wanted to help, but the cost of a dozen lemons wouldn't solve a problem of that magnitude. All of the money he carried wouldn't make any difference in the long run, if Lira even accepted payment for the lemons. But this family had shown Chism kindness. Unfortunately Chism couldn't think of anything that would help. If he could, it just might give him a bit of the glimmer Mave had experienced.

He glanced at the faces of his men. Mave's was still bright.

"Mave, do you have ideas for Lira until trade picks up again?"

Mave snapped out of a grinning daydream and asked, "Is someone helping you out here?"

"Of course," said Lira. "We have enough trees that they kept Mikel and I and all of our sons busy. You can imagine how much goes undone with the boys moved on and Mikel traveling."

"How many hands do you hire on a daily basis?"

"Two, usually."

"But neither is as valuable as Mikel, right?" Mave did not make eye contact with her as he spoke, but he seemed to see everything else for a fraction of a second at a time.

Lira shook her head. "And it's not always the same two. We have four young men who rotate."

"How many travel with Mikel?"

"Just one."

"How far can you rationally transport fruit with it still being fresh enough to sell?"

"Palassiren is almost a hundred miles," answered Lira. "If it wasn't such a large market, we wouldn't go that far. And we can only take fruit that far during cooler parts of the season when it stays fresh the longest."

Mave asked twenty-four more questions about the value of a wagon of fruit, the purchasing power of nearby towns and cities, the skill required to negotiate sales, and the price of other exports from Shey's Orchard. With the patience of an oyster, Lira answered his seemingly random questions.

Mave's focus left the vicinity without warning, and his lips moved like someone working to add numbers in their head.

Lira turned to Chism since Mave was obviously not present. "Is he some kind of merchant?"

"No," said Chism, "just a genius when it comes to the mechanics of operations."

"Production clearly isn't the problem," interrupted Mave. "During war times, there is money to be made by the fistful, you just have to get your fruit to where people gather, not where refugees pass. Your problem is distribution. If your distributors have dried up, it leaves the problem in your lap. It does you no good to produce if you can't distribute."

"That's what Mikel's doing in Stevva."

"No." Mave shook his head. His eyes were still not fully focused on the then and there. "He's peddling. Distributing requires more focus and organization. How many wagons can you come up with?"

"We have three, but only because no one around here has the coins to buy the two we don't use."

"Horses?"

"The one team plus an old nag," said Lira.

"Men willing to work?"

"It's not the willing men, it's the coin to pay them." Lira's shoulders hung much lower than when she'd first approached. Without seeming to notice, she'd hunched so far over that she was almost as short as Chism.

"Are there men who will work on commission?" asked Mave. "Meaning future pay when money comes in?"

"I think there are men who would work for orange peels and corn cobs. Shey's Orchard has grown since Chism was here, but the amount of work available hasn't kept pace."

"Okay," said Mave. His lips moved a little more, then his eyes came into focus and he drew air into his lungs.

"Get ready," said Chism.

Lira raised an eyebrow and leaned back ever so slightly.

Mave took off like a he-goat that had broken its chain. "Take on six men who are willing and stable to travel. Form them into two groups of three men each. On the road, three is a safer number than two by a factor of ten. You can ask me later how three men can seem like eight. One of them will be the merchant. He should know the other exports of Shey's Orchard as well as he knows circus."

"Citrus," said Chism.

"Citrus." Mave nodded and took another breath. "The other two men are basically muscle, but a brain to advise the merchant wouldn't hurt since he will have a lot of information to process and pick through. On a map, design four trade routes with a round-trip time of eleven or twelve days each. It will take some fine tuning to perfect this part. Each route will see a wagon once in a month, assuming four days' shore leave between trips for your men. One wagon will remain here as a backup and for repairs. Half of each wagon that leaves Shey's Orchard will be filled with citrus fruit, and the other half, minus supplies for the men, will be for other goods —mirrors, dates, honey, peppers, and the like." The word 'mirrors' brought Mave's giddy smile back. "The people who supply those goods will take all the risk of placing them on your wagons, as you will for your own fruit. When the good sells in other towns, one third of the sales price is yours. Of that money, four percent goes to your merchant man, and three percent to each muscle man."

Lira opened her mouth but couldn't squeeze a word in.

"Grower Mikel will stay here and continue with two men. He is a farmer and should do and supervise farming. You will continue to sell citrus to merchants that come to you, of course. Do not discount too steeply just because you're desperate to sell. You don't want them undercutting your men. How long until the citrus season ends?"

It took Lira a moment to realize she'd been asked a question. "Three weeks. Five if the weather cooperates."

"That soon? When does corn start?"

"Six weeks after we end."

"And corn goes until cotton kicks in?"

"Close enough." Lira nodded.

"And cotton leads to citrus. Good. So don't make any trips without one of those crops as the anchor, and don't make your cargo too predictable. That is to say, don't carry mirrors every trip, or raisins. You want people to know what's coming but also to look forward to something different. Once you establish this pattern, have the men purchase smallish amounts of bulk goods in other towns. Keep away from specialty items at first, such as mouth harps and silver goblets. You will need to start with workaday and eataday products that will not have trouble selling. Nails and wheat, not fine dishes and chocolates. Focus on the staple products of each town since they can be bought cheap. It should not be difficult to predicate what will sell and how much to buy. Remember that you are a distributor, not a merchant. Eventually you will need to hire more wagons and create new routes, but this plan should last through the first thirteen months, unless you're either superb or incompetent at carrying it out. Any questions?"

Lira's jaw worked, but she seemed to answer her own questions before asking. If her efficiency at running her house during the week Chism had spent with her was any indication, Mave's plan would be as easy for her as waking up in the morning.

Eventually, she asked, "What do we do when the corn growers and cotton pickers copy what we're doing?"

"Why don't you just grow your own cotton and make linen instead of paying them to do it?"

"Because we're citrus farmers," Lira objected.

"*Mikel* is a farmer," said Mave. "*You* are a regional distributor. The corn growers are corn growers and the cotton pickers are cottonpicking cotton pickers. They will continue to farm, and they'll prosper with a local partner to help them sell."

"How can we compete with merchants who have been doing this for decades?"

"How can an orange grower compete with a corn farmer?"

"We don't compete," said Lira. "Our customers don't overlap."

"Exactly. That's one of the reasons you'll secede. Merchants sell from a single shop; you transport goods from market to market. More importantly, you are leveraging the efforts of many men and earning off of each of their backs."

"I don't want to exploit anyone," said Lira, her hand coming up to touch her cheek.

Chism could have predicted such a reaction from her.

"Is providing men a wage with which they can feed a family exploding them?"

"You mean exploiting?" asked Lira. She shook her head. "Of course not. Not if they are willing to work and we take all the precautions we can for their safety."

"And they are not exploiting you by providing a living for you and Citruser Mikel."

"On the contrary," said Lira. She nodded and said, "I should write down the details I can remember and the ideas that came to mind while you were talking. I hate to send you off, but I feel them leaking out already."

"We'll be at the Dusty Tunic at lunch time if you need to talk to him anymore," said Chism. He reached into his purse and took out a thripp. "I need some lemons."

"For the hair," she said. "That explains it. You're more like your brother than I realized."

Chism chuffed a small laugh that surprised him. He hadn't done anything, but listening to Mave help deliver Lira and Mikel from their quandary had done something to him. Still the only similarity he saw when he looked at his brother was their lack of dreams.

People see what they want to see.

"I can't take your money," said Lira.

"Then I can't take your fruit," said Chism. He held out the coin, pinched between two fingers. "Hurry, before Mave's words are lost or jumbled."

She opened a hand beneath the coin, and Chism let it fall. "This is too much for a few lemons. Please pick whatever else you'd like for the road. The tangerines are especially sweet this time of year."

"Thank you," said Chism. "I'll visit the next time we pass through Shey's Orchard." Making promises seemed like a decent way to force his future self to do things he didn't feel like doing. His word was definitely much stronger than his drive.

Lira reached out her hands toward his face again but caught herself and wrung them instead.

"Mikel and I will watch for you."

Those with hats tipped them, and the men turned to walk away.

"Oh, Chism."

He looked and saw Lira in her doorway. "If you're going south, you won't find any more lemons. Wipe a thin layer of grease over some of them. That will give you an extra week or two. When those start to turn, you can squeeze the juice and keep that for another week. But even that much time won't give you hair like your Fellow's."

Ander smiled and bowed again. Chism waved his thanks and continued walking.

"Nice work," said Chism.

Mave's back straightened even more.

"They'll build you a statue here someday," said Ander, and Mave's step picked up some bounce. "Of course, no one will see it because it will be in the shadow of the Vorpal Knight's much bigger, much less handsome statue."

Mave's pride fell behind like the stepped-on tail of a lizard. Chism had planned to rebuke Mave for not addressing Lira as "ma'am," but Ander's comment had already robbed Mave of the feeling of victory.

It took 10,808 steps to reach the house of Steffen's family. A year before, Chism had done it in 9,404 steps. Somehow they made it all the way to front door without seeing any of the bruised and scarred boys who'd seethed like a tomcat colony the last time he was there.

"Hello?" called Chism. In a low voice, he asked Hatta, "Do you know their names?" He only remembered the mother's nickname—Burly. Even if he was rude enough, he didn't think he was brave enough to call her that.

"I generally don't entirely memorize unpleasant names of unpleasant people."

"Hello?" Chism raised his voice. They waited without result.

With as many people as they had, the whole family couldn't just be gone. Chism started walking around the house. Halfway around it, he heard a babble of conversation. He paused for a moment before making himself visible to the people behind the house. He dreaded the necessary confrontation with Burly and Steffen. Adding in the rest of the family was like getting all of his teeth pulled instead of just an aching one. His cadre paused behind him while Chism rallied his sense of duty enough to go forward.

"What is it?" asked Mave. His hand wrapped his sword hilt.

"Nothing like that," said Chism. He stared up into Mave's eyes until they locked. "Do not, under any circumstances, draw your sword here."

"I don't like where this is going," said Mave.

"Get used to orders you don't like," said Chism. "This won't be the last."

"Dung and dungarees," said Ander. "You're going to get us into a fight and tell us we're not allowed to win?"

"No blades," said Chism. "That goes for all of us." He moved forward, denying reluctance a chance to work its way back in.

The scene around the corner was worse than he'd dreaded. Forty-three people, ranging in age from babies to Burly, were sitting at mismatched wooden tables, reaching for food, slapping hands, elbowing, chewing, cussing, and generally acting like the rubes they were. They didn't even have the decency of having an even number. Or a divisible number.

"Whozat?" shouted a dirty-faced kid no taller than Chism's belly.

Thirteen adult faces, including Steffen's and Burly's, turned to face them, as did the army of scamps.

"Last time I saw you," said Burly, pushing back from the table, "you were pretending to be a runaway or farmhand or somesuch." She stood and wiped grease from her hands onto an apron that she probably hadn't changed since Chism had seen her last. "Now you're playing at soldiers and Elites?"

"I'd like a moment with Lemon—I mean, Steffen."

The family erupted in laughter, in table-pounding and taunts. Hatta let out a high-pitched laugh.

I really maved that one.

When Burly stopped laughing, she said, "Steffen's too much for a thirteen like you, but I have a few grandsons who'll strip off those blues and teach you to insult our kin."

Three eleventeen-year-olds stood on the benches.

"I get him!"

"No, I do! I kin beat both you."

"Only 'cause you bite!"

Burly slapped the table, and they shut their mouths. "If they're too much for you, there's always Brandine."

A copy of Burly minus thirty years stood and took a few steps toward Chism, her elbows swinging wide. She stared him down, bringing to mind the image of the water buffalo he'd seen in Darieus's museum.

"I just want to talk to Steffen for a moment," said Chism.

"Talk?" asked Steffen. "Wuzzat mean, Brandle?"

A young man Chism's age wearing a ragged coat with tails stood up. "Talking is that thing women do while they sew."

"Hmm," said Steffen. He sat down and reached for some meat.

Burly asked, "Z'there gonna be fightin?"

Chism shook his head.

"Who cares then?" Burly waved a hand dismissively at Chism and nodded to Steffen. "Go talk to him."

Steffen groaned. As he got up from the table he mumbled something about wasting his time with a tweedle who didn't even know his colors.

"S'alright," shouted a girl. "Neither does half of us." More laughter and table pounding.

Chism walked to the side of the house and waited. He didn't need the audience.

"Did you come back to tell me you finally learned orange from green?" asked Steffen with a sneer. "'Cause I really don't care." He had unevenly close-cropped brown hair, a crooked nose, and ears so swollen they looked like cauliflower curds.

"I came to invite you to join my squadron of Elites," said Chism in an even voice.

"You want me to play soldier with you?" Steffen's laugh made Hatta shuffle his feet in the dirt. "S'no Lira here to protect you if I decide to get really mean and poke you." He shoved a finger into Chism's chest and added, "F'you're a lieutenant, then I'm the Red Knight."

"Show some respect," said Mave, stepping forward.

Chism held a hand out and it ended up sandwiched between Mave and Steffen when Steffen rose to the bait.

"I might like this talkin' stuff after all," said Steffen, glaring at Mave. "S'always fun to add a little ugly to something so pretty."

"Mave," said Chism slowly. "Step back."

The muscles in Mave's jaw looked like they'd pop through the skin, but he stepped back. Steffen swiped at the Circle and Sword emblem on Mave's chest, but by some miracle, Mave didn't react.

"Some soldiers you've got here," said Steffen, looking over the four of them. "I've never heard of Tweedle Squadron."

"It's 113 Squadron," snapped Mave. "Until we earn a name."

"Ooh," said Steffen. "Can I be lieutenant tomorrow? Maybe Ma'll make cheese sandwiches for our rations." He started to turn back to his lunch. "S'a fake squadron and you all are playin' dress up with dang'rous costumes."

"I hear you're pretty good with a staff," said Chism. "Beat Tjaden, right?"

"S'right," said Steffen. He stopped, puffed a little. "I beat the Vorpal Knight."

Chism widened his eyes, as if in wonder and said, "And the only reason the fight was close was because of your broken wrist, right?"

Steffen lowered an eyebrow and gritted his teeth. He looked at Chism as if trying to figure out if Chism was implying what he thought. Apparently, he wasn't quite as thick as he looked or acted.

"Oh wait," said Chism, tapping one finger on his cheek. "That was Tjaden that had a broken wrist because your brother cheated. Guess I had my story wrong. Maybe you're not what I'm looking for after all." He turned away.

Before Chism could take a step, Steffen was in front of him, scarred face less than an inch away. The smell of chicken grease wafted down Chism's face. Steffen wasn't much taller but he was twice as bulky and probably ten times as strong. His shoulders were tight as if he was holding something back. Chism expected to be cold-cocked any second. He might not be quick enough to block or dodge, and if he wasn't, his chance with Steffen could be over like that.

When Steffen spoke, his voice was low and sounded like the growl of a bandersnatch. "You think because we worked together at Mikel's'zat makes us friends? You think I won't rip your ears off, shove em down your puny throat, and laugh when you choke on them?" His breathing was thick and fast. "My turds're meaner'en you, you smug little cockroach."

"Like I said," Chism breathed in a voice no louder than Steffen's, "I hear you're pretty good with a staff."

Long seconds passed before Steffen grinned and stepped away. "Staves it is." The grin grew into a toothy smile like a pit dog's. "We don't use any sissy padding here."

"Then I'll be careful not to hit you too hard," said Chism.

Steffen's face twitched in anger. "First, I'm going to break your ankle. Then your ribs, then your head." He swaggered to the backyard like a cock in the henyard. "Ma! S'gonna be a fight after all!"

Cheering sprang up as if a holiday had been announced. The children jumped over and away from the benches and raced, pulling and clawing, to a circle in the dirt a dozen paces away, jockeying for position in the front row. One of the men, Steffen's brother by the look of him, retrieved a pair of staffs taller than Chism.

"You strong enough for this?" Ander asked in Chism's ear as they walked to the ring.

"I've said it a thousand times—fighting isn't about size or strength."

"It's been less than a month since the Pit. You're still as scrawny as a baby bird."

Chism frowned and glanced back at Ander over his shoulder. "Your confidence gives me the strength I need to win, my trusted friend." In his own head, he thought, *Lucky ray, don't fail me now.*

"I don't care if you win," said Ander. "Better if this donkey continues to think we're fakes and we go on our way without him."

They reached the edge of the circle, and a small opening appeared to let Chism in. Before entering, Chism told Ander, "A three-man squadron is as useful as a pitchfork with one prong." He took one of the proffered staffs without bothering to test it against the other and walked into the circle.

Steffen stretched and jumped into the air to limber up. Chism already felt warmed up after his morning routine and the long walks of the day.

"What's your name, boy?" asked Burly.

"Lieutenant Chism, commander of the Elite 113 Squadron and Red Knight of Wonderland, personal bodyguard to Cuora, the Queen of Hearts."

The children hooted and bowed and saluted. The adults made comments to each other that Chism was glad he couldn't entirely make out.

"*Sir* Chism," said Burly with a voice full of sarcasm, "and Steffen—"

"Destroyer of fools," interrupted Steffen. "Grand Privy of the South Kingdom of Shey's Orchard."

One of his brothers chimed in. "Belching Champion of her Lady Volga's Table!"

"The Blue Dart of Flatulence and Purveyor of Brown Stains everywhere!" This came from a woman. It set the whole family laughing. Burly doubled over, clenching her gut. Two adults fell to the ground. Steffen stopped stretching long enough to stick a finger in each nostril. He bowed repeatedly around the circle, making flicking motions with his dirty fingers. Some children reached for the imaginary missiles and shoved them into their mouths. Others caught them and wiped them on nearby cousins or siblings.

Ander laughed openly, and even the upcoming match couldn't keep Chism from grinning. A true and honest fight was coming; the funk had a hard time competing with that.

When Burly recovered enough to speak, she motioned her family to silence. After a few unpleasant noises, they approached a version of solemnity.

"What're the rules?" boomed Burly.

As one, the family answered, "There are no rules!"

"Fight!" yelled Burly, and Steffen charged.

Chism wasn't ready, but he fell into a defensive stance and blocked the initial onslaught without even thinking about it. He hadn't sparred in nearly six months, since Phaylea's wall, and the staff was not his weapon of choice. But he was a professional and among the best fighters in the world.

He blocked an overhead swing that shook his bones and nearly cracked the staffs. The jolt reminded him that Steffen was not sparring. One lucky blow could maim or kill him.

The crowd chanted "Steh-fin! Steh-fin! Steh-fin!" as their champion continued his assault.

Chism remain in a defensive stance. Steffen was like a strong, angry child. He struck quickly and powerfully, but without poise or skill. There was no tiring Steffen, though. Chism's steps were small alterations of his stance, but his stamina quickly faded. The match hadn't lasted long but it was already time to stop toying with the larger man.

After blocking another two-handed swing, Chism kicked Steffen in the side. It was his first attack, and was barely enough for Steffen to feel, but it got his attention. He backed up into his own defensive stance and motioned Chism forward.

As Chism walked slowly forward he spun the staff. First, the Maple Seed, a two-handed, over-the-head rotation that any child could do. When jeers came from the crowd, he changed to a one-handed spin in front of him, the Fan. The observers quieted. When Chism began to spin the staff in a blindingly fast Figure Eight in front of him, it drew some cheers from the hostile crowd.

"S'nothin," said Steffen. The permanent snarl on his face grew more pronounced. "Even Ollie could do that."

There wasn't much of flair and flash in Chism, but the purpose of the fight was to impress. It would be a mistake to use anything less than everything in his arsenal to accomplish that. Switching to a form he called Bee in Butterfly, Chism expanded the course of the figure eight so it flicked in front of, to the sides, behind, and above his head. He moved forward and the staff appeared to be wings, moving faster than eyes could see. He let the motion appear to propel him forward.

The name-chanting started up again. "Chih-zum! Chih-zum! Chih-zum!" It wasn't as loud as Steffen's name had been, and an equally loud faction took up Steffen's name again.

Chism ended the display with a jab, which Steffen barely blocked. But he blocked it exactly as expected, and Chism was able to use the momentum in another strike. It hit Steffen's shoulder hard enough to knock him off balance. Chism did not let him regain it.

Blow after blow touched Steffen, from the flat top of his blocky head to the flat bottoms of his feet. If Chism had used a sword instead of a staff, nary an inch of skin would have been free of blood.

As the seconds passed, Steffen began to resemble a chicken holding a staff. A drunk chicken with no head. The blows came easily, Chism striking when and where he wanted. He began to tire from giving them long before Steffen tired of taking them. A final, sweeping strike took the legs out from under Steffen and the air out from inside his lungs.

When Steffen opened his stunned eyes, Chism's staff was poised a foot in front of them, ready to open skin and bone. Steffen released the staff he'd somehow managed to retain and raised his hands submissively.

Chism placed an end of his staff in the ground and offered a hand to his opponent. A quick handshake to move past the fight; Chism braced himself for the touch. Wordlessly, and still a little breathlessly, Steffen accepted.

As Chism pulled Steffen to his feet, Steffen loosed a fistful of dirt into Chism's face and bit down on Chism's forearm hard as alligator.

The scream of pain came from somewhere deep and primal. Chism had half expected a trick, but hindsight didn't help him see anything through eyes full of dirt and sand. Teeth in his skin and skin on his skin as Steffen wrapped an arm around Chism's neck gave Chism the strength to scoop Steffen onto his shoulders and slam him to the ground.

Through the pulsing burst of rage, Chism could practically see the stars in Steffen's vision. There was no fight left in the stunned young man, but there was plenty in Chism. He put a knee on Steffen's throat and said, "Yield!"

A squeaky croak was Steffen's reply. Drops of blood left dark trails from the corners of his mouth through the dirt that covered his cheeks.

"I can't hear you," said Chism, even though he knew full and well what Steffen had meant. He added enough weight to make Steffen's eyes bulge. "Did you yield?"

A firm voice came from over his shoulder. "Chism." It was slow and warning, like a conscience. Ander.

Chism leaned a little harder for a split second, then took back his weight. Steffen took back his breath. In between his opponent's gasps, Chism bent close enough to growl, "You aren't the only one who will do anything to win."

He took two steps back and watched Steffen cough and wheeze as he grabbed a staff and stood. Chism sent it flying into the arms of onlookers with a kick.

"Enough," shouted Burly, stepping into the ring. "S'one never did have enough brains to know when he's lost."

Steffen sputtered, "What's 'lost' mean?"

The better-dressed boy said, "Means you didn't win but you weren't lucky enough to die."

Ander was next to break the circle. "Get me a clean, wet cloth," he shouted, pointing at a teenage girl. She ran off, and Ander bent to inspect the bite.

"Feels like he bit my arm off," said Chism, gritting his teeth to keep from swearing. He didn't want to sound like the hooligans. Fresh blood pooled in the two half-circles of the bite.

"S'a nice one," said Burly, raising her eyebrows. "You look like you could use a scar or two."

"I've got more scars than I need," said Chism.

"Where's your well?" asked Ander.

"Just there," said Burly. "S'not the first one to need it after a fight."

"I'm sorry about that knee at the end of the fight," Chism told her.

"Ha! Don't be. He'd have done worse to you if you'd let him."

The scattering family members tapped, snapped, and called out as Ander led Chism to the well.

"Blasted good fight!"

"You won't fall for the bite again!"

"The Red Knight beats the Blue Dart!"

Ander ladled water over Chism's wound, turning the liquid pink as it fell to the gravel at their feet.

"Flummox and firkin!" said Ander. "This is going to be like stitching chewed beef."

A cough brought Chism's head around. Steffen was approaching, his face as sour as a pickle.

"Are we going to have trouble?" asked Chism.

A cough. A cleared throat. "No."

Chism relaxed his hands; didn't realize he'd fisted them. A sigh of relief nearly turned into a curse as Ander began to scrub the wounds. After he blinked away tears of pain, Chism asked, "What do you say? Want to join us?"

"Even though I ... ?" Steffen searched for a word and gave up. "Brandle, s'that one word again?"

"Lost."

"Yeah," said Steffen. "Even though I ... lost?"

Chism nodded.

"Why would you pick a loser? Legates never do, 'cept for blessed Tjaden."

"You love to fight," said Chism. "Fighting is rarely a useful skill, but when it comes time to put down the pen of diplomacy, I need a squadron who knows how to embrace a battle like kindling embraces a spark."

A different kind of spark flared in Steffen's eyes.

Chism went on. "You have a lot to learn about fighting, but with your spirit, you can learn. I honestly don't care if you turn out to be the worst swordsman in the corps of the Elites. I just want you to work and practice. To try. Follow my orders, honor the Circle and the Sword, and we won't have any problems."

"S'that even mean?" asked Steffen. "Circle and Sword's just a design Elites wear. Or maybe it's a fun way to spice up our fighting ring."

The speech Chism got from Captain Darieus at the beginning of training would most likely mean nothing. How to put it in simple terms?

"The Circle and the Sword means that nobles don't treat citizens like animals or property. It means that citizens work for their own support and pay a fair tax. It means that soldiers make sure everyone plays nice, even the other soldiers."

"Z'long as you let me fight, I can go for all that."

"Welcome to 113 Squadron," said Chism. "Meet Ander and Mave. Ander and Mave, meet the Blue Dart."

Ander chuckled easily, and a smile found Mave's face. It happened slowly, but even Steffen smiled. He looked like a bandersnatch trying to be friendly. It was a wonderful thing.

"Hurrah for 113 Squadron!" shouted Steffen, raising a fist in the air.

Everyone within hearing repeated the shout. "Hurrah for 113 Squadron!"

The sound of the cheer almost stirred up some pride in Chism. "You'll need a Fellow. No rush."

"Brandle!" shouted the Blue Dart.

"Yeah?" The well-dressed boy walked up. His clothes were old and torn but the tailed coat and filthy ascot made it look like he was trying.

"What're you doing for the next ten years?"

"Nothin."

"Wanna be my Fellow?"

"Does Neb fart under the covers?"

"C'mon, then," said the Blue Dart.

"If he's the Dart, what does that make you," asked Chism.

The boy tugged at the waist of his coat. "Some people call me Dandy. On account of I dress so nice."

"You'll get along great with my brother," said Chism. "How long until you can be ready?"

"Hey, Ma."

Burly raised her eyebrows.

"We're off." Steffen cupped hands around his mouth. "Dearest family! I shall miss you like I miss having chiggers." He gave them a sloppy salute.

They cheered and hooted and stuck out their tongues.

"Ready, Lieutenant."

"What took you so long?" asked Chism, and he led his growing troop away.

At the side of the house, Hatta joined up with them. Chism couldn't tell whether his avoidance of meeting the Blue Dart's eyes was pointed or not.

It mattered little. He didn't plan on keeping them together long.

21

Chism turned in before Mave got back from his outing with Lily. When Chism woke up in the morning and went out for his morning routine, Mave was on his heels. The smile on Mave's face was anything *but* routine.

After a hot, early breakfast, 113 Squadron left their blue uniforms with Tellef, except Steffen the Dart and Brandle the Dandy, who hadn't earned them yet. An early morning farewell party of Lily and her father waited along the roadside a few buildings beyond the Dusty Tunic. The mirror maker had a resigned look on his face. He'd probably be happy to see the back ends of their horses.

Mave dismounted and handed his sheathed sword to Lily. She took it without question and wrapped the strap of the scabbard around Mave's waist, then buckled it.

They must have planned it the night before.

Lily looked into Mave's eyes and said, "May your sword be true and your arm be strong."

Mave bowed and kissed her hand. Neither one of them said anything as he climbed back on his horse, blew a kiss over his shoulder, and then waved until she was out of sight.

"Will you both survive?" asked Chism when Mave finally turned around to see the road.

"I hope so," said Mave. "She's none too happy with you for taking me away."

"Ooh," said the Dart, cringing. "I'd rather make enemies than friends, but not with that girl. She knows how to hit where it hurts."

"Perfect," said Chism. "Does she expect you to become a Knight by attending balls and ceremonies and smiling at her all day?"

"She expects me to do whatever I have to," said Mave, "and that's exactly what I plan to do." He stared down at the handkerchief she'd given him.

They reached the Telavir Spoke and circled up. The original four would continue south; the Dart and Dandy, north. Ander had given them a small purse with a few large coins and a letter of commission. The coins would get them places with nearly anyone in the Interior. The letter would most likely get them nowhere. The Circle and the Sword counted for much, as did a company of companions. They had earned neither so far and would be traveling as a pair of lowly novices with only Chism's name on a letter if they needed it.

That fit Chism like an old traveling hat. The last thing he wanted was men and boys travelling through Wonderland thinking they were suddenly as powerful as King Markin.

"So what's your mission?" asked Chism to make sure they understood.

"Find the Jabberwock," said the Dart with a sour smile.

"And kill it!" added the Dandy. "Then find Jaryn—"

"And kill it!" said the Dart.

"Funny," said Chism. "Wish we weren't splitting up so I could keep hearing your hilarious jokes."

"Our mission, Sir," said the Dart, "S'to master sword fighting and staff fighting, then find you and the resta 113 Squadron somewhere in this wide Wonderland and try to teach what we learned."

"Our mission," said the Dandy, pointing at himself with both thumbs, "S'to keep the Blue Dart out of trouble."

Good enough.

"Remember," Chism said. "You are recruits. You have no special privileges or rights. Your behavior has to be at a higher standard than other soldiers', not lower."

"We'll be as well-behaved as pupils in a school," said the Dart.

"I'm sure you will," said Chism, and they parted paths, two afoot and four on horseback.

When they were barely within hearing range, the Dart called to get their attention. When Chism looked over his shoulder, the Dart shouted, "Enjoy your lunch!"

"That doesn't sound good," said Chism. He was tempted to fall back to the supply horse and find out what the Dart had done, but didn't want to give him any satisfaction. He'd be sure to check the oranges for ripeness with Ander before eating any.

When lunch time did arrive, they stayed in the saddle and pulled some dried beef from the supply horse's pack. Chism glanced at it and didn't see anything suspicious. The first bite set Chism's tongue burning like a mouthful of fire ants.

He couldn't even speak to warn the others. All four of them spent the next minute or two draining their waterskins and coughing and spitting. Chism looked more closely at the meat and noticed a fine white powder.

"White pepper," sputtered Chism. "The Dart loves pepper tricks." Speaking was difficult, so he decided to wait until they made camp to warn his small squadron to check their bedrolls for dead snakes or live scorpions.

"That's some recruit," rasped Mave.

"He's got grit," said Chism, wondering if he'd gotten more grit than he'd bargained for.

22

"Why are you staring at that house?" asked Mave after fifteen minutes of stillness and silence. "If we need supplies, I'll go ask if they'll sell us some."

"We'll be here until tomorrow morning," said Chism. "At least. Get comfortable."

Eight days had passed since they'd parted ways with the Dart and Dandy. They'd traveled on small roads to avoid White guards where the Telavir Spoke crossed the Fringe Road. With no way to know how it would pan out, Chism hadn't explained to Mave that they were after another possible recruit. Ander and Hatta cared little—one just wanted to hurry into the Western Domain, and the other wanted to do anything but hurry into the Western Domain.

Mave put his head back against the side of the berm and exhaled. He scratched absently at his two-week beard. Chism kept his head forward, eyes on the house like a cat watching a mouse hole. There was no sign of a beard to scratch on Chism's face.

A few minutes passed and Mave slid down to the river's edge. He kicked a rock into the flow, then another.

"Sh," said Chism, catching Mave in the next midswing.

Mave dropped his foot and began pacing. When the sound of

Mave's feet on the hard-packed dirt stopped, Chism peeked back and saw him sitting on a patch of flat ground. He was shaving a small stick into paper-thin slices. A pile of twigs of various sizes sat by his side.

Satisfied with the pile of shavings, Mave took his tinder box from his pouch. A pinch of tinder, the finest shavings, and plenty of small fuel within reach. He positioned the flint and raised his striking tool.

"Are you seriously making a campfire while I'm trying to be stealthy?" asked Chism. For some reason he'd assumed Mave had grown out of his habit of doing the worst possible thing.

Mave looked down at the pile of kindling as though he'd just awoken from sleepwalking. He swallowed and kept his gaze down as he tucked the tinder, steel, and flint away and spread out the other items.

"Mind checking on Hatta and telling them how long we'll be here?" asked Chism.

"Sure," said Mave.

While Mave was gone, a boy came out of the house, carried something across the grass to the smokehouse then went back inside. That couldn't be anyone but Baen, but he'd grown so much since Chism had seen him that he looked completely different.

"Sitting and staring," said Mave when he returned. "Like always."

Chism knew who he was talking about. "How much worse will he be after this snark hunt fails?"

"No worse," said Mave. "No better. We're stuck like this for the rest of our lives."

"There were a few minutes when you were talking to Lira in Shey's Orchard when I thought you might have found something."

Mave's blank expression didn't change. "It was just carryover from meeting Lily. There was no joy in the planning itself. Probably the same as when you fought the Dart."

The fight had been another in a long list of *almosts* since the targus.

"It makes it worse knowing some of these things should lift my heart and make Thirsty hum." Chism looked down at the silent friend at his hip. He felt nothing. Again. "And that some of them should make me want to run someone through."

"What about when the Dart bit you?" asked Mave.

Chism looked at the rough wound on his forearm. The stitches would be ready to come out soon.

"It hurt from here to infinity, and a glint of anger burst through the haze, but after I made my point, everything was gone."

Mave shook his head. "My wager is that the Dart turns out to be a monstermental mistake."

"Monumental," said Chism. "What are the odds that this nonsense with the targus works?"

Mave stared at the ground. His lips moved like he was chanting a prayer. "There are too many unknowns, but one in ten, we get caught in the Provinces. Three in twenty, the Domainers kill us. One in a thousand, they take us alive. Five in ten, we don't find the stupid thing. If we do find it, five in ten he eats us like a badger in a honeycomb. Three in ten we kill it. One in ten it poisons us even worse, though it oggles the mind how that could even be possible. One in ten it can fix us. And that's all assuming your brother's right about what he heard."

"You're kidding," said Chism. "You say there's only a fifteen percent chance we find It, and if we get lucky and make it that far we have a ten percent chance of getting anything useful from It? That's one and a half percent."

Mave nodded.

"It's the worst suicide mission in the history of Elites."

"It's very close."

"As bad as Wot's idiotic plan to escape from the Pit."

"Maybe worse," said Mave, "if you allow for margin of error."

"Neither of us would even consider that idiocy in the Pit, so why are we thinking about this one?"

"I've been wondering the same thing," said Mave. "I'm only here because you are. If there was anything else worth living for, it might be different, but there just isn't."

"What about Lily?"

Mave looked at the ground, then kicked at the dirt. "As much as I want to go back to her right now, it wouldn't be fair to expect her to live with someone like me. Not under these circumstances."

"So you should be happy even for a one percent chance of changing things."

Mave shrugged. "There's only one thing that makes me happy lately. And it's not planning a suicide mission."

"Well, we owe it to Hatta," explained Chism. "He lost more than any of us, and he had no business being in the Domain. You have no business there now. It's personal business, not Elite business. I have a hundred tasks you could do, risk-free, back in the Interior."

"I can't go sit sound and safe while you throw your life away," said Mave. "Where's the loyalty in that? If I wasn't so ... devoid of everything, I'd probably be offended that you mentioned it."

"I have no desire to lead a f—" Chism stopped himself. He'd almost said *friend*. "To lead a fellow Elite and a member of my squadron on a suicide mission."

"If the choice is mine, I choose to stay by your side. I always will."

The same boy came outside, dumped a small bucket behind the smokehouse, and went back inside. Then nothing happened for hours. Except watching and more lemon treatment for Chism's hair.

After midday, Leis hung some laundry, and the two smallest boys chased each other with sticks. Ander brought food and the rattle for Mave. Two hours later, Leis took down the laundry, and the same small boys stood side by side at the creek's edge and pulled up their tunics for a distance competition. It was quite possibly the exact spot Cactus had made water a year before. The younger boy won the competition and ran inside, cheering.

The contest was the highlight of the day's activity.

Night fell, and Chism and Mave joined Ander and Hatta for a dark, fireless night. Rain forced them into their tents.

Chism was back in the rain at the first sign of sunrise. The light was distant, muted. The first rays of the day wouldn't come for an hour. Maybe more. Mave crawled out of the tent not much later, and followed Chism to the waiting place.

"Do you mind watching?" asked Chism.

"What am I looking for?"

"Anything or anyone," said Chism, taking the stance for his first form.

"We have time. You can confer in me, you know. I might have some helpful feedback."

Chism held the stance and considered for a moment. "This is something I have to do, Mave. I will lean on you and lean heavily, but these decisions about the members of the squadron have to be mine." Somehow Chism knew that was true. Believed it anyway, strongly enough to almost know it. "To be honest, I can't even let myself think about it too much because I don't want to talk myself out of what *should* be. If you feel like you are in the dark, it's basically because I'm keeping myself there too until we are one step away."

Maybe he'd said too much, given Mave too much fodder to argue. It all sounded like nonsense when said out loud. That was probably the reason he kept it to himself for the most part.

Chism stared straight ahead, still prepared to begin his routine, but waiting to make sure Mave was done talking. After the space of eight breaths and nothing but silence, he brought Thirsty down quickly then raised it to the starting position. The small practice area, the darkness, and the rain were factors he wasn't used to. Chism did not welcome the change to his routine, but at least he wasn't sitting still staring at the house.

When he finished, he traded places with Mave. There was light enough to see into the yard, but the light illuminated nothing other than the familiar shapes of buildings and grass.

Another day like the first, only wetter.

Except that Mave was more impatient. Between their late lunch and darktime, he blew out 814 exasperated breaths. That didn't include his normal breaths—only the heavy, bored exhalations.

Chism still carried leather strips, but ever since the targus, rubbing them didn't relieve stress or keep his mind occupied like they once had, so he'd given up using them.

As Chism stood and gave up for the day, Mave asked, "Why don't you just go up to the door?"

"It's a test," answered Chism.

"Of my patience?"

"No." Chism stretched. He'd been sitting still for hours. "He must be mome. Off delivering honey with his father."

"Who?" demanded Mave.

The back door opened, revealing a slim figure framed by lamplight. He was pale haired and a couple of inches taller than Chism.

"Him," hissed Chism, ducking back behind the berm. He'd been home the whole time. How disappointing. "Where's your staff or sword?" Chism whispered toward the boy, who was much too far to hear.

The boy walked to the far corner of the house and picked up a thin stick. It was too frail to be a weapon, but could do as a practice staff.

To Chism's disappointment, the boy walked back to the door. As he went inside, Chism heard him ask, "Will this do?"

The door closed.

Chism sat and let out his own pent-up exasperation. "We move on tomorrow morning."

Mave was either too proud or too disinterested to ask why. Chism didn't care which it was. After a little dinner and a lot more rain, they climbed into the tents.

The rain had stopped by the following morning when Chism rose before day. He finished his forms while Mave watched the yard, then swapped places again. The aroma of fresh bread wafted to where Chism waited and watched. He regretted having to leave without tasting some.

A single beam of sunlight found its way across the horizon and through the blind to land on Chism's face, warming his cheek. An instant later, the back door opened, and Buckhairs, the slender boy from the night before, came out. He appeared to have no destination other than the center of the grassy area. After a minute of stretching, he went to the same corner he had the night before and picked up a stick shaped like a practice sword.

Chism's hands began to sweat, and his heart struck a faster beat. "First lucky ray," he murmured.

The boy walked back to the open area of the yard and stood in the familiar stance that started Chism's forms every morning.

Chism took his eyes away long enough to toss a small clod of dirt to get Mave's attention. He motioned him up to the berm.

The boy stepped and struck, then reversed the motion. Step, strike, reset. Step, strike, reset. Chism counted while he admired the precision of each motion. It was a beautiful thing.

During number thirty-seven, a little brother stuck his head out of the back door and shouted, "Mom says bring eggs when you come!"

It caught the boy off guard, and he stumbled, but then reset the motion. Chism continued the count, expecting him stop at fifty. He stopped at eighty-eight. Thirty-seven for the failed start. Fifty for training. One extra for excellence.

Buckhairs breathed frosty breaths into the morning air for a minute or two, then took the same stance. Instead of a simple strike, the form he repeated now included a parry, thrust, high swing, and reverse thrust. The footwork had to be precise or he'd trip and fall on his blade.

It wasn't perfect, but it would be soon enough.

"I could watch this all day," said Chism.

"Don't get creepy," said Mave. "We going to talk to him now? Kill him? Yell insults and run away?"

Chism gave Mave a sideways look and turned back to the boy.

"Is he some Provincial Elite or something?" asked Mave.

"He's only thirteen." Chism pulled himself away from his observation and sunk below ground level. Pride in the boy almost brought a grin to Chism's face. "He passed the test. Go talk to him. Ask what he's doing and why. Ask why he didn't practice yesterday."

Mave began to rise, but Chism pulled him down by his belt. "Wait until he finishes this pattern. No sense in making him start over. Oh, and leave your sword here."

They waited, the boy finished, the sword stayed behind, and Mave approached.

"What are you doing there?" asked Mave.

"Practicing my sword. Who are you?"

"Just a passer-through," Mave said mysteriously.

The feeling that Mave was going to mave up his task sunk into Chism's chest.

"Why are you practicing?"

"The festival's coming up soon, and there's a competition. The White Legate will be there. Are you a soldier?"

"Yes. Are you going to win the competition?"

"Yes, Sir. Are you here early with the Legate?"

"No," Mave said in a slightly questioning tone, as if it was only half a no. "Why didn't you practice yesterday?"

"I did, Sir. Are *you* the White Legate?"

"No, but I have the power to extinguish lies from truth. Are you lying to me about practicing?"

"No, Sir. Ask my father. We were traveling home from Telavir. We took honey to the market there. Do you want some warm bread with honey?"

"If Leis made it, I'll have a slice," called Chism, climbing out of concealment.

Buckhairs squinted, then his eyes went wide as he ran forward. "Sir Chism! You're back!"

Good, thought Chism. *He recognized me even though my hair is the color of a sick goldfish.* That comparison had come from Hatta.

"Hi, Buckhairs."

Buckhairs didn't do anything crazy like try to shake hands or anything.

Chism said, "Thanks, Mave. Will you go get Ander and Hatta?"

"Your hair's almost as orange as mine, Sir," said Buckhairs. His nickname came from the cowlick in his bangs that reminded Chism of two giant buck teeth. "How'd that happen, Sir?"

"Lemons. I have a long way to go."

"Let me get mother and father, Sir. They'll be aright angry if I waited too long to tell them you was here." He dashed into the house. Chism followed as far as the back door, stopping where he'd met Cactus, the old man who'd become his first friend.

After the trouble between the kingdoms and before his assignment to Scaled Tiger Squadron, Chism had come back to pay Cactus a visit. He'd made it only in time to mourn with Cactus's family.

So much for friendship, thought Chism, staring at Cactus's old chair. Old *empty* chair. Friendship was as intangible as rainbows and unfathomable as the stars. Might as well leave a thimble of milk out for a wish fairy as make a friend. It would do about as much good.

Leis stepped out of the back door saying, "What are you still doing out here, Chism?" A few new age lines showed around her eyes. Her face was squat but pretty. She herself was short, no taller than Chism.

"I've got some ... ," *men* didn't sound right, but neither did *friends,* "some traveling companions."

"They're welcome too, of course." Leis stood within touching distance, but wrung her hands in her apron to keep from hugging or other actions people normally did to greet each other.

A man's voice came from inside the house.

"Is he here to take him already?"

"Take who?" answered Leis.

"Hi, Lowan," Chism called to Buckhairs's father. "I hope you don't mind."

"What are the two of you talking about?" asked Leis.

"They gave me a squadron," said Chism. "I'm picking my own men."

"Oh, you're not going to stand here outside and talk about that." She brushed him inside without quite touching him. "Eram, wait for Chism's friends and let them in."

The house was overflowing with of the odor of fresh bread. Three and a half perfectly golden loaves were laid side by side on the table. Leis's three other sons had mostly finished the slices in front of them. They took a break from their bread to smile and wave at Chism.

"Look at your boys," said Chism. "Every one of them's taller than me already." That was far from true. Buckhairs was the only one taller, but he was also the only one older than ten.

"Sit down," ordered Leis as if she couldn't believe she actually had to tell Chism to do that. She cut a thick slab of white bread and asked, "How many more of you are there?"

"Three," said Chism, sitting on the bench next to the smallest boy.

Leis cut three more slices and added generous smears of butter that melted immediately. Pure, uncrystalized honey filled every nook.

Chism didn't wait for his men. He picked up his slice and took a bite. It was light and savory and sweet. Impossibly similar to the rattle. The home and family were nearly as snug and warm as the rattle as well; more hale than any place he'd ever been. Sitting at Lowan and Leis's table, he felt closer to normal than he had since the infernal targus had poisoned him. If not for the men to lead and his promise to Hatta, he'd just stay put. Keeping bees was as good a profession as any.

"Is the reward still up?" asked Lowan. He was a decade older than Leis, and while his smile rarely made it to his mouth, Chism saw it in his eyes almost constantly. He had the same pale hair as Buckhairs and sideburns bushy enough to rub both doorposts when he walked through.

"I was hoping you could tell me," said Chism. "Didn't you just get back from Telavir?"

"We asked around. You aren't important enough for rewards and such in Verinalia Province anymore."

"Maybe I need to go pick a fight with a duke there. One of my training partners, Rodín, is a marquis or marquess in Telavir." That was another noble Chism wouldn't mind picking a fight with.

"It'd be mighty decent of you," said Lowan. "At its peak, your head was worth twenty trips to market."

Chism held his hands out in an inviting gesture. "Anytime you want to try to take it."

Lowan chuckled and everyone enjoyed a couple more bites of bread.

"Been stung much lately?" asked Chism.

Lowan shook his head. "Only a dozen times in the last month."

"Almost every other day isn't much?"

With a shrug, Lowan said, "Everything's relative."

The door opened, and Chism's men came in with Buckhairs. Cold bread was delicious, but while it was warm, it was worth sneaking into the Provinces for, so Chism made the introductions short, and they all squeezed around the table. Leis gave up her chair for a spot on the bench with the boys.

"I didn't know you had a brother," said Leis, looking between the two.

Baen, the eight-year-old, pointed at Hatta and said, "Mr. Hatter got all the color and you got all the normal?"

Hatta grinned a polite grin. "We never have been much of a muchness." A curious expression crossed his face, as if he'd just learned something. "In fact I think accurately you could say that muchness is what neither of us currently has much of." The patchy hair growth on Hatta's face made him look older and less like himself than ever.

Chism didn't want the mood to darken too much. "We'll have to come back in the future. Hatta's usually much more colorful than this."

"Downright flamboyant," added Ander.

"It's a horrible thing to lose your splendid," said Hatta with a sad half-smile.

Chism was too far into his next bite to say anything to dispel the heavy silence.

"Where are you headed, Sir?" asked Buckhairs, his eyes full of wonder.

"Putting together a squadron," said Chism. "That and taking care of a personal matter."

"And?" Lowan's raised eyebrows almost matched his sideburns in how far they jutted out.

"I want him in my squadron."

"He's barely thirteen," said Lowan. "You know that."

Chism nodded. "And you know he's something special."

"Leis? Eram?" Lowan looked at them. "What do you say?"

It took Chism a moment to realize that Lowan was talking to Buckhairs when he said *Eram*.

Leis bit the inside of her lip and watched Buckhairs, her eyebrows drawn in an intricate up-and-down across her brow that spelled worry. Buckhairs swallowed and looked down at his bread. He took a sip from his cup that made him cough lightly.

"I can't promise to watch over him every minute," said Chism. "In fact, the first few weeks of training, we won't even be together. There will be difficult training, high danger, and you won't see him for months or years at a time. Elites are reserved from frontline battle, but we're used like scalpels in very tight situations. This I can tell you: if there is ever a chance to give my life in place of his, I won't hesitate to do it. There may also be a time when we as a squadron must complete a mission that practically guarantees suicide but is necessary to protect the kingdom."

What am I doing? Making promises and invitations before I run off to get eaten or killed. Or both.

"Not very convincing," Ander said, moving his head in a weighing motion. "But accurate."

"I don't think that's why Eram's concerned," said Lowan.

"Well, it's why I am," said Leis.

"Out with it, Eram," said Lowan.

"Like I was telling Sir Mave," started Buckhairs, but Mave cut him off.

"Just Mave. 'Sir' is reserved for Knights. Someday, perhaps, but not today."

"Yes, Sir," said Buckhairs. "A White Legate is coming to the festival in two weeks. Couldn't I just wait 'til then, and if he picks me, I can join you as a real Elite?"

Chism took his time chewing and swallowing the bread in his mouth, again wondering how he could make promises without knowing if he'd be alive in a week. In a month.

Duty. Was it to his post or to this boy? Sometimes it was so hard to see where it lay. But he'd have to cross that particular bridge later. Buckhairs met Chism's eyes and held them.

Chism said, "Mave and I are Elites. You will be too if you make it through my training." He picked up the mug in front of him and took a slow drink of water. "We will always be the squadron of Elites who didn't have to do it the same way as everyone else—didn't have to win local competitions, didn't have to go through the Academy. If their validation is more important to you, 113 Squadron is not the right one for you."

One at a time Buckhairs met his parents' eyes. Leis shrugged as if to tell him she wouldn't make the decision for him.

Lowan wasn't as hesitant. "You practice every blasted day. Rain. Snow. Holiday. Sickness. I'm lucky to work with creatures I love, but it's a rare thing for anyone to love their work." He sucked his teeth for a moment, then spread his hands. "Someone wants to pay you to do what you already love to do for free."

The smallest boy piped up. "Will someone pay me for peeing really far someday?"

Leis blushed, but the men and boys chuckled.

Buckhairs wiped his hands on his pants, sat up on his bench, and looked at Chism. "Your opinion matters more to me than the Legate's or the other soldiers' or even Queen Palida's herself."

"Queen Cuora," corrected Ander. "If the kingdoms don't unite again, you will be a Red."

"It matters little," said Lowan. "When I was born, this land was considered part of the Interior. At some point a bored noble looked more closely at a map and decided a road made a better border than some dry riverbed, so he built the Fringe Road and all of a sudden we're loyal subjects of Far West Province. The tax collectors wear different colors, but little else changes. By the time Little Pisser here has kids, this could be Domain land, the way things are going."

"Not if there's aught I or my squadron can do," said Mave.

"Have you made up your mind, then?" asked Chism.

Buckhairs nodded. "Yes, Sir. I want to be in your squadron, Sir."

"Hurrah for 113 Squadron!" shouted Ander.

The room repeated his cheer. Leis wiped her eyes, and Lowan shook his son's hand.

"If there is someone around here you trust, you can pick a Fellow to go with you," said Chism.

"How do I pick, Sir?"

Ander said, "You choose someone with wisdom and great hair. Those should be the two main factors, followed by handsomeness."

Chism shook his head. "I was going to say humility, but that would make me a hypocrite."

Mave put his face down and covered it with a hand on his forehead. They couldn't avoid talking about Fellows forever, no matter how hard it was for Mave, but Chism decided it didn't have to begin immediately.

"I'd like you to leave in two days," said Chism.

"Where are we going, Sir?"

"Have you ever shot a bow?" asked Chism.

"No, Sir."

"Good. I want you to find Ollie, Fellow to Sir Tjaden."

"The Vorpal Knight, Sir?"

"Yes," said Chism. "His squadron, the Grimblades, should be back in Palassiren. They should be there for at least a month."

"What do I do when I find Ollie, Sir?"

"Give him this letter and learn the bow," said Chism handing over a letter from his pouch. "There may be archers better than Ollie, but I don't know who they are. Take advantage of the Academy and learn everything you can—not just how to shoot, but about bows and arrows themselves. Which are best for which climates? How do you use them against cavalry from a downhill position? Learn things I don't even know to ask about, because you will be the archery expert for 113 Squadron."

"What about the sword, Sir? Is Sir Tjaden going to teach me that?"

Chism shrugged. "We're all going to learn the sword. But we already have a Master in that area. With your precision and aptitude for repetition, on the bow is where I need you." It was more of a feeling in Chism's gut than logic, but after saying it aloud, he felt even better about it.

"I want to learn everything, not just the bow, Sir."

"All Elites do. It's our biggest weakness. We will all learn as much as we can, but it will be our Masters who make us Squadron First."

"Squadron First?" asked Lowan. "That's a high goal, especially for a bunch of ragtag boys."

"Yes, it is," said Chism.

Mave said, "No one ever changed the world by aiming for mediocracy."

"Medioc*rity*," said Chism. He turned to Buckhairs. "A year from now, no one this side of the Domain will bother you. Until then, you need to be cautious. If you can make it as far as Shey's Orchard, a small town fifty miles up the Telavir Spoke, talk to a woman named Lira. She will be sending wagons and goods to regions as far as Palassiren. They'll be happy to welcome an upstanding companion or two."

"Tonin still goes to Shey's," said Lowan. "You can go with him."

"If you're lucky, he won't make you ride in the water barrel like he did with me," said Chism.

"No fair!" said Little Pisser. "I never got to ride in the barrel."

The next oldest, Prion, said, "I'll roll you into the creek later today if you want."

"Neither of you will do any such thing," said Leis. "Now finish eating."

Chism obeyed, finishing his slice of bread and two more. When he claimed to have picked her son for his squadron only so that they would have access to the best bread in Wonderland, her lips tightened and trembled.

Though he'd spent longer than he'd planned talking and luxuriating in the warmth of the family, Leis was reluctant to let them leave so soon. Chism felt his own twinge of reluctance.

In the Pit, three things had been stolen from him and his men: space, food, and light. Leis and Lowan's house had as much of those as he ever wanted. It wasn't a large home, but he knew no one there would touch him. The food was the best he could think of anywhere in the kingdom; he wasn't exaggerating when he told Leis that. And the light came not only from the open windows and the fire in the fireplace—it shone from every member of the family.

Yes, Chism needed to leave soon. Duty could only force him to do so much, and the longer he stayed, the more he risked his mission.

"We need to be on our way," said Chism. Even if he did decide to linger, except for Ander, they were not the sort of companions this family needed. He had no desire to poison the family's well of happiness.

After short goodbyes, Chism penned another letter while the others packed camp and prepared the horses. It was to Queen Cuora, asking her to take charge of the Dart, Dandy and Buckhairs if anything happened to Chism. It told of their strengths as soldiers and assured her that they would be valuable members of the Red Army. He sent a short third letter, addressed to Mully, the armorer and quartermaster, instructing him to outfit whatever weary soldiers arrived in the name of 113 Squadron.

Ander took the letters to Buckhairs along with enough coin to reach Palassiren.

When he returned and they'd mounted their horses, Mave asked, "Where to now? Any more lemons to pick?"

Chism shook his head. "I was hoping to come up with more possibilities by now, but the Dart and Buckhairs are the only ones I felt strongly about. What's the point anyway, if we're off to be killed or captured?"

"To the Domain, then?" asked Hatta. His mind had apparently blocked out the unpleasant words of Chism's question.

"To the Domain," said Chism.

"To our dreams," said Hatta, and he put heel to horse.

23

With black market furs, Domainer coins, varying beard lengths, and smuggler's maps, the four plunged across the border into the Western Domain in an area with no roads and no signs of cities or towns. According to men they'd questioned in Far West Province, there were no Domainer towns within two dozen miles. For an hour they rode vigilantly, ready to run or fight at any sign of Maners. A shallow river blocked their path so they stopped to wash off road dust and change from civilized clothing to the furs and leathers worn by men in the Domain. All three besides Chism had decent starts on a beard. Nothing that would impress Maners, but they might be able to blend in if circumstances were just right.

"We made it through the Provinces," said Chism as he and Mave pulled off their tunics and laid them on the riverbank. "Our chances of success just went way up." After washing up they could find a place to stash their Wonderland clothes and trimmings. And Thirsty.

"To about five percent," said Mave.

"That's five times as good as they were before," said Chism with a shrug.

Hatta and Ander kept watch in the shrubbery, one upstream, one downstream. Chism unstrapped Thirsty and laid it carefully onto his tunic, then added his pants to the pile.

Mave stripped down to his unders then took a step into the fringe of the river and looked pleasantly surprised.

"Warm?" asked Chism.

"Warmer than you'd suspect in spring."

"You mean expect?"

Mave paused and considered. "I'm not sure."

"We're not suspicious of the warmth of the water. We don't suspect it of anything."

"You suspected it of being cold."

Chism shrugged as he walked into the chilly water. "You might have a point with that one, but I still think it's a stretch." He took a deep breath then put his face in the cool water and scrubbed.

When he stood, Mave asked, "What's that scar mean?"

"Nothing," said Chism, turning his back away from Mave. It might be the biggest lie he'd ever told.

Mave took the hint. "If by some miracle we do make it out of here and through Far West again, where's our next stop?"

Chism debated whether to answer, but with a five percent chance of success, he decided it mattered little. "We'll probably pick a few more lemons before we leave the Provinces."

"Please tell me you're talking about citrus fruit," pleaded Mave.

Chism shook his head.

"More kids?"

"Maybe," said Chism. "I haven't decided for sure yet."

"I've been thinking," said Mave. The water covered his knees. That seemed almost as deep as the river would go. He placed his palms flat on the water's surface as if they floated there. It was a distracted movement, and Chism waited for him to spit out what he was thinking. "I'm not sure I agree with what you're doing. You should put some thought into the members of the squadron instead of picking up random kids along the way. There are plenty of soldiers and even Elites who would be willing to join 113. Are you scared you won't get respect from real soldiers?"

"I can earn respect from people I want it from. Just because some Legate thinks a man fights a decent tournament doesn't mean I want to be stuck with him for ten years."

"So you're choosing people you like? As in, the Dart? Seriously?"

"First of all, do you think the Dart is someone I look forward to spending time with?" *I'd sooner spend time with my brother*, Chism thought. "You're too pretty. We need the Dart's grit and toughness to balance you out."

"What does that even mean?" Mave splashed some water out into the center of the river.

"I'm not looking for fifteen replicas of 'the perfect soldier'. We need balance and variety that complement each other."

"I agree with that," said Mave, not looking up at Chism. "We both know I'm not the conventional Elite. A group of experts is clearly superior to a squadron of soldiers broken from the same mold. But still, you agreed to build and lead a squadron. You should give it some honest thought and effort."

"What makes you think I haven't thought about it?"

"Buckhairs and the Blue Dart are unproven. I find it hard to have faith in them or anyone else like them."

"And what makes—"

"Two leettle feeshes over here!" shouted someone from the east bank.

Chism's eyes darted to Thirsty, six paces away. A fur-clad man with short beard and short bow stepped from behind a thick serpentine bush and stood next to Chism's things. If Thirsty could act without Chism's hand, it could cut the man down at the ankles from where it lay.

"Stay where ye be." He held his arrow drawn, ready to fire. In his beard were a couple of small chits.

"There's one of him and two of us," muttered Mave. "I'm not

going back into the Pit." Mave knelt slowly in the water. Chism saw his hands close over a pair of fist-sized rocks.

"Don't do anything stupid," warned a voice from downstream. Three bearded men stepped up to the bank a dozen paces away. Two of them held bows, one a mace. Another man joined the first one they'd seen. Five versus two. And three bows versus zero. Ander was somewhere out there. Against so many men with ranged weapons, there was almost no chance for Chism and Mave to self-rescue, but Chism held tight to hope. Ander was resourceful, not to mention ultra-experienced.

"Why don't ye drop rocks back into water?" yelled one of the Maners.

Too quietly for the men to hear, Mave said, "Not going back in the Pit." He kept hold of the rocks.

"Lizards and gizzards, man!" Ander appeared, pushed forward by three more Domainers. "The point of your sword doesn't help me walk any faster."

"Move yeer feet, not yeer mouth," ordered the Domainer. He had a white-streaked beard that reached halfway down his belly. The vest he wore was made of skunk pelts that matched his beard. He wore six chits and carried at least four blades that Chism could see. "Get in water," he said calmly, signaling with his polearm, a fiendish curved blade at the end of a short staff.

Ander swore as he splashed his way into the water and the skunky Domainer leader strolled to the spot on the shore nearest Chism. Two Maners upstream, three near Chism, and three more downstream. And Chism with nothing but his unders.

Mave slid over to separate Chism from Skunky, but there were two other groups of Domainers. As if turning away from Ander's splashing, Chism twisted his face away from the closest Maners. The longer he could keep from being recognized, the better.

"That is Red Knight!" shouted a young Maner with a bow. "I seen his scar on wall of Phaylea!" He pulled his bowstring more tightly and held the arrow on Chism.

"What are ye saying?" asked Skunky, bringing his polearm up into both hands. "He's much too old."

"Not whitehair man," said the young Maner. The hand holding the arrow trembled. "Heem." He used his beard to point at Chism.

"Nay," said Skunky. "I seen the boy Knight after Pit. His hair was black, not copper like yeer chit."

The young man went cross-eyed trying to look down at the speck in his beard. "Look at back. Same thirteen scar I seen that night."

Skunky blinked twice. He squinted and stuck his head forward. He shook his head, tapped one temple with the palm of his hand, and stretched his eyes open wide.

"Vaylee's beard!" He stroked his beard thoughtfully. "Manifest wonder, who ever heard of raid so successful before even leaving Domain?"

The young man said, "I heerd him and five men brung ten thousand ferucents."

The leader made a clucking sound in his throat that sounded impressed. "How many men have ye today, Knight?"

Chism didn't answer. Hatta could never affect a rescue, but by some miracle he hoped his brother might be overlooked and escape back to the Provinces.

"Tell me, and I spare them," said Skunky. "Keep secret, and we kill any Wonderlanderman we see on sight."

"Better to die," muttered Mave. He still crouched like a protective mother beast in front of Chism.

It was hard to argue with that. Then again, it was harder to wager with Hatta's life.

Under his breath, Chism asked, "Is there any way out of this? Without doing something stupid?"

Mave looked from one group of men to the others. Eight armed against three unarmed.

"I start throwing rocks, you dive and make a swim of it. Five times in a hundred, you make it."

Those were the same odds of success before the Maners had shown up, and it had gotten them here. If he followed Mave's new plan, Ander and Mave would die for sure. That was not an option.

"Enough talk," said Skunky. He held up his hand with the fingers spread wide. "I give five seconds to tell how many men I will soon have to ransom. Five." The thumb dropped.

Chism still didn't know what to do.

"Four." A finger joined the thumb.

Was it better to die or go back into the Pit?

"Three."

And should he gamble with Hatta's life?

"Two."

Chism opened his mouth to answer, still not knowing what he'd say.

The word "One," came out of Chism's mouth before the Maner could say it. He pointed in Hatta's direction.

To the downstream men, Skunky said, "You and you, go find man. If you find more than one, kill all." He turned back to Chism, Mave, and Ander. "You three feeshes, out of water slowly. No rocks, no trouble."

There were still four bows on Chism and his two men. The axe and polearm didn't worry him; if he could reach the shore and fight, he liked his chances. But the water wasn't deep enough to disappear in and he couldn't run fast enough through the water to close the distance without getting more arrows through his thighs or even more vital body parts. The scar on his leg was still raised and rough. Looking at it made much of the pain from the old injury return.

In a whisper, Chism said, "Go along for now, Mave. It's our only hope of escape. Phaylea is days away and there are only eight of them. We'll find our escape somewhere between here and there."

Mave was still clutching his rocks, and scanning. Why did Chism have to convince him? It should be enough to tell him the plan and have him follow it.

As if reading Chism's mind, Mave said, "If that's an order, I'll do it. But I'll die before they throw me back in the Pit."

From the shore, Skunky ordered, "You, handsome boy, drop rocks or taste arrows."

"It's an order, Mave," said Chism. "I rescued you in their capital before. I can get us out of this too." The situations were entirely different, but they both needed a reason to hope.

One rock splashed into the water, then the other.

"Now," said Skunky, "handsome boy and oldtimerman, stay in water. Red Knight, thank you to slowly walk to shore."

Ander huffed, "Old. I'm young enough to get myself into this nonsense. Superannuated is more like it."

As Chism took his first slow step toward the shore he retorted, "Old enough to know you should shut yourself and do what they say." The slow pace gave Chism a chance to work on escape ideas. Even though the Maners seemed to be taking every precaution, he kept watching. Two of the arrows stayed on him while two stayed on Mave and Ander. There was no way they could all miss from such close range.

Only one Maner seemed relaxed as Chism approached the shore—an upstream Maner holding the mace. He was in his mid-twenties, wore round spectacles, had a curly beard with two large chits in it, and smiled at Chism as if they both knew a secret. The second time Chism glanced up at him, he added a wink to the smile.

Wacky, deranged barbarians. They lived for rigmarole like this.

"Close enough," said Skunky when Chism was ankle deep in the water. "Kneel."

The order to submit all over again to the Domain created a crack no thicker than a hair in the funk that plagued Chism. A sliver of anger and hatred shot like a slice of light into the Pit. The intensity of the fury would hardly register in the old Chism who overflowed with spit and vinegar. But in the dark room Chism had lived in since the targus, the memory of ascending from the Pit and seeing all the Maners pity and judge and scorn him was vision to the blind. It was a beacon to a man who'd been adrift at sea. Chism focused everything on it.

Just let me take one step closer to you. The situation was similar to being chased by militiamen through the snow while he fled from Jaryn. If he could create problems for the angles of the arrows, he would have a chance. Mave would certainly spring into action if Chism initiated resistance. Ander would too, right?

"I see stupid decision on your face, Knight." Skunky's voice was cautious and warning. "But I have heard you are wise one. We will see if rumors are true. We will see if legend of Red Knight is true."

Who am I? Chism asked himself. That old spit and vinegar version of himself would have attacked already. Maybe he would have survived? Maybe Ander or Mave would have, but not all three. Was it worth sacrificing one—or two—so that the others—or other—could live? If there was a way for Chism to take all four arrows so that Mave, Ander and Hatta got away, it would be an easy decision

"What choose you, Knight? Living or dying?"

Living was better. Not for himself, but for his men. Chism forced one knee onto the river rocks, then the other. Cactus would be proud, but Chism mourned his forfeited spunk.

"This is good," said Skunky. "This is wise." He tossed a small sack toward Chism, who snatched it. "Put bag over head."

There was no reason to ask why. The Maners were taking every care possible. With no ideas how to use the sack to escape, Chism complied. The world went dark.

"Now, hands behind back."

Chism obeyed. Footsteps came toward him in the water. If he was going to act, it had to be immediately. The Maner steps splashed closer.

Life was risky, war was riskier, but the odds were too poor to put his men's life up as ante under the circumstances. A rope wrapped once, twice, then again around his wrists, rough and tight. It was tied off then the sack was yanked from Chism's head.

Skunky said, "Now please to walk to dry ground and lie face down."

Chism hurried to his feet. He didn't want to give the Maner who had tied his wrists any reason to help him up by touching him. No sooner was he lying on the sharp rocks on the bank than the Maner bound his ankles and cinched them up to his wrist cords tighter than necessary.

Like a hog lying in the dirt. If he ever escaped and got his emotions back, this would go near the top of the list of things to avenge.

"Good," said Skunky. "Next, handsome man. Same as Knight."

Following the same slow pattern as Chism, Mave came forward and knelt in ankle-deep water. Instead of sending the man who'd tied Chism, Skunky came forward carrying rope in one hand, his polearm in the other. They didn't bother with a sack over Mave's head.

The Maner leader stood behind Mave and dropped the rope into the water at his feet. He gripped the polearm in both hands and brought the haft down sharply across the side of Mave's head.

Mave melted into the water, bonelessly, face first.

He'd drown in seconds. Chism struggled against the ropes but there was no give, no way to reach Mave and drag him out of the water. Ander took a step forward.

The arrows on Ander flinched and Skunky said, "Stay, old man." In no hurry, the skunk-clad Maner slid his weapon over his shoulder into a sheath on his back. He bent and picked up the rope, then almost as an afterthought put the fingers of his other hand into Mave's hair and lifted his head out of the water.

Dragging him by the hair, the Maner said, "That is for not obeying orders. You listen to *me* now, not Knight! If you are smart, you learn. If you are idiot, we repeat."

You're the idiot if you think he can hear or learn anything when he's unconscious.

But at least Mave's face was out of the water. He coughed reflexively, weakly.

Skunky let him fall on the rocky bank. The other Maner took the rope and wasted no time trussing him up as Chism was. With each breath and cough, water trickled from Mave's mouth. He needed to be rolled onto his side or have his stomach squeezed or something.

"Mave," said Chism forcefully. The ropes hadn't stirred Mave; Chism's voice didn't do it either. Drowning might be the least of Mave's worries after that blow to the head.

Hatta came through the brush in front of the tip of a Maner's spear.

"Just do what they say, Hatta."

He nodded and in less than a minute all four Wonderlanders were tied like hogs.

Three of the Maners retained their bows. Two men lifted Mave —one by an elbow the other by a knee, so that he was sideways like a travel bag. The jolt made Mave's eyes flutter and his coughs spark in intensity. A huge knot had already risen on the side of his head.

"Where am I going?" spurted Mave as soon as he could talk. He looked up at the Maners with wide, confused eyes.

"Just cooperate, Mave," said Chism.

"Why am I tressed up?"

"Trussed up," said Chism. "We've been captured."

Mave rapidly scanned the area. "How did I get so ... empty?"

"Don't fight back!" shouted Chism as Mave went out of view behind some bushes.

"Where am I going?" repeated Mave from a distance.

The Maners would be back soon for Chism. They'd pick him up with their hands and carry him as they had carried Mave. Chism felt like he'd die if they touched him for so long. He didn't even have clothes on to protect him from their hands.

"I have a request," said Chism.

Skunky laughed sharply and said, "Request. This I must hear."

"Will you have your men carry me with that branch there?"

The Maner leader looked at the arm-thick branch.

"It will give them a buffer from me so they don't have to touch me."

"Yes," said Skunky, "for Red Knight I will do this."

There was probably a 'but' or 'if you will' in there somewhere, but Chism didn't force the issue. Water rushed by as time crawled. The two who had carried Mave away returned. Two more Maners followed on their heels, men Chism hadn't seen yet. Where had they come from? That made at least ten Maners they'd have to escape from.

Under Skunky's instruction, the Maners slid the branch under the ropes that bound Chism's ankles and wrists, then lifted him. The sinews in his shoulders felt like they'd snap under the pressure. The muscles in his legs were stretched to tearing point. But nobody was touching him.

The other two Maners picked up a similar branch and used it to carry Ander. Skunky followed along with at least one of the bowmen. The other five stayed with Hatta.

The Maners skirted some bushes but weren't as concerned with keeping Chism's bare skin from being scraped and torn by them. The tearing touch of the desert plants was infinitely better than being carried by actual hands. The path they trod down as they wound through the brush made it clear that the river bent sharply just upstream from where the encounter took place. Chism cursed himself for not scouting the area better and for letting his guard down.

Ander's escorts took a different route and they ended up arriving to their destination faster. From the other side of some scraggly bushes, Chism heard Ander exclaim, "What the brute is wrong with you sadists?"

Chism rounded an ironleaf bush and saw what Ander was

talking about—at least twice as many Maners as they'd seen at the river. But that wasn't what stirred Ander. On the back of a wagon sat a cage, not even tall enough for Chism to stand up in. They'd already deposited Mave inside.

Ander went on. "Who goes around with a cage on a wagon? I mean, seriously, there is something wrong with every one of you."

At the wagon, Skunky had his men pause before lifting Ander inside.

"You have big mouth," said Skunky. With the butt of his polearm, the Maner struck Ander on the mouth. Blood immediately ran from his split lip. "Big mouth like animal. Keep mouth shut or I will teach you to shut it." He motioned toward the cage with his long beard and his cronies heaved him in.

"Where am I going?" asked Mave, staring at one of the bars.

Chism didn't answer; he was too busy wondering what treatment was coming for him and Hatta. Knot on the head, cut lip, or worse?

Nothing. Apparently Skunky was pleased with Chism's compliant behavior. Cactus would be so proud to know that out of the three, only Chism had held his temper.

Skunky leaned down and looked blandly into Chism's face. The stench of skunk still clung to the pelts he wore. "If you try to run, we will cut off foot thumbs."

There was no skin to skin contact as the Maners dumped Chism in the cage with the other two. It was just big enough for the three of them to lie on their sides without touching. He didn't know what they'd do once Hatta came.

But that wasn't the biggest concern. Counting the eight men he'd seen at the river and the ones here with the horses and wagons, there were at least nineteen Maners. That many would have no problem guarding four prisoners in an iron cage.

"Why do I feel so empty?" asked Mave.

Perfect. Just when Chism needed Mave's brain the most, it was scrambled.

They should have run or fought before it was too late.

Bother Cactus's advice, thought Chism, grieving for his lost spunk. It just went to show that friends were as useless as dreams.

24

Another cage. Smaller than Chism's cells in T'lai and Palassiren and smaller than the Pit, though more breathable than any of them. Chism did his best to collapse inward with his naked back outward against the bars so the other prisoners' body parts wouldn't touch him. Wearing only his unders, Chism was vulnerable everywhere. But even if no one inside the cage violated his space, Maners could easily poke him through the bars. Chism's neck was getting sore from constantly swiveling.

He was supposed to be a hero of the realm making the most of fate-granted time. Some leader he turned out to be. Less than a day in the Domain and the fool's mission was over. If only Queen Cuora could see her brave and noble Knight curled up in the corner of a Maner's cage, cringing away from the fingers and legs of the men he'd doomed.

Nothing in his future but the Pit. And at the end of a year, life as a slave. If he was lucky maybe he'd keep his big toes.

Chism wiggled his fingers and toes to keep blood moving through them. He and the others were still tied at the wrists and ankles, but the rope connecting the two bonds behind his back had been removed, allowing Chism to sit up in a small enough area to avoid the others.

Two guards watched him from opposite sides of the cage. After two hours another pair of guards took their place. The lock on the cage was large but rudimentary. If the guards ever slacked and Chism could find a small tool he might be able to pick it.

And if they caught him trying to pick, it would be the end of his big toes. When Chism had made the decision to comply, he'd never expected the Maners to be so well prepared to take hostages.

The one bright spot in the dismal night—Mave was asleep so Chism didn't have to listen to *Where am I going? Why am I tressed up?* and *Why do I feel so empty?* over and over again. Mave's chest moved with his breathing and once in a while he mumbled something unintelligible, so at least he was still alive.

A weak torch burned behind Chism, lighting up him and his men, and blinding the guards to the rest of the night. Without the torch they would only see outlines and Chism might be able to slip his ropes. He stored the idea to extinguish the torch if they ever left it too near the cage.

Chism however, wasn't night blind. Behind one of the Maner guards, he saw the branches of a tall bush move. No wind rustled the air or any other leaves. No sound accompanied the motion, not from leaf, not from gravel. Nothing else so much as twitched or breathed. Whatever man or animal came toward the wagon was a skilled woodsman. What- or whoever it was couldn't be any help to Chism. Nothing within twenty miles had any intent but harm for him. He hadn't even told anyone about his plans to come back into the Domain.

The movement in the leaves reached the near edge and out slid the Maner with round spectacles, the one who had smiled and winked at Chism from the river. Specs. He was only a couple steps away from one of the guards.

Specs adjusted something in each of his hands then threw something all the way over the cage and into a tree. The far guard looked at the sudden noise and Specs brought his other arm up quickly. A rock flew at the distracted guard's head and hit him square in the forehead.

Before the guard in front of Chism was able to turn to look, Specs smashed the back of his head with the butt of his axe haft. That guard would be lucky to live through it. Specs ran past the cage and set something next to Chism without looking at him. He hurried to the rock-struck guard, bent, and tied a gag around his mouth.

Chism looked down at what Specs had placed in the cage. A knife with a bone handle. Chism stared at it in shock. The events were too odd to be real. He had to wonder if he'd fallen asleep.

Specs appeared at the cage and stuck a key into the lock.

"Take knife," he whispered.

"Oh." Chism twisted around, picked up the knife and reached for Ander's ropes. Hopefully Ander would wake up gently, not spouting gibberish out of his dreams like he sometimes did.

The sharp knife freed Ander in no time. Ander took the knife and cut Chism's ropes then started on Hatta's.

"What now?" asked Chism as the gate door creaked open.

"I suggest run," said Specs. The voice was familiar, but everything in the night was strange and unpindownable.

Thoughts of a trap ran through Chism's mind, but he pushed them out. There was no reason for Specs to entice them to run, since they were already prisoners. And if it was a trap, they wouldn't hurt the guards so badly, right? More importantly, the last time Chism had declined to attempt an escape it had landed them in the cage.

"What about you?" Chism asked. "The other Maners will know what you did."

"Perhaps." Specs still smiled that easy smile. "I will worry about me."

Hatta was awake and silent. Mave as well, but only because

Ander's hand was over his mouth. The old Fellow was speaking quietly in Mave's ear.

"No time to waste," said Chism. With the knife in hand, Chism climbed down quietly and his men followed just as silently. The night air was more brisk now, or perhaps it just seemed so with them moving around nearly naked. The path would tear their bare feet up eventually, but it would be worth it for the chance at escape.

In a low crouch, the four ran along the wagon path back toward Wonderland. Eleven steps into their flight something spread out in the air in front of the path, coming toward them.

"Stop," said Chism, skidding.

The other three didn't react quickly enough. They ran straight into a net, tripped over each other, and tumbled to the dirt as Maners sprang onto them.

Chism veered and picked up speed. If he could get away, there was a chance to come back and rescue—

Something sped through the air toward Chism's knees. He jumped, but weighted ropes caught his ankles, clacked as they entwined, and took his feet right out from under him. Chism fell like a practice dummy, barely breaking the descent with his hands. The knife flew out of his grip. As he struggled to disentangle his legs, a net landed on him. Two Maners followed quickly, one kneeling on the back of his neck and the other on his lower back. Both men wore leather pants, which made the contact bearable while still unpleasant. He didn't mind having his bare chest ground into the dirt and gravel as long as they didn't touch him.

Skunky approached from the area the first net had come from. Specs and two other Maners came from the cage direction.

"Red Knight is no match for qilumis," said Skunky, smiling proudly. He looked over at Specs, who stood at the edge of the fray. "Good work, Zeemi. Now we cut off foot thumbs."

Zeemi. Chism's neighbor from the Pit. No wonder the voice sounded familiar. A so-called friend had set up the escape just so the Maners would have an excuse to cut off their big toes.

If a man hadn't been kneeling on his neck, Chism would have cursed Zeemi, who stood in the corner of Chism's vision. Cursed him then struck out for revenge, no matter the consequences.

Skunky cupped his hands around his mouth. "Aymatungula! Wake! Take what Wonderlandermen have forfeited!"

The response was impressive. Within seconds the entire camp had gathered, seventeen men holding five torches. All of them except the two guards who Zeemi had subdued. Everything about the scene was so asymmetrical it nauseated Chism. He tried to focus on how quickly the Maners had responded. They were good soldiers. If the things Chism had heard in the rattle ever came true, he'd have men who could respond so quickly at any time.

Of course, two of his men—Ander and Mave—would never move as swiftly as the others. Not once they lost their big toes. And again, the fault fell to Chism. Why had he ever let Cuora insist on making him a leader? Even Hatta, who never wanted to hurt anyone, would lose his toes in addition to his already reduced muchness. Chism should have left him back in Wonderland. What had he been thinking?

Skunky came forward, tossing a knife end over end, catching the hilt each time. Moonlight and torchlight glinted off of the knife edge. The hilt was intricately braided metal. He stood near Chism.

"Red Knight should be first. Please to know I find no pleasure in this, Knight." Without any more words he knelt on the side that Chism faced and began to disentangle his legs.

Chism tried to struggle, but the slightest movement threatened to break his neck as the man kneeling on it added weight. His feet were free, but the—what did Skunky call the ropes with weights at the ends, qilumis?—were tangled around his knees and the net covered everything from there up.

Behind their leader, nine Maners spread out to watch the punishment or ceremony or whatever it was. Probably the barbarians' favorite kind of entertainment. They bent, craned, and knelt for the best view. Only Zeemi stood aside, out of repugnance for the toe-cutting or out of shame for his betrayal, Chism didn't know.

THE NINE ... fell asleep. One second their eyes were wide, the next they were closed. One second they formed a twisted wall of watchers, the next a pile of sleepers. A torch fell at the base of a tumblethorn bush and lit the scene rapidly.

Skunky shot up, raised his dagger and told the other men, "Do not let Knight escape." The fire spread outward, a wall of light along the path where Chism lay.

Everyone went silent. The night itself went silent. Only the river and fire spoke but they did not tell what the night hid.

The sound of men falling came from the direction of Chism's men.

"What happened?" croaked Chism.

Skunky kicked Chism in the ribs. "Silence."

"They just dropped," said Ander. "All four of the men guarding us. All of a sudden they all went bootstraps over beltbuckles. We're still tied up tight."

If nine fell, plus four more, plus the two Zeemi dropped, the only Maners left were Skunky, Zeemi, and the two holding Chism. The fire from the fallen torch continued to spread. In some places it lit everything like noonday, while in others its smoke obscured the already dark night.

"Why do I feel so empty?" mused Mave. Chism was already used to ignoring the statement.

The situation had to be handled carefully. Ander was the only one capable of putting up a fight, but he was netted with Mave and Hatta. If Skunky thought escape was unpreventable he might do something drastic like stick a knife into Chism's spine and run. Or instead of running, pull the knife out after stabbing Chism and cut his own throat. With the barbarians anything was possible.

As if the Maners weren't a big enough threat, the fire had jumped the path and now spread toward Chism and his men.

Skunky tried to watch all directions at once with his wild eyes. If Chism could just get free, he wouldn't have any problem fighting off the few Maners remaining, but the longer nothing happened the more weight settled onto his neck and back. Skunky went around in circles, moving closer with each step to where Chism lay. His boots scuffed the gravelly dirt, the only noise Chism could hear over the cracking fire.

Some motion remained to Chism's arms and legs. If the spinning Maner tripped and took out one of the men restraining him, there would be a chance of escape. Just when Skunky came close again, Chism slid his right leg out and hooked the Maner's foot. Skunky's other foot joined the tangle and he came tumbling down.

Instead of crashing into the back-kneeling Maner, he came down onto Chism's legs.

"You!" said Skunky as he scrambled on the ground toward Chism's face. "It is you doing this." He pointed his knife at Chism's face. "Who is it? What is it? Tell me or I end this now!"

Of course. Chism had been so intent on finding a way to rescue himself and his men, he hadn't even considered what was causing the Maners to drop so suddenly. Bringing Skunky down to his face was the worst possible thing he could do.

Way to think before acting, he told himself. If he would have just waited.

"How does such sorcery happen, Knight?" shouted Skunky. The tip of the knife dug into Chism's nose. It broke the skin. "What hidden powers do you wield?"

THERE WAS ONLY ONE EXPLANATION.

Targus. Chism had seen men fall just like the Maners were doing, but if Skunky hadn't figured it out already, Chism couldn't tell him. The Maners might have some knowledge about how to deal with the creatures and Chism wouldn't give him any advantage. He held hope that the targus was targeting the Maners, trying to help the Wonderlanders. All of which was based on Hatta's interpretation of It's strange words. If Chism had thought of all this *before* tripping the Maner, there would be enough distance between Chism and the Maner for a targus to target one without hitting the other.

But if Hatta and Chism were wrong and the targus was as ruthless as its reputation said, it wouldn't matter if Skunky's knife took Chism's toes; they could very well be lost to a targus before morning came.

But that was hours away and the fire was minutes away, if Chism could even breathe that long under the increasing pressure on his neck. Then there was the problem that would be resolved within seconds—it had a razor point and a braided metal hilt and dug deeper into the skin of his face with every one of Skunky's rapid breaths.

"You will tell me, or you will die!" The knife point moved from Chism's nose to his throat and didn't waste time before penetrating skin.

Chism still felt like it was a bad idea to reveal the targus. The animal hadn't shown itself, and there was probably a reason.

"This is last time I ask," said Skunky in a flat tone. That emotionless voice coming from Maners in the past had meant they were done negotiating and ready to act.

The weight of everything still held Chism down. If Skunky did kill him, the targus could just spray the lot of Maners and end the situation.

"Kill me," croaked Chism in a forced whisper, "and you ... *will* die." His breath wheezed as he sucked in more air. "That is a promise." It was hard enough to say those words with a knife at his throat and a knee on his neck.

"Ha! You know nothing of the Indomitable if you believe we fear death. A death together with Red Knight is death I am proud to die. I should have embraced such death from beginning." Skunky pulled the knife back. "Goodbye, Knight."

A shadow flashed through the corner of Chism's vision, struck Skunky squarely in the back and went rolling across the gravelly dirt.

Chism strained his eyes, expecting to see a targus tearing parts off Skunky's body, but was shocked to see Zeemi struggling hand to hand with his commander. Even though Zeemi had the first strike, he was no match for the long-bearded Maner.

In seconds, Skunky had manipulated himself out from under Zeemi and twisted around so that Zeemi's neck was cradled in Skunky's legs. The fight was over. He'd kill or incapacitate Zeemi and they would be back to where they had been seconds earlier. Chism could barely breathe, much less struggle against the men kneeling on him.

Skunky held the choking grip long enough for Zeemi's eyes to roll back and for him to go limp, then he disentangled and straddled the body.

"Traitor. Pigboy. Shameful, disgraceful death for you." Skunky pulled a large rock close.

Chism yelled as loud as he was able. "I curse you!" He had no idea what it even meant, but he had to try to help the man who'd risked his life for him.

"Booger on your curse," said Skunky, struggling with both hands to lift the large stone. He got it a few inches off the ground ... and went to sleep, falling over on top of Zeemi. The stone fell harmlessly to the ground.

Both men holding Chism down grunted in shock. Would they step in where Skunky had been and end Chism's life, ignoring all the consequences except for the glory? Would they just hold him there until the flames surrounded and began licking them?

Not if Chism could do aught about it.

"Why will you die, Indomitables?" asked Chism barely loud enough to be heard over the spreading fire. Smoke burned his pained throat when he inhaled. "I am ... the Red Knight. Son ... of Vaylee. I command the very night."

They didn't move. That seemed like a good sign since he actually expected the pressure to increase more. The heat of the fire blazed against Chism's bare skin.

"Would the Red Knight come into the Domain with only three men and no plan? Do you think I will allow myself to go back into your Pit?"

The man on Chism's neck shifted his weight nervously. Both of the Maners had to be feeling the intensity of the fire.

"I will not allow you to die," said Chism. "That would be a kindness and I will not grant it to the other seventeen. They will suffer, without death and without glory. Run now and save yourselves from their fate."

The knee on his neck almost lifted all the way off.

"Run!"

Both men broke. Chism breathed lungfulls of smoke-filled air and watched them flee into the night. One stuck to the road but the other tore straight through the burning shrubs. Chism rolled away from the heat towards the center of the path, then shook off the net and qilumis. Stumbling painfully to his feet, Chism trudged toward his men.

"You command the very night?" asked Ander slowly.

Great. Chism would never live that one down.

"I didn't know that about you," said Hatta. "The night seems very large for a sane brother of mine to command. Now if you were mad ...."

"Forget you heard that," said Chism, coughing out smoke. With every breath and cough, pain stabbed his ribs where Skunky had kicked them. Blood dripped from his nose and ran down the front of his neck, but he was free. "Let's go before we burn up."

"Where am I going?" asked Mave.

The question actually made sense after Chism's order, but most likely it was just the repetition of the question that had been going around.

"Go not far I think you should not far go." The voice was coarse like the stone on stone from a mill.

Into the firelight stepped a targus.

25

The targus dragged no headless snake along. No other headless animal for that matter, but it had just incapacitated fourteen barbarians without even being detected. There was as much peril in the stumpy body as in an entire Elite squadron. Chism and his men were in no shape to fight, even if that had been the reason they had come.

"Ander and Hatta," said Chism calmly, "go find our belongings."

Mave wore a confused look on his face but his eyes were focused on the targus. "How did I get so empty?" He started walking toward the targus. Apparently during the fray they had freed themselves from ropes and net.

"Mave, stop."

"How did I get so empty?" Mave didn't seem to have heard Chism. His tone became angry. "How did I get so empty?"

The targus saw Mave coming forward. Monkey lips drew back, revealing long, white teeth. It took a stance that accentuated its muscular body. "It does not like to be threatened it likes it not."

Chism had to stop Mave before he got to the targus, but both men still wore only unders. There was no way to restrain Mave without touching him skin to skin.

"Ander," called Chism, "a little help."

Ander must have heard the desperation in Chism's voice because he backtracked at a run.

"Mave! Stop!" ordered Chism. For all the attention Mave paid Chism's shouts, he might have been a hundred miles away.

Ander arrived and stepped in front of Mave, holding him back with both hands. What a relief. Chism wouldn't have to touch him after all.

Mave swept Ander's hands away, put a foot behind Ander's leg, and shoved him to the ground, all without appearing to see the Fellow.

Mave's hands were clenched and his eyes seemed to see only the targus and a solution. He was only two and a half steps from the targus, who growled threateningly.

"How did I get so empty!"

No option remained for Chism except the worst one.

Five seconds! he told himself. *I can hold him for five seconds.* He lunged and wrapped Mave's neck in the fold of one arm and tucked his hand into the fold of his other elbow.

One!

Mave threw an elbow back into Chism's gut, then the other one. Chism's injured ribs exploded inside his chest.

Two!

So much skin. Arms, neck, chest, back. Chism wanted to die. He wanted to break Mave's neck and be done with it. If he didn't stop Mave somehow, they might all die but it would be better than this.

Three!

It burned. It stung. Chism could practically feel his skin blistering.

Mave flung himself up and back. Both he and Chism left the ground. They came down on Chism's back. All the air left Chism's chest, rocks dug into his back, and his damaged ribs shattered, but his arms were locked tight. The pressure of Mave's body on his only added to the horribleness.

Four!

Chism's whole body poured sweat. His soul poured enough sweat to drown itself. Vomit threatened to squeeze up through his constricted throat. Instead he screamed his agony at the top of his lungs and cranked tighter on Mave's throat. Lightheadedness bordering on unconsciousness made it difficult to maintain his grip. He didn't know if he could outlast Mave.

"Five!"

Mave went limp. Chism released and tried to squirm out from under Mave without touching him more than necessary.

"Get him off! Get him off!" Chism's voice was a shriek.

An eternity later, Ander rolled Mave away. Chism shot to his feet and backed away from everyone. His whole body shuddered as he tried to brush away the memory, but it was inside him, under his skin, and rooted into his brain. Crawling and sinking in. He scrubbed with his hands but it only spread the sensation over more of his body.

Maybe the river would wash it off. Maybe the fire would sear it. Anything was better than the taint of someone else's skin on his. So much skin, so much contact.

Chism's gut clenched, and vomit erupted from his mouth. He tried to get some air into his lungs and ended up choking and coughing.

His breathing still wanted to race despite the muck in this throat. Tears clouded his sight before running amok down his face. His whole body wanted to run until he was far enough away that he would never see another person. It was the same feeling he'd had when he blacked out in the Pit, but this time it was too much. He'd die for sure.

Chism fell to his knees and gasped wildly. The world went black on the edges. He closed his eyes to steady himself on the unstable ...

"I found it." Hatta's voice. "I mean Es. I found Es."

Chism put a hand down on the dirt to stabilize himself and

everything else. He closed his eyes and held the earth to try to keep it from spinning. The gravel was warm. The smoke smell and heat from the fire reminded Chism where he was and what had been happening. Again, he considered finding the hottest flames and submerging himself to decontaminate his skin.

The world glowed and flickered when Chism cracked his eyes. For a few breaths he let the shimmer and roll of the earth ease into a rhythm he could synchronize with. Breath by breath he reattached to the world.

While Chism struggled to find strength inside himself, there was Hatta, walking up to the targus like a fearless child walks up to a wolf. Courage when Chism was nothing but dread.

As Chism settled into the flow of everything, he watched.

Hatta. "Is that you, It?"

The targus. "It is me is It."

"We have your uncle."

"It knows the location of your dreams their location knows It."

Hatta looked at Chism, smiled like an idiot, then set down the burlap-wrapped bundle and untied it. He unwrapped Es like a porcelain doll and stood it in front of It.

While Ander worked on tying up Mave again, the targus walked a slow circle around the stuffed carcass. Side by side, the signs of age were obvious in the dead targus. The corpse had wrinkles like a raisin. The feathers around the neck and groin were frosted white. By contrast, It's feathers were as dark as Chism's hair before the lemons.

It smelled the preserved carcass, picked at skin and feathers, and touched its uncle with its lips in a gesture that was less a kiss and more like a taste and a gesture of submission in one. Chism wondered if the preserved animal would come back to life.

While this went on, Hatta folded his arms, then unfolded them. He removed his hat, ran his hands around the brim, and replaced it. He rolled a cuff in the right sleeve of his jacket, then unrolled it and rolled it into the left cuff. He fidgeted in a dozen other ways before the targus turned to face him. It finally seemed satisfied.

Hatta asked, "Kindly may we have our dreams back?"

"Have not your dreams I do not have."

"What?" The sharpness in Hatta's voice matched the pointed focus of his eyes. He was as angry as Mave had been. "You said if we bring Es's body back, It would give us our dreams back it would."

"Hidden are your dreams are hidden."

"Where?" said Hatta. "We'll go as far as it takes." He stepped toward the targus, and the targus stepped toward him. Another step, and another. With each one, Hatta bent further at the waist. One more step by each and there was barely room enough between their faces for the targus to reach one stumpy finger into its mouth and place it behind its bottom teeth.

"My dreams are under your tongue?" asked Hatta.

The targus shook its head slowly. "They are in here are they." It removed the finger, wet with a pearly liquid, and traced an arc along Hatta's left eyelid.

"My dreams are hidden inside my eye? I'm very close to my eye. I think I would know if—" Hatta unbent suddenly at the waist and blinked. He closed the wetted eye and smiled with half of his mouth. He opened the closed eye and smiled with the rest of his mouth. "There they are! I can see them! Hear them! I can feel them all the way out to the white edges of my toenails!"

Hatta hooted, stretched his arms, and wiggled his fingers. "I'm amazing! I'm perfectly, entirely splendid!" Tears ran down Hatta's face as he ran to Chism. "You can see it, right? It's the most muchiest I've ever felt!"

It was obvious something had changed to make Hatta ecstatic. And while Chism *knew* that it was good and right and nice, he didn't feel any of it. Better Hatta than Chism, though. Not only because they were brothers, but because just as Chism was the professional soldier, Hatta was the professional feeler. Hatta knew what to do with all the feely things. Those ... emotions and such.

"You have to try it!" said Hatta. He looked at the targus. "It, he has to try it has to he has to!"

It gave Mave a distrustful look, then walked slowly toward Chism. Even after weeks of searching and hundreds of miles, Chism had no faith that anything would ever change. The pit he was in was deeper than any Maner Pit. The world was too deep and dark to ever get out.

Chism slid backward without standing, just like he used to do in the Pit.

It continued to prowl forward and when he was just a step away from Chism, he stuck a finger under his tongue again. When he pulled his finger out, Chism saw even more clearly the opalescent swirls in the liquid at the end of the stumpy finger.

The cure would never work on him. Magical healing and emotional avalanches were not how Chism worked. Certainly he was immune to such unfathomable nonsense.

It held the finger toward Chism. It could easily reach Chism's eyelid, but seemed to be waiting for permission.

Something surfaced. A ... feeling. One of the first Chism had experienced since the last run-in with the targus. It was *not* a feeling Chism knew well, and he struggled to put a name on it. Somehow he knew what to call it; the struggle stemmed from his willingness to face it.

Fear.

Fear of the touch of the targus and fear that he'd fail to be healed. With such little experience, he didn't know how to deal with the feeling. If he failed, what then? A life of nothing but duty for the sake of duty?

The fear stood like city walls between Chism and all the things he wanted. More than the unobtainable things from the rattle. Those were nothing but dreams. All Chism really wanted was to be an Elite but there was that wall and no way over, around, or under it. His feet and hands felt planted in the ground. That wall would always prevent him from doing, getting, being the things he wanted.

Hatta was there, leaning close to Chism, whispering. "Fear lies, brother. Lies are one of its strongest powers. Don't dare believe it. Fear hates it when good things might happen to you."

Chism pulled his eyes away from the targus and his mind away from the wall. He turned to his brother, feeling a desire to hope but just barely. So much could go wrong, not just today or in the past, but in Chism's entire future. That wall.

"Brother." Hatta's voice was quiet but firm, and he didn't continue until he had Chism's full attention again. "If you're going to be afraid, be afraid only of your fear."

That was unexpectedly sound advice coming from a madman. Chism looked inwardly at the wall of fear and felt a small door open at Hatta's words. The door was so small, much smaller than Chism himself. Smaller than Chism by far.

But what made Chism so big? If something as ephemeral as a feeling could stop him cold, he must not only be small, but bordering on inconsequential. The door however was supremely important. It was the pathway to all the things he wanted. Even if it was a likely path to eternal failure, it was something.

As much as Chism didn't want to attempt the door and fail—try anything and fail for that matter—maybe Hatta's words made sense.

"Fear is guaranteed failure," Chism whispered. He gritted his teeth, closed his eyes and took a step through the door, certain that he was too large to squeeze through such a minuscule opening. Outside of his mind, his head inclined forward.

Wetness brushed his right eyelid. It slid across without any of the pressure of touch.

Nothing changed.

Chism opened his eyes and waited.

Still nothing. Hatta exuded joy. Enemies lay prostate at Chism's feet. Nations in both directions seethed with pre-war. The very world itself burned. But inside Chism there was less than nothing. At least when he'd hoped for success and healing he had a lifeline. Even that was gone now.

Whatever Hatta was going through might be merely in his imagination. It wasn't the first time. More likely, the dream-restoring spit only worked on people like Hatta and not like Chism. It had only taken seconds for Hatta's muchness to manifest and Chism had waited much longer, minutes perhaps. His chin fell to his chest.

Failure felt even worse than he'd expected. Chism wasn't just broken, he was broken forever.

26

Chism dragged the back of his hand across his vomit-smeared face then forced himself to look up. Maybe the targus cure would work on Mave. There was no reason to think he would be immune like Chism.

Ander sat on the ground next to Mave, holding a rope wrapped around Mave's wrists. Mave looked more confused than he had since the head injury.

Through the strong odor of smoke—warm bread and honey.

Chism looked around for the source of the smell. Someone must be cooking in the pre-dawn morning. He saw nothing but fire, shrubs, sleeping enemies, glimpses of river, and rocks. Maybe the aroma came from his vomit, but it had been days since they'd run out of what Leis had sent with them.

Not just bread and honey—*warm* bread and honey. It was unmistakable. Was it possible that one of the Maner bushes gave off a bread and honey odor when it burned? That would account for the warmness.

But it was more of a feeling than a physical sense of smell. And a taste as clear as if Chism had a mouthful of it melting on his tongue at that exact moment. He exhaled and the sensation continued; it seemed to come from inside of him. Along with thoughts of leading a victorious squadron—no, an army. And protecting people, all the people. And everything else he hadn't felt for twenty-eight days.

"Is that the future I see?" asked Chism.

The targus took three steps back. "The future is your highest dreams if you are powerful enough to make your highest dreams be the future."

Hatta was sorting through the contents of one pocket. "If you're anything like the current me, you're amazing, Chism." He tucked strings, buttons, a rusty ring, and a smooth rock away then walked over to where the horses stood. In a voice too quiet for Chism to hear, he spoke to them while holding his oversized hat in both hands and resting his chin on the horse's neck. Tears ran down his face and into the horse's mane.

The targus looked sideways at Mave, grave enough to spit at any moment. Ander still held the rope behind Mave's back in case he tried anything else.

"I apologize for him," said Chism to the targus. "He's not right. Yesterday he got hit in the head and it knocked him silly.

Hatta added, "I don't know if you have dreams, but it can be very hard for us humans to lose them."

The targus's face relaxed slightly. It calmly watched the scene like a person observing a pack of tame animals.

"Will you give Mave his dreams back?" asked Chism.

"I will consider it will I. He will act reasonable will he?"

Chism knelt next to Mave and addressed him by name. "Are you ready to calm down?"

Mave looked over with eyes slightly crossed, still trying to make sense of the world.

"How did I get so empty?" The fight was gone from his voice.

"Do you want your dreams back?" asked Chism, pointing at the targus.

The creature stood a few paces away. When Mave turned his

head toward It, his eyes focused like a falcon's. For half a second, Chism thought Ander might have to tackle him.

Then Mave's shoulders slumped. He nodded.

"That is better is that." Step by slow step, the targus prowled forward. It ran one wet finger over Mave's right eye, then stepped back as carefully as it had stepped forward.

"Give it a few seconds to take," said Chism. "I'm sorry I choked you. That wasn't the best choice I could have made. Things never go well when I'm forced to touch someone."

He didn't expect Mave to answer with anything but the standard three statements he'd been using since Skunky had clobbered him.

Only a few seconds passed before Mave started to answer, slow and resigned. "Your choice wasn't as poor as my decision to attack It." Pressure and speed built up in his words like a cart rolling down hill. "I just felt so frustrated that we came all this way and risked so much and I didn't understand how it had happened but I knew that I didn't feel anything but I couldn't explain any of it so something snapped and I was ready to tear open his head and find a way to fill myself somehow. But it's back—everything's back! I can see the future too; I'm a Knight and I'm leading an army and the Domain is ... " His words grew so fast and jumbled that Chism couldn't make any more sense of them.

All of a sudden, Mave stopped talking and jumped to his feet. "I thought I was loyal before, Chism, but now I really owe you everything." Ander had unbound his wrists and Mave put both hands on Chism's shoulders then looked down into his eyes.

In one motion, Chism slapped Mave's hands away and shoved Mave back two steps.

With surprise and hurt on his face, Mave said, "I would do anything for you."

"Start by keeping your hands off me." He tried to brush away the touch, but it was stuck to him. "I thought we crossed that bridge already."

There had been something different about the contact. It didn't burn as sharply as it usually did when people touched him. Chism had reacted before he even had a chance to consider, but he still didn't want the lingering feeling.

"If I can please have your silence please," announced Hatta. He'd retrieved the rattle from Chism's pack. He shook it twenty-two times, listening as if hearing a secret. When the sound faded, he listened just as intently to something else, but there was nothing to hear except the roar and crackle of fire and the quieter flow and murmur of water.

"What are you listening to?" asked Chism.

"My dreams," said Hatta. "The ones that are inside my head now. Your silence, please."

Chism exhaled a frustrated breath as quietly as possible, resigned to pay the price for being with his cured, mad brother.

Hatta shook the rattle twenty-three times, and then listened to nothing. The rattle again. Nothing again. He looked at the targus and said, "My head says the same thing as the rattle."

"They do if you say they do," said the creature, unimpressed.

Hatta walked over to the targus and placed his ear near It's mouth.

"Is the same magic in your mouth that's in the rattle?"

The targus slowly shook its head. "It is no more magic than the wind in a seashell's magic it is not."

"But there *is* magic in a seashell," said Hatta. "It's a tiny ocean with waves and water that never dries out. I've heard it in there."

Still watching Mave closely, Ander explained, "What you heard was air bouncing around a small space combined with a filter of the outside world. Trust me, I've taken enough of them apart—there is no water. Your mind just told you it was the ocean."

"Your mind told you to hear dreams told you did your mind," said the targus with a hint of a smile.

"No," said Hatta. "It was dreams in the rattle. The others heard them too. Tell them, Chism."

It was a winless conversation, so Chism steered it away. "What about the other soldiers who were with us? If we bring them here, will you give them their—" He paused and restated, "Will you fix them?"

The targus tapped its teeth and thought for a few moments. "Have a small container do you have?"

"Like this?" asked Hatta, producing a tiny vial with a droppered lid from one of the inside pockets of his coat.

"Yes yes," said the targus. He held out his hand. Hatta stepped forward, and the targus said, "Open. Please open."

Hatta did so and held out his hands, palm up, one with the vial and the other with the dropper.

The targus pinched the dropper with the caution of a mother removing a splinter from a child's hand. It worked its jaw like a snake swallowing something larger than its mouth. It opened its mouth and placed the dropper under its tongue where its finger had been. A pearlescent liquid with shaded spirals that swirled but did not mix eddied in the dropper when he removed it. He held it toward Hatta.

If Hatta's face was any judge, the swirls of the liquid were an impressive array of colors. He seemed to think the targus was simply showing off something pretty.

"The container hold out," It said. "The container."

"Oh, pardon me. It's just been so long since I've quite seen colors." Hatta awkwardly wrapped both hands around the tiny vial and held it out.

The targus pinched one, two, three drops into the vial. It worked its jaw again, stuck the stopper in its mouth, and then pinched one more drop into the vial.

Mave glanced rapidly from the vial to the targus to the air to the ground and to everything in between, then back to the vial.

The targus pointed at the tiny glass jar with one stumpy finger. "Give one drop per human one drop give."

Chism stepped forward for a closer look at the liquid in the vial.

There seemed to be more to what the targus spit had done than just peel back a thick layer of funk. Chism wasn't just healed, he was ... improved. Not only superior to the Chism he'd been when he woke up that morning, but superior to the Chism he was before he ever met the targus. "This does more than just take away melancholy."

"Yes, yes," said the targus with a smile that showed the sharp tips of its teeth. "You will see soon will you see."

"One drop for each man, on their eyelid?" asked Chism.

"Yes yes. Said that already that I said."

"Your speech is strange to us."

"Strange?" The targus made a clicking sound in its throat and palmed its temple. "You begin to speak on a subject and by the time you finish I have forgotten the subject on which you began to speak. Strange. Do you pay pennies for words, pay pennies do you?"

"No," said Chism. "I just don't like to waste time with long conversations."

Hatta stepped up next to Chism and asked the targus. "Would you have another drop of that? If the colors are this bright with one drop, imagine two!"

"For you I do not have any for you."

Mave joined the growing half circle. "Serrill can't use his. He's beyond hope."

"Beyond hope he may be beyond hope, but beyond saving he is not beyond saving."

"Would you sell more drops?" asked Mave. "Something like that in the right market could be extremely ludicrous."

"Lucrative," said Chism.

The targus shook his head. "I have no need for your money have I no need for. Years it takes for one drop to make one drop it takes years."

"So, more than a decade to make all the drops you just gave us!" Mave's eyes began to dart again. "What exactly does it do?"

The creature must have realized the direction Mave's mind was going. With a sly smile it said, "Rash one, you do not get ideas about murder and theft, or murder and devouring ideas I will get about you, rash one."

"No, I ... it was just starkly curiosity," said Mave. "I feel better and all, but for one drop it's just so very latent, or portentious—what I mean to say is portent."

"Potent," said Chism.

"In more time it will more potent become will it in more time." The targus slowly scratched its neck with one hand. "Your minds take a long time to see; take much time do your minds."

"Speaking of time," said Chism, "we are short of it. Even if we hurry, we might still be gathering a squadron while everyone else is fighting a war."

Hatta took another step toward the targus. "Um, if I might be bold enough to be more bold. You wouldn't be able to spare a drop for Ander, would you?"

The targus looked at the white-haired Fellow.

Ander waved and said, "Hello. I'm Ander."

"I did not make any bargain with you a bargain I did not make, but helped bring back Es you did help bring back." It tapped its chin for a moment in thought. "A half drop is acceptable is a half drop?"

"More than a year of your savings in exchange for a duty I would have done for none is a bargain in my eyes," Ander said. He walked forward and bent so the targus could reach him.

"Close your eyes, them close."

Ander closed both eyes. The targus tapped both eyelids as if testing to see if a griddle was hot. He did not smear as he had the others.

Hatta patted Ander on the back, smiled at him, and said, "Mind of a cobra, heart of a kitten."

As they all watched Ander, waiting for him to come alive, Chism remembered Zeemi, without whom Chism would most likely be dead. Zeemi was still sleeping and Skunky was still on top of him.

"What about him?" Chism asked, pointing at the Maner. "Zeemi, the one with the spectacles."

The targus didn't look at Zeemi. "Ask sooner I thought you would sooner ask."

"I would have died if he hadn't intervened."

"My fault that is not my fault. Sleeping is my fault is sleeping. Wake him I will wake. Again, dreams he will dream again."

Hatta was watching the exchange closely. "Will he have splendiferous gifts like we do?"

"Like his gifts will the gifts of his be like." The targus walked slowly to Zeemi. It wetted its fingertip then anointed his right eyelid. The touch was longer than Ander's had been, but it only touched the one eye. Chism wondered if the specific eye made a difference. It had touched opposite eyes on Chism and Hatta after all.

The targus walked to the preserved corpse of its uncle. "No longer men I do not wish to see men any longer." It picked up Es and walked unhurriedly into the brush. Chism felt the same way about targus as the targus did about humans.

Chism looked at Zeemi after the targus disappeared and found him following the targus with his eyes.

"Help him out," Chism told the other three. "Get that skunky Maner off of him."

Ander and Mave obeyed, dumping Skunky roughly to the ground on the far side of Zeemi.

"Hoping to not get killed here." Zeemi held up both hands open and empty.

"You're safe," said Chism. "I owe you."

The Maner stood up slowly and said, "Maybe we are even." He tapped the two chits in his beard, the ones Chism had bartered from Wot way back in the Pit. Combined with his small grin, the spectacles Zeemi wore gave him a peaceful look. But there was something special about Zeemi that Chism couldn't identify.

"I thought you'd be older," he told Zeemi, who couldn't be more than twenty-six or –seven. "Those chits seemed so significant."

"I thought Red Knight would be more ... more ... with hope of still not getting killed do I dare say taller, older, and bearded?"

A powerful intuition in Chism's gut made him say, "I need you in my squadron, Zeemi."

Mave and Ander both dropped their jaws and stared at Chism.

"What are you saying?" asked Mave. "He's a filthy Maner. Undoomable, or whatever."

"He's not an Indomitable after what he did," said Chism.

"True," said Zeemi. "But invitation seems rash. Even for friend."

"We're not friends," replied Chism. That had no bearing on anything, so he added, "It's no more rash than fighting your own squadron or whatever you call each other."

"Exactly!" said Mave, stomping one foot. "He can't be trusted."

Chism hadn't taken his eyes off Zeemi. "I appreciate your input, Mave, but this is my role, not yours." Mave's job was to think tactically, not assemble the squad or lead it. Chism knew it in the same way he knew that the Domainer should be with them.

"Zeemi, I wish we had more time for you to decide, but as you'd say, booger me if I'll spend a minute longer in the Domain than I have to. Which is it: Indomitable or Wonderlandersoldierman?"

Zeemi smiled. "I don't need time. What I need is new army. Booger on Indomitables."

"Welcome to 113 Squadron," said Chism.

"Welcome to Wonderlandermanning!" exclaimed Hatta.

Mave swore. Chism looked at him, trying to decide if he owed Mave an explanation. Mave still had the giant knot on the side of his head, but apparently the targus spit had healed the damage from Skunky when it cured the melancholy.

What Chism needed was compliance, not explanations to his own men. "Mave, find our tunics and pants. The rest of you get horses ready. These Maners will probably sleep until morning. We'll be back in Wonderland by then."

As he started looking for clothes, Mave muttered, "With luck the targus will come back and gouge himself on Maner toes and eyeballs."

Gorge, thought Chism. He agreed with the sentiment.

Mave went on, "I'm tempted to drag that skunk-bearded Maner into the fires."

"Tempting," said Ander. He picked up a flaming branch by its cool end. "With your permission, Sir Chism, I'll see to it that that cage never holds another Wonderlander."

The horses appeared to be nearly ready to ride so Chism nodded. Ander wedged the firebrand between the wheel and wagon frame then quickly sought out another and placed it in the opposite wheel.

Chism went straight for Thirsty. And the clothes and other Wonderland items. As soon as Chism touched the hilt, Thirsty began to purr. Quietly. Barely audible over the crackling of the fires.

Don't do it, Chism told himself. *There's not time here to take it in.* Deep down Chism suspected the matter had less to do with logistics than it did with possible outcomes if Chism revealed his best friend, only to find a dead piece of metal. Yes, best to get his men out of the Domain before setting himself up for a potentially devastating revelation.

At his horse, Chism took a slow breath, gritted his teeth and carefully climbed into his saddle. The exertion was excruciating, but the forward momentum of the morning made it tolerable. Chism paused to take one last look at his enemies lying helpless in the dirt and the cage that had held him being lapped and laughed at by flames.

May it ever be so, thought Chism. With his own newfound muchness, it seemed as if it always would be. As further proof of the prophecy's validity, one of the Maners started sliding like a headless rattlesnake into the brush. At last one Maner would provide the eyeballs and toenails for a targus feast tonight. Too bad it wasn't Skunky.

Chism straightened and heeled his horse lightly. Sounds of his men following came from behind.

"Was the sky so purely obsidian before we lost our dreams?" asked Hatta to no one in particular.

Mave made a noncommittal noise. "Looks the same to me, but I've never had such a deep understanding of battle strategies."

"No, I'm sure of it," said Hatta. Chism heard him inhale deeply. "I can smell the obsidianity, and if the hooves of the horses weren't so heavy, I might be able to hear it."

"No one can hear and smell colors, brother," said Chism. Better to put an end to his nonsense before it got out of hand.

Hatta reined his horse to a stop and bent an ear toward the sky. "Perhaps if *I* could, then that statement might not be worth stating." At some point Hatta had tucked some tiny flowers into his sparse beard.

Ander rode up next to Hatta. "Close your eyes and bend forward." He waved part of his horse's mane under Hatta's nose and asked, "What color is this?"

"Burnt sand," said Hatta.

"Try something that doesn't smell like horse hair," said Chism. The other men had pulled their horses up to watch. The moon was mostly full so even people who weren't Chism would be able to see well.

"Keep your eyes closed," said Ander. He pulled a feather quill and a piece of paper from his pouch and held them under Hatta's nose. "What color?"

Hatta's face scrunched in confusion, his eyes stilled closed. "Hmm. Perhaps it doesn't work because I smell carmine and cornsilk."

"Those aren't even colors, are they?" asked Chism, watching Ander's reaction.

The Fellow seemed both pleased and surprised. "I would have said red and off-white, but he's even more accurate."

Zeemi silently produced a single chit. He waved it in the air at the side of Hatta's head.

"I hear the color copper," said Hatta. "Tarnished copper."

"That is proof for me," said Zeemi.

Chism started riding again and the others followed. He asked Ander, "Can you smell colors too?"

Ander shook his head. "No, but I have a million and one ideas in my head. Wish I was in the workshop, not riding a horse between two hostile nations."

"I've experienced many shades of madness," said Hatta, "and if I have my choice, the melancholy one will be the last I ever revisit."

"Maybe I can't speak," said Ander, "but after watching you all, I'd rather spend a year being digested by a barbantula than go through what you did."

"I'd rather go back into the Pit," said Mave. "Any dreams we had there were unlikely to ever come true, but at least we could aspirate."

"Aspire," said Chism.

"What about you?" Ander asked Chism. "Feel like a new man?"

Chism nodded. "I don't really plan on doing anything different, but at least I can enjoy the things I do now." He wished it were morning already so that he and Thirsty could practice their morning routine and collect lucky rays of sunlight together.

Hatta pulled his horse up in front of Chism, blocking the path. His eyes and mouth were wide open. "How did you do anything without your dreams? Doing nothing was laborious; I can't fathom doing something or everything!"

Chism wanted to get back to Wonderland, not sit around in the Domain wasting time on feelings and fluff. "I just did what I had to do, even though I didn't feel like doing anything." But that was only part of it. He and Hatta couldn't be measured against the same standard. "I guess I don't have as many dreams as you do, so It didn't have much to take. Or hide, or whatever It did."

"I'm amazing now that I have my dreams," said Hatta, "but you don't even need your splendid to be amazing."

"Three cheers for Lieutenant Chism!" shouted Mave. Ander and Chism shushed him.

Back to babysitting, thought Chism, pushing around Hatta and into the lead so he wouldn't have to talk anymore. With his right arm pressed against his ribs the cadence of the horse was bearable.

The branch of a rockleaf bush spanned the path. The gray, heavy-leafed plant was rare in Wonderland, and Chism looked at it from base to top. One thousand four hundred and fifty-five leaves. He knew it with the same certainty that he knew a full-fingered hand had five fingers. Sure enough to bet his life on it.

In the past, he could instantly count up to a hundred, maybe two hundred if the items were laid out in some sort of pattern. But nothing near the number or random arrangement of leaves on that plant.

He pulled his horse to a stop, dismounted gingerly, and grabbed a fistful of sand. The others watched, curious. Chism opened his fist and allowed all of the sand that would not lie in a single layer to fall.

"What do you have?" asked Ander.

"Sand," said Chism. "Six thousand eighty-nine grains." The indivisible number was like sand in his unders so he brushed a speck off the edge of his palm. "Six thousand eighty-eight."

"Interesting," said Hatta. "Shame you didn't get a useful talent like me, but at least you got something."

The others' faces seemed to echo Hatta's remarks—*Why would anybody in the entire world care about counting grains of sand?*

Chism couldn't answer, but he could've stayed and counted all night long. And smiled and felt the joy and relief he never thought he'd feel again.

If it weren't for duty.

He took one more look at the sand then brushed his hands together and mounted his horse. What this new talent meant and what it was good for, he had no idea, but he couldn't wait to see where it led him. Below the surface of his newfound talent and his regained purpose, a fiery loathing for the Domainers still simmered.

They would pay—for the Pit, and the targus, and for the drowned kitten Chism had been when they raised him from the depths. The Blood Red Knight would collect his due, every penny and pound.

27

For half an hour they rode hard. As hard as Hatta felt the horses could safely run in the moonlight. The air was clear, the night was bright, and purpose like a thunderstorm drove Chism. He discovered that he knew how many steps his horse took without having to count each one. He knew how many steps it had been since he left the Maners and the fires behind. He knew how many since the rockleaf bush. There were more numbers going on in his head than humanly possible, but there was no jumbling or confusion. They were as sharp as a million shards of broken crystal.

How many days was I in the Pit? The answer came immediately: one hundred thirty-three.

Chism smiled and made a fist with the hand that held his ribs. He glanced at the other men and found them smiling to themselves.

At the Vlitta River they reined in the horses and Chism led his men across the ford where they'd entered the Domain.

"Welcome home, men," said Chism.

They grumbled agreement and Ander said, "You'll have to drag me by my toenails to get me to leave again."

"Tempting," said Chism. To the group, he added, "Take ten minutes to make yourselves look like soldiers." They would have to work fast to clean up and shave that quickly, but the squadron had a lot of preparation to do and not much time. Chism didn't plan on giving them much rest until after the war came and went.

The horses drank and grazed while Chism's men followed the orders. Zeemi borrowed a tunic from Mave and a pair of worn-out trousers from Ander. As the other four pulled out razors to rid themselves of the beards they'd been cultivating, Chism considered binding his ribs, but there was something more important that needed doing first. He put a hand on Thirsty's hilt and slowly drew it.

The encouraging hum greeted him immediately. Chism closed his eyes and felt it resonate through every bone in his body. The bond was back; his friend was back. An hour earlier Chism's insides had been an empty palace entryway. Vacant and immense. With his companion back, it was a tiny cottage with warm bread and honey, a meal with caring people who didn't try to touch him. It was small, but cozy. As comfortable as anything he'd ever experienced.

Though it had been Chism who'd been healed by the targus, somehow Thirsty was the one who'd been made whole. No one else ever heard Thirsty hum or purr, and Chism suspected it might be entirely in his head, but it didn't hurt anyone for Chism to have such a close relationship with his sword, so he never fought it. Why would he when Thirsty was as therapeutic as the rattle.

Chism gripped Thirsty's hilt with one hand, swung it on both sides of his body. The pain in his ribs didn't compare with the joy of the reunion. He put both hands on the hilt and did two quick strikes. Nearly as bad as he had wanted to do nothing after the targus poisoned him, now he wanted nothing more than to spend the rest of the day reacquainting himself with his truest friend. Daylight would arrive in a couple hours and he could pause then long enough for his routine.

A dark spot on the back edge of Thirsty caught Chism's eye.

Looking more closely, Chism found two other spots that would rust soon if not attended to. He fished his whetstone and oil from his pack and sat down on the rocky river bank to care for the blade he'd neglected since before the Pit.

"I never claimed to be a good friend," he muttered as he stroked Thirsty's edges with the stone.

Even the guilt couldn't bring him down. He was home, practically. Healthy, probably more so than ever. Confident that justice would come to his enemies. Hopeful that he might just do a decent job as lieutenant.

Surprisingly, even leadership didn't scare him at the moment. He had to wonder—since he had heard all sorts of grand leadership things in the rattle—did that mean he wanted it all along and never realized it? Because he still didn't think he wanted it. Nevertheless, after what he'd done for the last month, how hard could it be to lead fifteen men? No one was asking him to do more than that. The soldiers he should pick were firm in his mind where they had been uncertain a day earlier.

Thirsty was healthy again. A little neglected, but Chism could continue to nurture it while they rode. How wonderful it was to have a friend.

Life could not be better. Chism had far to go, but considering where he'd been, everything was perfect.

A single word, a voice he recognized, undercut his emotional summit.

"Greetings."

The sound materialized out of the air directly in front of Chism, but no one was within twenty paces of him.

"Cheshire," said Chism, disappointment dripping from the word. He considered how easily Thirsty could permanently put an end to his encounters with Cheshire. Even though Cheshire had good intentions and had never done anything to hurt Chism, spending time with the whimsical creature was as grating as standing next to someone constantly grinding teeth.

"Hello," answered the Cheshire Cat, fading into view. His obnoxious smile appeared first, as usual, followed by his head and striped body. "Is there someone else you'd rather see right now?"

"A long list of people," said Chism. "In fact, I'm having a hard time thinking of more than three people who aren't on it."

Footsteps approached and seconds later, Mave, Zeemi and Ander appeared, all holding weapons.

"We thought we heard talking." demanded Mave, scanning the area.

"It's just Cheshire," said Chism.

"Who?" asked Mave.

"Do you mind showing them?" Chism asked the Cheshire Cat.

"By no means," said Cheshire, and he began to fade out.

"Men, meet the Cheshire Cat. Cheshire, I believe you already know everything, so I won't waste my breath with introductions."

"Hello again," said Ander.

Mave stared at the spot where Chism had last seen Cheshire. "Oh, it's just a ... cat."

"No," said Chism. "Don't get him started on that. He's not a cat and neither is a catfish. And a stick insect isn't a stick."

Mave just looked more confused, but Chism didn't want to spend all day going around in verbal circles, so he told Cheshire, "What do you want? We have places to go."

Cheshire appeared again, eyes brighter than before. "Ooh! What kind of places? I want to hear all your plans for your new talents and such."

"I'm going to get more recruits." The definite ideas of where to go and who to get, excited Chism.

"Then what will you do?" asked Cheshire.

"Then back to Palassiren."

"Why?"

Letting his exacerbation show, Chism said, "To join the defense force. The Domain's going to invade soon."

"Sixty days," interjected Zeemi. "Perhaps more, perhaps less."

Perfect. They were already short on time and Cheshire wanted to waste what little they had.

"Sounds delightful," said Cheshire. "Gathering your little chicks and defending the realm and such, but if that's the extent of your plan it won't be enough."

"Hello, Cheshire," said Hatta, looking in the general direction.

Cheshire blinked out then in again as he said, "Hello, my friend."

"What do you mean it won't be enough?" Chism asked.

"Unless of course you want Hatta, and Lira, and your perfumed-dubbed inevitable, and Leis and all her little bread-eaters to become slaves or Maners."

"What are you talking about?"

Cheshire was looking out over the river. He went on as if he was having a pleasant conversation with himself. "What? The best squadron in Red Wonderland? Yes, I think Squadron First would do. I'm quite sure of it, most likely."

"Cheshire!" snapped Chism.

The creature turned his head leisurely to look up at Chism.

"Who are you talking to?" asked Chism.

"You, of course," answered Cheshire as if the question was foolish. "Why? Are you not hearing? If I were you instead of me and you, as I, were talking to me as you, I'd most definitely listen closely to ourself."

"If you want me to understand, speak more clearly."

"Did you hear things in the rattle?" asked Cheshire casually.

Chism wouldn't mind giving details if his men weren't around. He simply said, "You know I did or you wouldn't be asking."

"Well, if war were to happen without the right man as the first of Squadron First then those things inside the rattle would never happen outside of the rattle. There is a soldier, whom I happen to know, who is as essential in the upcoming as his brother was in the previous."

It felt to Chism as if the Cheshire Cat was stacking heavy duty on him without giving him the understanding of what the duty consisted of. Suddenly Chism was ten years old, trying to protect himself and an older brother without the slightest idea of how it should be done. That had ended up with a dead father and two half-mad brothers on opposite sides of the kingdom. Was it even possible to do worse with the task currently ahead of him?

Chism muttered, "I never asked to be a leader."

"Yet," said the Cheshire Cat, "you insisted on being the best."

How could the cat know about his conversation with Serrill? "Just tell me who I need and I'll get them."

"Even if I wanted to or could, which I likely might be able to but won't, I wouldn't. You think you've been gifted a gift for no reason?"

"I think you make my head spin on purpose," said Chism. His mind felt like a child's top. "I can count things. That'll come in handy."

"I have an unhandy gift. I can lick my elbow." Cheshire lifted one leg and demonstrated.

Frustration made Chism's grip on Thirsty's hilt get tight. Thirsty wasn't the right tool for this job, though, so he sheathed it.

What else do I have at my disposal, wondered Chism, thinking back on Mave's first lesson. His men watched, waiting to see what he'd do. Hatta just stood there smiling his mad smile. What was it he'd said back in Palassiren? *"Nonsense is a language which I speak."*

"Hatta?" said Chism. "Can you translate?"

"Yes, most indubitably probably," said Hatta. "What Cheshire seems to be saying that you aren't hearing is if yours is not the best and first squadron in Red Wonderland you will fall and Red Wonderland will fail, except I spoke that last part backward. Kindly reverse fall and fail."

Chism took a moment to unscramble Hatta's words. "The best squadron?"

"Yes," said Hatta. "He seems to feel that Squadron First would be satisfactory."

"Oh is that all? Just gather a bunch of new recruits and become Squadron First in two months. Why not give me a difficult task?"

Zeemi's eyebrows rose sharply. "You are truly man of miracles if this is not difficult task."

"No, Zeemi," said Chism. "It's called ... nevermind." He didn't have time to explain the subtleties of sarcasm. The lemons, or the soldiers he had in mind could never accomplish Cheshire's task.

Maybe Knights would do. Sir Hamran, Sir Gwillym, and Sir Tjaden would be a powerful foundation to build a squadron around.

Chism asked, "Should I start with the other Knights?"

"Inquesting someone besides yourself is a splendid good way to fail! The only you in the kingdom, and hence the only one capable of your task, is you," said Cheshire. "A king at a feastday would never go asking food from a pauper."

Chism looked up at his brother.

"What Cheshire would be trying to make you understand is that you have what is needed to succeed and you shouldn't ask someone else to give you what they have because it's worse than what you already possess."

The thing that bothered Chism the most was that he couldn't just ignore Cheshire and shrug off the warning. Every time Cheshire showed up it was at a critical moment and he'd never been wrong. At Hatta's mercury mining shanty Cheshire had urged them to leave. In the Kirohz Valley, Cheshire practically led Chism to the exact spot in the parlay where he needed to be to threaten Duke Jaryn, allowing Hatta to work his magic. And then, after the targus had poisoned Chism, Cheshire appeared just long enough to tell the brothers to stay together and because of the advice they eventually found the targus and were both healed.

If their history together wasn't enough, something inside Chism knew that what Cheshire had said was vital and true. The gut feeling was as instinctual as hunger and as visceral as the urge to sleep at night. But it made no logical sense, and that worried Chism.

"Last time I saw you, I kicked you," said Chism. "Why would you come help me?"

"Is that what's happening?" Cheshire's eyes went wide with perplexity. "I thought it was *you* helping *me*. Wonderland has been my home longer than yours, after all." He stood to stretch and faded from Chism's view.

Good riddance, thought Chism. They had wasted enough time. Chism gathered his things then stood and walked toward the horses. Mave and Zeemi tore their eyes away from the spot where Chism had seen Cheshire, and followed.

No one in the kingdom or anywhere in the world for that matter would believe that Chism and the soldiers he had in mind could become Squadron First. Not if they had a hundred years to do it. But Chism's gut said differently. If he could gather the squadron he had in mind, they would change Wonderland and change the world. Maybe *would* was too strong a word. *Might* change the world. It was a better chance than anyone else would give them.

"Mount up," said Chism. "When I'm done with you, you might just change the world."

All that fate granted time might count for something after all.

THE END

Chism and his plucky recruits return in Book 3 of the Knights of Wonderland Series—
White Knight

ABOUT THE AUTHOR

Daniel Coleman lives in a small town, with his medium-sized family, and a large cast of fictional characters. The only things he enjoys more than writing are spending quality time with his family and watching them reach new heights in their endeavors.

For updates on future releases, sign up for his newsletter at www.dcolemanbooks.com, or like his Facebook page. facebook.com/authordanielcoleman

Made in the USA
Monee, IL
15 October 2023

44645826R00164